29

a novel by
vera west

For all of us who are not afraid to try again.

PROLOGUE:

Everyone says that sex is a mind-blowing experience. It starts with a shared smolder between two chemically compatible beings and ends with crumpled sheets and sweaty, sated muscles. Happy endings; every woman wants to feel it and every man wants to give it. We're taught to believe that physical attraction is the precursor to lasting happiness, but my view of the romantic world has always been different.

My mother hadn't had a prince charming. She had a career. She had me. She had years of piled-up lonely nights but she was happy enough. My mother was fearless. She didn't care what people thought, even though she was aware that they were definitely thinking; categorizing her as another women who couldn't "keep a man around" or "make a man happy." She still didn't care what they thought and her fierce strength led me to decide at a young age: if it was good enough for her, it was good enough for me too.

Now, I'd be lying if I told you I didn't want love—it's hard to not want something that the whole world is telling you that you should— but I'd also be lying if I didn't confess that I'd settle for just good sex. Love was complicated, risky, uncontrollable, but sex, that could be arranged. It could be timed. It could be tweaked. I wasn't waiting for romance. I deserved my feel-good now. Forget the hollow, empty promises; just give me an orgasm.

Which leads me to the problem area of my sexual manifesto: the first time I had sex.

We'd met in college our freshmen year. He was cute, he showered regularly and he was completely into me which was enough to make me interested in *him* and open to explore noncommittal possibilities. I'd seen movies. I *knew* how this worked. He was supposed to want something fun, I was supposed to want something more and eventually he would end our adventure before it got too serious. It was the perfect plan that never made it to fruition.

Clyde didn't want sex from me, he wanted more, and I found myself in a twilight zone where gender roles were bullshit and guys had feelings too. That wasn't my only problem. Clyde had been my first and I hadn't anticipated that I wasn't like other women.

I wasn't normal.

My body didn't work right.

My name is Piper and I'm not able to reach an orgasm.

PART ONE:

Kiss me;
but don't mean it.
satisfy, but
leave my soul be.
That way is *best*.
I'll still breathe
—barely, but bravely—
when you're gone.

1

White papers littered the floor of our Harlem apartment like a fresh layer of winter snow.

Berea, my best friend since the invention of such, stood on our couch doing some weird dance as she fanned out the hundreds of printed applications. They were responses to my social media solicitation: I was looking for twenty-nine applications to help me validate my belief that women could have healthy, noncommittal, non-emotionally driven sex. I was going to prove that men weren't the only ones entitled to string-free pleasure.

Over a decade ago, my mom (Evette) and I started an online magazine in our cheap, roach-filled studio. It was late on a school night and I'd been scarfing down my portion of a split pack of ramen.

"I need a job where I can set my own hours, make extra money and we're still be able to spend time together."

I slurped a noodle off my spoon as I thought. Evette was always looking for additional ways we could make extra money. She already had a second job and I had a little hostess job at a local diner and it *still* wasn't enough. It was never enough.

"I don't know," I muttered in defeat.

"Think, Piper—let's brainstorm, let's weigh out our options."

I sighed.

"Come on! You're the one with the young brain here. Can't you think of *anything?*"

"Like what?" I asked.

"I'm asking you, kiddo. Just start naming things off."

"Anything?"

"Sure!" Evette insisted. "We're storming here! What is something that you like to do that we could also make money from?"

"I like to write," I said. I had handfuls of diaries, filled to the brim with complaints, dreams, memories, secrets, poems, even a short incomplete story or two. It was the one thing I could do for myself without anyone's help and I reveled in the independence.

"All right," Evette said, nodding. "Keep going. How can we turn that into dollars?"

"I could start writing more, and maybe we could sell it?"

Evette's eyes widened.

"Mom?"

"That's brilliant, honey! We could start an online magazine."

"What?" I asked, confused.

"It's perfect, we could let people subscribe to our website and then they can view the articles. It'll be a lot of work, but maybe you could have your friends from school write pieces too—we wouldn't pay them, of course, but it would be good practice for college."

And that was how *Galaxy* was born. I blurted out a half-baked idea and my mom turned it into an empire. We were a powerhouse team, Evette and I; we wrote, we edited and we both promoted *Galaxy*.

Spending even more time with my wacko, eccentric, weird mix of feminist-yet-traditional mom was not very high on any teenager's list but I actually loved it. Instead of playing sports or going to parties, I stayed home writing. We gave everything over to our creation and it took care of us. Eventually, Evette was able to work just one job and all our focus was on *Galaxy*. Life as we knew it changed and we had something even better than poor-love—we had rich-stability. Now, I was twenty-eight. Galaxy was a thriving, reputable online magazine and pulling in enough revenue to support a good- sized staff including summer interns fed to us by a local university.

Even though I was destined to one day rule *Galaxy,* I still couldn't suppress my need to prove myself to the world and my mother. I had a need to do something that set me apart from Evette. I was desperate to reinvent my writing style and I had a killer plan for a piece that only Berea knew about.

I needed twenty-nine willing candidates to go out with me, and if we both felt the *vibe,* we'd sleep together. I'd ask them a series of questions before and after and I'd also journal how I was feeling before and after. Eventually, at the end, I'd create twenty-nine different articles about sex, and the whole piece would be featured in *Galaxy's* debut print edition next April.

The number twenty-nine had a bit of sentimental value for me. This April 29th was my golden birthday and I couldn't give up the idea that it was a going to be a magical--nothing could go wrong, throw caution to the wind—kind of day. That day felt like good luck and no one in their right mind turned down luck.

Unfortunately, I'd come up with this battle plan six months *after* my twenty-eighth birthday, so I only had half a year left to pull it off. I'd been worried at first, fearing I'd bitten off far more than I could chew, but with hundreds of responses I was feeling giddy with assurance. I could pull this off and when I did, it would change everything. I wouldn't be Evette's best employee anymore, I'd be *me.*

"What a workout," Berea exclaimed, as she gathered up the papers we'd strewn everywhere. "Have you made any decisions yet? I know one person who would *love* the opportunity to get some smoosh-smoosh time with you."

"Never again," I answered quickly. I knew she was alluding to Clyde, our best guy friend who couldn't get over the fact that I'd given him my virginity but not my heart. He had this I'll-just-give-her-time mentality, but I knew time wouldn't make a difference. I just didn't *want him.*

Clyde hadn't always been so needy and intense. At one time, he'd been the welcome third wheel to Berea and me, but one college night when I'd gotten a little too buzzed and a little too friendly had changed everything between us. It'd been my first time (not his) and even without an orgasm it had been fun. I liked him, but I hadn't felt anything other than enjoying the way he responded to me. I let it happen a few more times but each time nothing happened for *me* and eventually he realized.

Clyde wanted to talk, I didn't, and somehow we melted into this weird unrequited love friendship. He occasionally did date other girls, things would be normal for a moment, and then he'd started looking at me like he wasn't satisfied. He tried to force conversations, eager to understand what he'd done wrong, asking for another chance, but I always shrugged him off. Clyde was hurt by my robotic responses and ultimately always became defensive, telling me that other women loved him and that it was me who had the problem, not him. I agreed with him, knowing that it probably was me, but that always pissed him off even more and he'd argue back that I was cold, unfeeling, my heart too icy to be thawed. It was in those moments that I feared he was right because deep down I wanted to feel what everyone else did when someone touched them but I had to accept that I was powerless to change reality.

Even with Clyde's emotional love-fueled outbursts, he was still a good friend to Berea and me. I'd gotten him a job as a marketing intern at *Galaxy* (perhaps out of guilt) and he was phenomenal at it. We'd quickly hired him into a permanent position and he was flourishing. He'd been working there for a year and lucky for me, there'd been no more talk of an *us*. I hoped it stayed that way and prayed daily that he found someone who could appreciate him.

"There's an inquiry by a woman," squealed Berea, bringing me out of the past and back to the present.

"This door only swings one way," I replied, without looking up.

"No seriously, look at this!" Berea insisted, waving the application under my nose, "It's from a woman, but she is *offering* up one of her male employees. She wants you to interview this guy and create some hype for her company."

"What kind of company?" I asked as I skimmed the application.

"Porn."

I quickly nabbed my phone and dialed the provided number.

"It's ringing!" I squeaked nervously to Berea.

"Top Hat Productions, how may I direct your call?"

I quickly found the applicant's name. "Kendyl, please," I stammered clumsily.

"Sure! One moment, please."

There was soft classical hold music followed by a high-pitched beep when the line was answered.

"Kendyl speaking, how can I help you?"

"Hi, I'm calling in response to an application submitted on Chirp to be a part of an expose on—"

"Yes," Kendyl interjected excitedly. "You're Piper Ezrah from *Galaxy*, right?"

Shit.

I was silent, stalling, trying to give my brain a chance to formulate a half-decent response. I thought I'd been so careful. I hadn't wanted my affiliation with *Galaxy* known until the piece launched.

"Your secret's safe with me," Kendyl said, cutting right to the point. "We'd love to get some exposure for our new actor, Levi Gallant. Mainly, I'd like you to interview him; a little good publicity could reap valuable benefits for my company and my actors. If you'll include the interview with Levi in your piece and mention Top Hat, we'll fly you out here for a weekend."

That was quite the offer and I couldn't refuse.

"I think I could arrange that," I said, trying to feign coolness.

"Fantastic! Levi is doing some modeling gigs right now but he'll be shooting his first movie with us in a month. I'd like you to meet him on set. Is a month too far away?"

I quickly went over a calendar in my mind. It was the first week of August now; a month would put me roughly at the same spot in September. I could schedule all my other interviews and make this one my last. Then, the rest of the time I could spend writing and editing.

"Actually, that would be perfect," I agreed.

13

"Great! I'll be in touch with the details."

My heart pounded in my chest. I was doing this. I was really doing this.

2

WEEK ONE:

I walked into the Hayes University's library. It wasn't far from where I lived, just a couple train stops away from my apartment, and the subway exit took you practically to the library's front door. I was on time and meeting my first applicant. Ironically, this was the university that *Galaxy* was partnered with for its internship program. It had let the applicant pick the location; hopefully, that hadn't been a mistake.

I knew it was him right away because, luckily, he looked just like the picture he'd sent me. Number one looked a little nerdy but non-greasy—like a stereotypical nerd: he'd be cute if he took his glasses off, let his hair grow out a bit and stopped having his mom lay his clothes out for him each morning.

"I'm glad you could make it," number one greeted me as I sat down across from him at a wide, solid-oak studying table. He had his books spaced out in neat little stacks. I skimmed the titles; a hodgepodge of randomness that gave me no clue to what he might be studying.

"Hi, Adrian, right?"

"That is correct. Thank you for being so prompt," Adrian said in the most monotone voice I'd ever heard.

"It's always professional to be on time."

"It's appreciated, I assure you."

God—it was like talking to the first fully functioning piece of artificial intelligence.

"Did you review my application?" Adrian queried as he begun to gather up his belongings.

"Yes—and I thought you would be perfect for an interview."

"Interview?" he echoed, as if the word was an incorrect form of binary code.

15

"Yes, I'm going to ask you questions about your sex life."

"Forgive me; I thought this was more about experiencing coitus rather than talking about it?"

Nope. Halt. Last train to vagina town had just departed. Not even a remote chance for *coitus*.

I got out my tablet and a stylus and feigned making notes.

"You're more comfortable with having sex than talking about sex?" I asked, in a clinical tone.

Adrian's eyes shifted to my paper.

"What are you writing?"

I ignored his question. "Surely, due to the nature of my posted request, an interview isn't unexpected?"

"No, it's not entirely unexpected, and yes, I'm more comfortable having sex than talking about having sex."

"In your opinion, which gender is less likely to become attached to their partner during repeated sexual encounters?"

A crimson flush flared at the base of Adrian's neck, rapidly spreading to his cheeks.

"What?" he stuttered.

"How regularly do *your* partners reach climax?" I continued on.

He took his glasses off and closed his eyes; he looked completely exasperated. I couldn't help it—admittedly it was wrong of me. Adrian was probably an honestly nerdy guy who'd thought this was a booty call request disguised as a project. I took pity on him.

"I'm sorry, Adrian, I just got an emergency text. I'm needed elsewhere. Perhaps we can finish this another time?"

He put his glasses back on and opened his mouth to respond but I was already taking strides away from the table.

"It was nice meeting you!" I called over my shoulder.

"Sorry to interrupt you, but were you interviewing him?"

I felt a light pressure on my arm and turned around. A lean, classic hipster styled college student (loose beanie, plaid shirt, dark jeans, combat boots included) had caught up to me on the steps. Her skin was

16

tan just light of brown and her wavy hair was longer than a pixie cut but to wild and conformed to be considered a crop. She was cute and I immediately envied her easy style and confident that let her approach someone she didn't know on the fly. I'd paused before answering her; unsure if I should lie or be honest. If I told her the truth then I'd have a hell of a lot of explaining to do.

"I'm Amy," she continued before I'd even responded to her question.

We shook hands and she lingered one long almost-seductive moment before letting go.

"Piper," I final answered back, "and yes, I am working on a project that requires applicants."

I know I shouldn't have been listening in on your conversation but it was so *juicy*. Are you writing a piece about sex?"

I smiled timidly feeling like I'd been caught with my hand in the proverbial cookie jar.

"Something like that."

"Do you need a female participant?"

I blushed. I had a mix of emotions ranging from curious to scandalized but the overwhelming hesitation that I wasn't emotional ready for any additional sexual exploration won over.

"No, thanks though."

Amy smiled not in the least put out. She wished me good luck and went about her business. I wondered if she'd only been teasing me a little flirtatious test sprung from curiosity to see what I might say.

I trotted down the library steps quickly, wondering if every person was going to be like this. I ran over the wording of my request in my mind. I'd asked for the applicants to be willing to discuss sexual acts, then give unbiased answers, state their ages, professions, estimate number of partners. I don't believe I'd said anything about test runs, but in my mind it'd been a real possibility that I was open to. I must have eluded my thesis idea, or perhaps it was just that when a woman talked about sex she must surely want to have it.

That statement was both truth and not true for me. I felt my chest tighten in anxiety. Did I really want to sleep with twenty-nine different men? I'd use condoms, of course, or rather make them use condoms, but now that I was out here meeting people that number felt ginormous. Irony; I'd romanticized my idea to *un-romanticize* sex. When I'd come up with my plan, it had seemed wild, bold, fun, even brave, but now it just felt *invasive.*

Stay calm, I told myself firmly. *You're in charge of your body and this essay.*

I lifted my chin; my inner monologue pep talk was already sinking in. I didn't have to sleep with people to discuss sex. I'd just evolve my thesis idea into something tangible. It would still be an interesting piece, and unlike anything *Galaxy* had ever printed. Failure was not an option.

WEEK FOUR:

"So," Clyde asked with a cheeky grin. "How has your 'project' been going?"

Clyde had been mysteriously extra chill lately, so much so that I'd accepted his offer for lunch. We'd met at Peaches and Plums, a little fresh-fruit store that had an upstairs diner with simple but amazingly tasty food. It was just down the street from *Galaxy* and a favorite spot of the whole staff.

I snorted.

"Horrible."

"How many men have you seen?"

"Like four?" I held my hand up as I counted them off to him. "Number one thought we were going to just go off and bang, number two had this long hair that was covering his face like some kind of escaped convict."

"Was it stringy and greasy?"

"Yes! I don't think I ever saw his full face; grunge king for sure."

"You might need to start bringing mace with you," Clyde suggested.

I laughed, but Clyde's expression was completely serious. He looked genuinely concerned. My brain flashed a warning sign. Feelings were a slippery slope, especially for Clyde.

Avoiding eye contact, I carefully answered him.

"I think you're right," I agreed, "I don't know what I was expecting but so far it's definitely been an experience."

"Have you slept with any of them?"

I unintentionally choked on my drink.

"God, no," I said quickly. "After the long-greasy-haired guy, there was another named Ethan. He had this annoying catch phrase he kept saying. Then this other dude, named Frank, kept zoning out like he was some kind of stoner; he couldn't focus for shit! Seriously, none of these people I'm meeting are—" I paused, searching for the right word.

"Your type?" Clyde asked, attempting to finish my sentence.

19

"Yeah, they're horrible. I'm not attracted to any of them."

"I'm sure it'll get better eventually," Clyde said, trying to be supportive. "You're not really going to sleep with a bunch of them are you?"

"It's all for research!" I exclaimed teasingly, but he didn't seem to appreciate that.

"What are you trying to prove, Piper?"

"You'll have to wait and read the expose!"

"Seriously, you really want to be intimate with that many people? What if you catch something?"

I gave him an over-exaggerated wink.

"Condoms," I said.

"What if they end up wanting to see you again?"

"Maybe I'd want to see them again too."

Clyde stared at me blankly. I knew that look. We were headed into romantic waters.

"I am single," I reminded him, quietly.

He shoveled a big spoonful into his mouth and didn't justify me with a response.

"Clyde, you promised," I warned.

"What?" he said defensively. "I can't *care* about my friends unless I'm fucking them?"

"Clyde!"

"I'm sorry," he said quickly, lowering his voice back to a normal tone.

I eyed him suspiciously.

"You're running out of chances. If we can't even be friends—what's the point?"

"You don't mean that," Clyde said with an expression that mirrored a kicked dog.

"I do," I assured him. "Relationships are hard, but friendships should be the easiest type of relationship a person can have."

I got up, dug a twenty out of my wallet and tossed it on the table.

"Thanks for lunch," I grumbled.

I'd barely been at my desk for five minutes when our internal messaging system pinged me.

BEREA: How was lunch?

Awful, I typed back.

A response quickly popped up.

BEREA: Of course it was. It is Clyde after all. Why did you even go? If it's all of us that's one thing, but one-on-one lunches are always risky business.

I don't know. Lonely? I wrote back.

BEREA: Don't do that, you know how he feels about you. He can't help himself, but if you don't like him you have to help yourself. Don't lead him on.

A best friend like Berea was almost always right. I clicked my pen nervously. I could see Berea's desk from where I was. The office had an open-floor concept. Instant messaging was the only way you could have a private conversation, that is, unless you were in Evette's office. Out of my peripheral vision, I saw Clyde stride across the floor to his desk. Berea looked up at him and he gave her a sad smile.

I typed Berea a response.

He said he wanted to be friends. I was just trying.

BEREA: Well, stop trying! You guys can't be buds, no matter what he says or how many times you try. Did he make you feel like a slut for working on your project?

ME: Yes...

BEREA: You're not! Men separate sex from emotion all the time, but when we do it it's a monstrosity.

ME: Clyde's just frustrated and hurt.

BEREA: Don't defend his sex shaming!

"If only I could get that kind of concentration from you all the time. You must be pinging Berea."

Shit. I quickly minimized the window. I'd been so engrossed in my conversation with Berea that I hadn't even seen her walk up. I wondered how long she'd been reading over my shoulder.

"Afternoon, Evette," I said grimly.

"Now what is this about slut-shaming?"

Fantastic; she'd been standing there for at least five minutes.

"Just some article I read online. It's becoming common for men and women to be judgmental about a female who enjoys herself sexually."

"Familiarizing yourself with the goings-on of young women today, or have you been participating in activities with a high judgmental risk?"

My annoyance with her was rising rapidly, but I quickly checked it. When your boss was also your mother, the line of insubordination was ultra-thin.

"Look, Piper," Evette continued, "I know you're excited about this love-sex controversial piece you're doing, but let's keep it classy, all right? We want to keep our office and work professional. Now, I've given you a lot of leeway with doing a major piece for the launch of our first quarterly print edition, but I'm starting to think I need to sit down with you and hear a little more about your—*ideas*."

"We've already discussed the basis of my thesis and we agreed I'd send you proofs for approval well before the content deadline," I reminded her.

"You'll be managing the departmental content, like we discussed, but I'll be reviewing the entire print edition," she pushed, correcting me. "This is our name on the line, Piper, we can't afford any mistakes. This is the only legacy I'll be able to leave you."

Just like that the ultra-thin line between home and work threatened to vanish altogether and I was getting pissed off. The launch was in six months. We had plenty of time to finalize the pieces, cut things out, redo things if need be—mother or not, boss or not—babysitting my every editorial move was completely disrespectful.

"I'm aware," I said, practically snarling.

"Just to make sure you understand the severity of launching a new product, I'm going to allow some of our staff writers and even interns to also submit pieces to me."

"What, more than what they're *already* writing? The plan was to take the best pieces from the past quarter, use a few new pieces and then feature my expose."

"Scared you'll get out-written?"

I was fuming but I wasn't backing down. I wasn't going to lose my temper and let Evette undermine me in front of all of our staff.

"Fine," I said in the most even tone I could muster.

"I'm going to ask Berea to work on a piece that blends writing and photography. See what she comes up with. We can use it for the next quarter or for the debut print copy if your expose doesn't work out," Evette said.

I couldn't look at her. I was barely hanging on to my sanity.

"Still coming over for dinner Friday night, Piper?"

I had an unbearable urge to blare "NO" in her face like a fog horn. Instead, I gave her a noncommittal shrug and began pretending to be vastly interested in my computer screen until she took the hint and left.

When she was safely away a new message from Berea popped up.

BEREA: Did your mom just chew you out?

ME: How could you tell?

BEREA: Your resting bitch face is at maximum force.

I looked past my screen to Berea and she gave me a little smirk that cut through all my frustration. Her best-friend skills were strong. I stifled a laugh.

BEREA: You could always start your own magazine or finally start that small publishing company you talk about every time you get a little drunk. It's not like you don't have the skill or the contacts.

ME: No way! Also, Evette wants you to work on a piece to replace mine if I drop the ball.

BEREA: Seriously? That's not even necessary.

ME: Boss's order.

BEREA: She's been getting really domineering lately.

ME: That's an understatement.

BEREA: Maybe it's time to discuss your role in the company. She can't "mom" you forever. This is as much your legacy as hers.

Berea was right. I needed to be more than a glorified assistant. I had ideas, I had skills, I had talent, but Evette just didn't see them or didn't care. That's why I wanted to do this piece so badly. I needed to prove to her that I was her equal.

Towards the end of the day my phone buzzed. I figured it was Berea texting me something too saucy for the internal chat system. But it wasn't. It was an alert for a private message on Chirp from Mathais, applicant number five, the smart twenty-something from Michigan who'd moved to New York for college and never left. He was making sure we were still meeting tonight.

I sent him back a quick message confirming we were still on to meet at the Bitter End at eight, tomorrow night. I felt encouraged that he had called it an interview in his message, but just to be sure he *understood* my intention I added—a little ironically—a sixty-nine character disclaimer.

MathmaticalConstant: Are you aware that this is a discussion of sex and not an offer for sex?

SmittenMitten: I'm aware, but what if you swoon?

MathmaticalConstant: I don't usually, so we should be safe. By the way, your username is ridiculous.

SmittenMitten: It's punny though, right?

MathmaticalConstant: Nope, it just rhymes. ;)

I smirked judgmentally at my phone—he might just be the first normal person I'd agreed to meet.

"I assumed you were from *Michigan,* also known as 'the mitten' by some Michiganders."

Mathais smiled over his coffee before taking another sip. We'd both been on time, so much so that he'd actually held the door for me as we came in. We recognized each other from our Chirp profile pictures and chatted easily in the cafe line. I was right in my assumption that he was *normal.* Oddly enough, Mathais was definitely someone I could see myself being friends with. Standing in line with him to get coffee felt like the most natural and relaxed thing I'd done in months. I figured I'd better enjoy this interview because I had a feeling I wouldn't get this lucky twice.

We sat there, smiling at each other like idiots, but it was somehow anything but awkward.   He was taller than me, probably almost a perfect six foot, if I had to guess. His skin was warm beige, darkened by a combination of ethnicity and sun. His eyes were a dreamy hazel. Mathais was very attractive, dashing even, in a relaxed sort of way that made me want to scoot my chair closer to his, hook my legs over his lap and just listen to him talk.

What the hell, brain.

I cleared my throat.

"You ready for the questions?"

"Sure—are you doing this for a dissertation or for undergraduate work?"

Mathais smirked.

"Trying to figure out how old I am?"

"What made you respond to my post?" I asked.

"I thought it was bold and worth responding to. What made you change your mind about sleeping with each applicant?"

I shifted my eyes back to my paper and darkened a doodled dot unnecessarily.

"What makes you think I changed my mind?"

"In your original explanation it sounded like you were 'open' to seeing where things went if the attraction was there, but when I messaged you over Chirp you very deliberately made sure I knew that this was *not* a booty call."

A man who actually remembered what you said to him; he'd warned me I might *swoon.*

"I should have been a little more careful how I worded it," I confessed.

"I'm sure you've attracted some wallops."

"I've only met with a handful of the people who've responded so far, but, yes, a lot of them assumed they were guaranteed something."

"I'm not sure why people assume discussing sex is a precursor for getting sex. Honestly, you'll probably get better results from just talking to people about their sex lives anyway. What did you want to learn from this experience?"

Mathais' eyes looked genuinely interested, but those lips—they looked deliciously mischievous. I swallowed and took a sip of my chai, a feeble attempt to regain my focus.

"Mainly, I want to prove that a woman is capable of separating sex from love, but I'm open to discussing anything relevant. I realize now that forcing people to only talk about one topic wouldn't create a good discussion."

"Everyone can separate emotion from sex but some people just don't want to."

"Why do you think that is?"

"I don't know," Mathais answered honestly. I liked that he didn't try to give me some grandiose bullshit answer. Actually, I liked him in general. There was something edgy and real about him, at least that was the vibe I was getting.

"Do you prefer to have sex with or without an emotional connection?"

"Depends on what I want in the moment," Mathais answered.

"You mean what you want from the woman you're with?"

"Yes—but eit'
want release; wh
be the easiest a

I liked +
understand
seduced. F
tempted
was sur
"
very

I took a deep breath and swa
before tossing the container in
Nevada, and were making
like those five weeks from
evaporated.
The rest of the in
beginning to fear th
and my motives f
would wake m
crazy pipe dre
"I can'
My
accom
brib
be

owed the last gulp of bottled water
the trash. We'd just landed in Las Vegas,
ur way through the packed airport. It felt
when I'd first talked to Kendyl until now had

terviews had been flat. I'd learned little and I was
at I'd undoubtedly romanticized this whole process
r doing it. Maybe I was hoping that I'd find a man who
body up and show me that I wasn't broken. It was a
am but I couldn't stop hoping it would come true.
believe we're here!" Berea squeaked excitedly.
own airfare had been paid for by Top Hat so I "bribed" Berea to
pany me by buying her ticket. Honestly, I hadn't really had to
her, it was Las Vegas after all and neither of us had ever been here
fore. We were both ecstatic to be here and planning on exploring the
city in our free time. I was feeling pretty optimistic about the interview;
a porn star had to have some kind of sexual insight, right? Maybe—not
sure if I'd have the guts to do this—I was hoping they'd be able to help
me understand my own problem. I was probably grasping at straws, but
if you couldn't talk frankly about sex with a porn star, who could you
talk about it with? It couldn't hurt to try.

As we neared the exit I spotted a woman about our age holding a
sign with my name on it.

"I'm Piper," I announced with a little wave.

"You're from New York, right? Bet the weather change is a
shock?!" she teased amiably. "My name is Claire, I'm Kendyl's assistant.
Our car is right out front. Do you need help with your bags?"

"I think we can manage."

"It's about an hour's drive to the studio from here, but I have some snacks in the car. Kendyl thought she'd give you a tour of the building and then we'd all go out to dinner. I believe you're going to be here for two days? Levi's schedule is open tomorrow for the interview, but tonight we can just all relax and have a good time."

"That sounds good to me!" Berea chirped.

"Wow, a limo?" I asked, surprised.

"Our actors love rolling around in style, and trust me, cranky actors are not something anyone wants to deal with."

I scooted across the leather seat, hauling my overloaded carry-on in behind me.

"I think your article idea is really interesting," Claire added once we were all loaded in and the car begun to pull away. "Women aren't given enough credit. In my line of work I see a lot of things, and it's mainly men who fall in love first or at all!"

I nodded in agreement, enjoying the small stroke to my ego. It was empowering that another woman (other than Berea) thought the topic was worth exploring.

We drove past a block of large pole barns with studio labels and then pulled up to a larger one that had a bit of landscaping that made it feel more like *the* entrance instead just another set. Inside, the space felt like it was ripped out of an Ikea "hipster" section. The style of the room was urban industrial with a slight sense of entitlement flickering off the smooth, colored metal benches and bright caged lights. I liked it.

Kendyl was seated behind her desk and she greeted us excitedly as we approached. I was surprised to see how casually dressed she was. She still looked nice, even trendy, but definitely business casual in skinny jeans, a loose flowing top, and ballet flats. Her hair was long, layered and surprisingly brown instead of blonde. Perhaps most surprising yet, Kendyl had normal sized natural boobs. I guess I'd expected the owner of an adult movie production company to be overly sexualized.

"I'm sure you're tired," Kendyl said. "Levi should be wrapping up soon. Would you like to see him in action?"

"YES!" Berea almost screamed beside me.

"God, he's delicious to watch. Let's see if we can catch him before he's done," Kendyl added with a wink. My curiosity wasn't just piqued, it was quivering in anticipation. I'd never watched anyone have sex before. It was the kind of naughty, dirty, once-in-a-lifetime experience I just couldn't pass up.

We followed Kendyl back outside and hopped into a golf cart. Somehow, Berea convinced Kendyl to let her drive and we sped at an ungodly speed through the studio neighborhood.

"These barns are easy to put up and we have a team of carpenters that just build the sets. Claire loves interior design so she creates all of our different sets for the movies," Kendyl explained. "She's fantastic at it. I'm surprised I haven't lost her yet to some bigwig company. We made it just in time. The lights are on above the door, which means they are filming, so we will have to be super quiet. Once we're inside, I'll get you some headphones so you can hear everything clearly. Let's go!"

He was naked already, straddling a petite blonde clothed only in an oversized button-up blouse. As soon as I saw him, a shiver ran through me, my breath snagged in my throat, my heart fluttered, my stomach clenched in excitement; my body came alive.

His partner's hands were resting against his forearms, and I held my breath as I watched him bend to kiss her. Her whole body rose to meet him. I caught a glimpse of white lace underwear as the loose blouse slipped up her thighs. Her lips parted and the moan that seeped out from between them was loud enough for me to hear sans headset. This was definitely *not* scripted.

I watched enviously as her hands latched possessively into his hair. He broke the kiss long before she was ready for it to end. A knowing smile teased against his mouth—he knew she really wanted him, that this wasn't just *acting.* Leaning down to kiss her, he pinned her hands above her head and began a subtle kneading roll of his hips. He was

30

taking his time, working her up with each teasing touch. He was priming her.

I felt a nudge on my arm; it was Berea offering me a headset. I quickly put it on, curious to hear if the sounds were matching up with their heated body language.

"Do you want me to suck you off?" the blonde asked eagerly.

He smirked.

"Don't believe that's in the script."

"We're allowed to improvise, honey, I can *feel* that this isn't your first time filming this type of sex."

"What type would that be?"

"Sensual. It's almost like making love. It's good. Usually I just get rammed like a bumper car. God, where'd you learn that little move with your hips? It's making me feel *crazy.*"

He gave her another sly smile.

"How about we talk a little less?"

"These are just shots. It doesn't matter if we talk. They're going to edit it out."

His mouth dragged down her body until his lips were level with her sex. That lace setup she had on was hardly underwear and his tongue easily moved it aside as he took her with his mouth. He traded her words for moans and she was in full compliance, pushing herself hungrily against his face, as close as she could get.

He went to work on her, never stopping or slowing. Ecstasy came alive in her face. Her lashes fluttered as her mouth opened and her back arched as she cried out. He pulled back, unconsciously using the back of his hand to wipe her wetness from his face as he watched her come down from the high he'd given her. Her heavy lashes could barely open but she spread for him, wanting him to take her fully.

I shifted on my feet, accidentally bumping my hip into something. Whatever I'd bumped broke the air like a marching band symbol. It crashed loudly onto the floor. Levi's head snapped towards the sound and our eyes locked.

As we watched each other, I swore I saw a blush creep across his honey beige cheeks. I was trapped in his bewildered gaze. I couldn't look away, even though a little voice told me staring was even ruder than knocking something over while actors were filming in a studio.

"CUT!" I heard the director roar. "WHO KNOCKED SOMETHING OVER?"

"It's all right," Kendyl soothed. "We got more than enough footage. Once you're dressed, Levi, there's someone here that'd I'd like you to meet."

Through the headset, I could hear the blonde's frustrated protests.

"Sounds like it's a rap," Levi said, offering her an apologetic smile.

"Do you want to meet up—"

Levi cut her off. "Deb, you know how this works."

I took the headset off, oddly satisfied that the blonde bombshell had gotten turned down.

"Lord have mercy," Berea whispered in my ear as she fanned herself dramatically. "If that man can't make you hum, then we might want to get your engine checked out."

"He's wonderful to watch, isn't he?" Kendyl asked.

I'd forgotten Kendyl was still there. I agreed, nodding politely, completely unsure of what was the right thing to say. I'd never critiqued someone's fucking abilities before. I just hoped she hadn't heard Berea's comments exposing my own sexual hang-ups.

I felt the air change and looked past Kendyl to see Levi coming towards us. He'd gotten dressed, rather quickly, into dark jeans and a smooth charcoal grey sweater. His walk was pure relaxed confidence, which for me is even sexier than blunt verbal confidence. There is something about a man who just *is,* and Levi's walk said it all. I couldn't stop myself from biting my bottom lip as watched him move. His energy, even from a distance, made my body tingle.

"He can wear the shit out of some Levi's. Do you think his mom was foreshadowing when she named him?" Berea whispered.

I choked on a laugh but recovered just in time.

"Are you the one I've been waiting to meet?" Levi asked me, with unfaltering eye contact.

"No, I've been waiting for you—to finish the scene you were doing."

I'd barely recovered from that Freudian slip. *Get it together, girl!* He's just one extremely attractive man, not a god.

"You're not the writer who is going to quiz me on sex?"

"No. I mean, yes, I am the writer."

He offered me his hand to shake.

"Levi Gallant, pleasure to meet you."

"I hope you've washed those," Berea commented.

"Always," Levi answered smoothly.

Kendyl squeezed in between Levi and me.

"I have a friend at the Moderato Andante," Kendyl chirped, "and she got you some decent suites, not top floor, but free is *free.* You can gamble a little, relax, and then tomorrow you and Levi can do the interview. The best part? There is a fantastic in-house restaurant just a few blocks from the hotel. Hope you don't mind, but I made us reservations there for dinner. I know you must be starving, but did you want a quick tour of the filming grounds before we head off?"

"Are there any more films in progress?" Berea asked shamelessly.

"Maybe, let's do a quick sweep and see," Kendyl said with a smile.

4

We made it to dinner about three hours later. I hadn't been hungry when dinner had been suggested, but by the time we'd toured he studio and dropped off our bags at the hotel, I was ready to throw down.

As we were seated at our table, I awkwardly attempted to scoot my chair forward but kept getting the legs caught on the restaurant's carpeting. I could feel Levi watching me and my cheeks and neck grew hot as I inched my chair forward like a choppy snail to the table. I was off kilter and nervous with him being so near and it wasn't that I wanted impress him, I just didn't want to look like an idiot. I was worse than a fish out of water and I was quickly humiliating myself.

Levi got up, striding quickly over to my chair.

"Forgive me for not being chivalrous sooner," Levi said in a low voice behind me. I felt my chair glide forward to the perfect distance from the table.

"Thank you," I whispered, self-conscious for so many different reasons: needing his help, being so attracted to him, being so confused about being so instantly attracted to him. I was sure the list would keep growing.

Kendyl gave me a wicked smile. "How's your *research* going?"

Berea snorted and answered for me before I could even take a breath.

"Horrible! The wording of her original request made it seem like she wanted to sleep with anyone who applied, so all these inexperienced horny dingbats keep inquiring. It's like pulling teeth to get a good discussion going."

I cringed, reddening from head to toe.

"Is that right?" Kendyl asked. She tapped her nail on the tablecloth like a cat flicking its tail mischievously. I wondered what she was thinking. I knew she wanted exposure for her company, but was there

34

another point to all of this? Was I a mouse? Had she brought me here just to laugh at my inexperience? God, I wasn't normally this uncomfortable around people. I just felt so *vulnerable* being around *him*. He had changed the tone of everything.

"That's a shame. New experiences are always so fun," Kendyl concluded, with a final tap of her manicured nail on the table.

"I knew we were going to meet, but I didn't get a chance to research you or your magazine," Levi continued, ignoring Kendyl altogether.

"It's your mother's magazine, right?" Kendyl asked.

"Actually," Berea said firmly, "it's both of theirs. They founded it together when we were teenagers."

"That has a charming 'mom and pop' kind of feel to it, doesn't it?"

"More like *grass roots*," Berea said, correcting Kendyl again.

I made a silent prayer thanking God for besties. Levi smiled at me and I shrugged, barely containing my own smirk. That was my Berea, she'd correct you if you were wrong, didn't matter who you *thought* you were.

After our food was served, it was evident that Berea and Kendyl had this weird rivalry going on—constantly correcting each other, one upping, complaining—you name it, they did it. Then it got even worse—they started *liking* each other.

Their conversation went everywhere—current television shows, Hollywood gossip, viral internet videos, makeup, humanitarian issues—but never to anything even remotely close to *networking*. It was as if they were really becoming friends. It was twilight-zone bizarre. But on the flip side, Levi chatted politely with me, inquiring a few times about different aspects of the work I did at *Galaxy*, but for most of the meal we both just listened to Berea and Kendyl. I tried not to look at him too much, but I found myself studying him, his reactions to other people, his mannerisms. He was so poised and guarded. Just like on the set. He interacts but there's no reaction. He's very careful and he gives away nothing.

I didn't eat much of my food; I mostly just shuffled it around my plate smooshing it together, pulling it apart, praying we'd escape to our room soon and trying not to stare at Levi. The bill never came and then when Kendyl ushered us to get up, I realized that this wasn't the kind of place that handed you a bill. Probably wise, since the food was so horrid, if there was a *physical* bill no one would pay it.

We headed out towards the front of the restaurant. It was almost nine now and the floor was packed with beautiful, expensive-looking people waiting to be seated. I looked down at my own casual outfit: dark tan suede flat boots, form fitting jeans that I'd like to think flattered my thighs, loose flowing top and my favorite aviator glasses and go to crossover leather bag. I'd be normal in New York; here—not so much.

"What are your plans for the rest of the evening?" Levi suddenly asked.

I turned to face him, surprised that he was asking and oddly hopeful that he was going to invite me somewhere.

"Not sure," I said honestly.

Berea tapped me on the shoulder.

"Kendyl is offering to show us around. She knows a couple of fun spots where we could play the slots or catch a show?"

"I don't know—"

Berea stepped back, pulling me with her and away from the others.

"If Kendyl is offering to take us out, we should go!"

"Go, enjoy yourself. I'll be fine," I said quickly.

"We're just here the weekend and it would be horrible of you *not* to let me have fun, even if you're not interested, but are you really okay with being alone? Won't you get bored?"

"Go!" I repeated, "Have a good time. Enjoy yourself. I have some work I can do."

"You *brought* work?"

"When is there ever not some type of writing that needs to be done?"

"Fair enough," Berea said, conceding with a smirk. "Fine, but don't be mad at me later because you chose to be boring and stay in."

"I promise to never throw this back in your face," I vowed.

Berea gave an excited squeal and skipped back to Kendyl.

Levi fell in line beside me again.

"You really just want to go back to your room to get work done or were you just tired of Kendyl?" Levi asked.

I looked over to him and smiled. We stood there for a moment and then I finally gave him a noncommittal shrug.

He smiled.

"That's what I thought," he said. "I'll walk you back to your hotel."

"I didn't even say anything," I insisted, half-heartedly defending myself.

"You didn't have to. I can read you surprisingly well, considering that we've just met."

"No, I don't think it's surprising at all. You're the type of person that notices everything about everyone."

He laughed.

"Is that right? How would you know?"

"Because I can read you surprisingly well, you know, considering we've just met," I teased.

"Really, though," Levi insisted. "Why do you have that impression of me?"

"It was the way you were with the woman on the set."

"What about it?"

"She clearly wanted you but you didn't seem that interested, at least not in the same way she was."

"It's acting," Levi reminded me.

"Don't try to play me," I said with a laugh. "You read her perfectly and she clearly had an orgasm, but from what I could tell, you weren't into her at all."

"That's right," Levi agreed, bumping my shoulder flirtatiously, "someone bumped into something off set and the scene was stopped before I could get *into* anything."

I muttered an apology that just made him laugh even more.

"It's fine, Piper," Levi assured me with a sly smirk.

The way my name sounded when he said it gave me chills. It was wrong that he could be so much of *everything.* He made my brain feel completely discombobulated.

"You're right, by the way," Levi added. "She isn't my type. To be honest, no one in this industry is."

"Well, you're definitely *America's* type."

"What a compliment," Levi said, clearly amused.

"I'm sorry. I honestly did mean that as a compliment but it came out sounding horrible."

"You're forgiven—but I wasn't actually offended."

He stopped walking and I realized we were already standing in the hotel lobby.

"Thanks," I stammered awkwardly, "for walking me to the elevator," I felt like I had to say something.

"You're welcome. Are we meeting tomorrow for me to be interviewed?"

"Yes."

"What time?"

"Whatever works best for you," I said quickly.

"I'll come by around noon?" Levi suggested.

The elevator dinged and the doors automatically opened.

"Sure—thanks again," I said, giving him an awkward good-bye wave and waved for the attendant to hold the elevator for me. Just as the doors eclipsed closed, I saw Levi peek over his shoulder at me one more time. Was he regretting not asking me out? No, I was just delusional due to jet lag.

"Miss? What floor?"

"Twenty-nine, please," I stammered.

Shit. I'd forgotten anyone else was even in the elevator. He was a bellhop, taking up someone's luggage in a long golden cart. How had I missed *that?* I mumbled to the floor and in my peripheral vision I saw him smile as he reached over and pushed my number.

5

PROBLEMATIC LOVE:

I did something incredibly unique—at least for me—today. I watched a porn scene being filmed and it was incredibly erotic.

Why did I like it? No idea. Why did it turn me on? The answer to that is an even bigger *no idea*. All right, that's a cop-op, so I'll try to give an answer.

I think I liked it because you're envious the whole time, it's the ultimate tease. You want to be them or at least you want to be a person in the situation. It's like seeing a fantasy in the flesh. It's completely unexpected and so captivating. Maybe that's why people like watching porn because you can vicariously live through the actors.

Ironically, being on the set wasn't even the best part.

It was even more interesting to watch the interaction between them. I was expecting to see mutual sex where both parties are getting something out of it, but I was surprised that Levi (the male porn star) seemed detached. He made her want him, but he gave her nothing of himself.

Perhaps I'm naive, but even when sex was your job I assumed you'd at least enjoy it. No one was forcing him to do porn and he did have an erection, but still being with her touched nothing in him. I'm not even sure if it would have even led to him reaching his own climax—the scene ended before we got that far.

This sounds incredibly sexist, but I never thought I'd see a man have sex when he really didn't want to. This really may just be a *job* for him.

I'd showered, changed into my some loose, non-sexy sleepwear and got to work when I'd gotten back to my room. I figured I'd write a little and then maybe whilst typing away I'd come up with some extra questions I could have Levi answer during the interview tomorrow.

I'd written almost three mini columns, blogs, rantings, not really sure what you would call them, when my phone buzzed.

RANDOM NUMBER: Are you still up? This is Levi.

I read it and was immediately flustered. Just one text and my brain began stuttering as it tried to come up with some cool-chic-witty response. I quickly added his number but when it got to his name I typed a nickname instead. My phone buzzed as soon as I hit save, with another message.

ADONIS: Want to go grab some real food?
ME: We already ate.
ADONIS: Don't lie. You thought that food was disgusting.

I smiled down at my phone. It was true.

ME: What did you have in mind?
ADONIS: Meet me down in the lobby in five.

You should just say no, my boring brain told me. *You don't really know him that well.*

It took all of half a second for me to tell my brain to sit down and shut the fuck up. I was in Vegas, and he was the most god-like man I'd ever met and I was hungry. Why not get dinner with him?

Excited, I slipped my clothes from earlier back on; mildly gross, but necessary. I'd only brought two outfits and a set of comfy clothes for the flight back. I ran to the bathroom. Dampening my hands, I quickly applied a light layer of product, trying to freshen up my curls, but I got frustrated and threw my hair up into a messy bun.

I grabbed a jacket, my purse, my hotel key and briskly flew down the hallway. Levi was facing the opposite direction of me but even at the sight of him my stomach flipped. I could feel the panic bubbling. What was I doing? He was so out of my league. Levi turned around, smiling when he saw me.

I twisted my hands in my coat pockets nervously. I took a very deep breath and told myself to woman up.

"I almost thought you weren't coming," Levi said as we walked out of the lobby, "but then I remembered girls are always late."

"Sorry," I apologized quickly.

"It's fine. I'm only teasing."

Before I'd even walked through the doors, I caught the hunter green paint glimmering in the hotel lights of a car parked directly in front of the entrance way. It was a '77 Pontiac Trans-Am Brewster Green, black leather; all soul. I discreetly wiped a drool drop away from my mouth.

"Of course you'd have my favorite car," I muttered unbelievingly.

"Are you judging me, Piper?"

"Yes," I answered without censor. I immediately clamped my hand over my mouth.

Levi roared with laughter.

"I restored it myself if that makes it any better. Is it really your favorite car?"

"Yes!" I said again. Then, for fear of sounding like a mindless parrot, I added, "My mother and I lived in this tiny, tiny apartment for a while and car auctions were the only channel we got. I've loved this car since I was ten."

"Do you want to drive it?"

"No!" I shouted too loudly and then laughed at my own dramatic response.

42

"One day you should," Levi said as he opened the passenger door. I was about to insist again that I really didn't want to drive it when I realized he was actually opening the door for me. I slid a hand over the interior as I got in; perfectly smooth—just like him.

Levi reached over, took my coat and purse from my lap and tucked them behind my seat. The car roared to life. He pulled out of the parking lot slowly, but as soon as he hit the street the acceleration thrust me back into the leather seats.

"Had to show off at least once tonight," Levi said as he eased his speed back to legal.

I watched Levi as he drove through the Vegas strip. His tendons flexed as he maneuvered the car. He shifted gears with ease, in complete control, palming the wheel whenever we turned. I understood now why men and cars were so sexy, but that didn't make me feel any less of a basic bitch. I was growing increasingly more physically attracted to him and pretty sure that I was in danger of becoming a swooning romance-novel-cover heroine.

I was most ashamed of the fact that I didn't actually mind.

"You never told me where we're going," I said.

"Right—sorry! Just outside the strip is this great diner that only locals appreciate; burgers, shakes, fries—classic American food."

"I love fries."

Levi grinned.

"I knew we'd have a lot in common," Levi confessed.

We parked in a paid parking ramp and then headed back out to the street. I was glad I had left my coat in the car; it was still pretty warm out—the air was dry and hot—the blazer would have made me sweat, and smelling like hot onions was only sexy for ogres.

The diner was tucked just around the corner from where we'd parked but I was thankful for the blast of frosty air- conditioned wind as we walked in.

"You must like the heat," I commented as I led him to a booth.

"No, not really."

"Then, why stay?" I questioned.

"Work," Levi answered simply.

"There are other places to *work*. Aren't there?" I would assume so but, then again, Las Vegas was the home of debauchery in the States.

A middle-aged plump woman rolled over to our table. She leaned in close to Levi and gave him a maternal kiss on the cheek.

"How've you been, Darby?"

"Right as rain; who did you bring home to meet me?"

"This is Piper; she's a writer from out East."

"You better be sweet to my boy," Darby warned with a wink. "What can I get you both to eat?"

"Are you ready to order?" Levi asked me.

"Almost. I'll go after you."

"I always get the same thing," Levi said with a smooth smirk. "Sure you don't want more time, Pi?"

I had formally hated that nickname. When Evette had been my mom, long before *Galaxy* existed, she used to call me Pi. Usually it was coupled with a horrible rendition of "Sugar Pie Honey-bunch" in an attempt to cheer me up, but the way it rolled off Levi's tongue—I was shocked at myself. I'd known him not even twenty-four hours and I was already willing to let him call me anything he wanted.

"I'll have an olive burger, chili cheese fries, extra ketchup and a diet," I ordered.

Levi smirked.

"What?" I asked defensively. "I have to have diet because I'm allergic to corn syrup."

"Bring two shakes too, chocolate for me."

"It's all-natural ice cream," Darby reassured me, "no artificial sweeteners."

"Then I'll have a strawberry malt."

"Change that to a chocolate *malt* for me as well. I didn't mean to stare," he added when Darby was gone. "You just make me miss home."

"How's that? Aren't you from here?"

"No," Levi explained, "I'm actually from Michigan. I moved out here five years ago."

"Really? I'd never have guessed, but I'm not from Michigan."

"I know, but there's still something about you that reminds me of home."

I felt like that was a really sweet, honest thing to say to someone. I twisted the edge of my napkin.

"So, what is your usual meal?" I asked.

"Same thing you ordered, but with a Sprite."

"This isn't how I'd imagined you'd be like at all."

Levi gave me a curious, slightly alarmed look.

"How'd you imagine me?" he asked.

"I don't know, but it seems unfair that you're so fuckable *and* likeable. Usually it's one or the other." As soon as it slipped out, I wish I hadn't said it quite like that. I looked over at him nervously but he looked neither shocked nor offended. He just looked like he was thinking about what I'd said, as if my opinion mattered. Of course it didn't. The likelihood of us seeing each other again after this weekend was slim. Maybe that was why I was being so blunt.

Darby set the shakes down neatly in front of us and Levi immediately ate the whipped cream in one scoop.

"I had questions I wanted to ask you at dinner, but that meal was sort of a disaster. For the record, Kendyl chose that place to eat, not me," he told me.

I nodded in agreement. I chewed up the delicious cherry that had crowned my whipped cream.

"It's because it's that fancy shit that no one really ever eats. Whenever we have any type of business dinner she always wants to go there. It's horrible; she is too ridiculous to realize that expensive doesn't equal good all the time."

I raised an eyebrow at him. "Tell me how you *really* feel."

Levi laughed.

"Too honest? Sorry, you're just one of those people that everyone feels comfortable with."

"No," I disagreed, "I think it's just your perception of me. Everyone else thinks I'm too cynical."

"Tell me about your work," Levi said, leaning back in the booth.

I smiled and shook my head no.

"I've been trying to keep the details under wraps," I said coyly.

"My lips are sealed," Levi promised.

"Really? Go-Go references?"

"A good song is a good song; I don't care who sings it. How about this," Levi added, twirling his napkin on the table. "I'll ask a question and then you can ask me a question."

"Only work related?"

"I can accept that as a ground rule."

"Will we still do the interview tomorrow?"

"That's fine with me, " Levi confirmed.

"All right," Darby said, as she neared the table. "I've got both of your charmingly identical orders ready to be gnawed on."

My eyes widened. The portions were epic. I was pretty sure the greasy-fried aroma was making me drool.

"Looks good, right?" Levi said.

I nodded and reached for the ketchup bottle.

"You're not one of those *ladies* who won't talk and eat, are you?"

"As long as you're not one of those *men* who is grossed out when a piece of food escapes my mouth."

Levi bit into his burger with hungry zeal.

"Ask me a question first," Levi said between chews.

"How often do you come here?"

"That's really what you want to use your first question on?" he asked.

"No—," I said, dunking a cheese-covered, chili-glazed fry into the pond of ketchup I had created on my plate. "What made you decide to become a porn star?"

"Money. Explain in detail the thesis of your writing project."

"That was dirty," I said. I'm sure it was barely audible because I'd taken a strategically large bite out of my burger thinking I'd have time before I'd need to talk again, but I'd be a good sport and play the game.

"You promise not to tell?"

"Of course, Pi."

I pointed a fry at him.

"I'm serious," I said.

His smile felt like a challenge.

"Stop stalling," Levi said.

"I'm doing an expose on the theory that women can have sexually satisfying sex without getting emotionally involved with their partners."

"Repeated occurrences?"

"Yes."

"Same partners?"

"Not necessarily."

"Your turn," Levi said.

"I gave you a better answer than you gave me. Plus you asked little sub-questions."

He smiled, waving a hand at me to continue.

"How did you know you'd like being in the porn industry?"

"Money. Were you trying to prove your theory by having sex with various partners?"

"Nope; no more information until you answer my questions. You're two in the hole right now."

"Fair enough—what were those questions again?"

I gasped in feigned disgust. "You're not even listening to me?"

"Ah, I remember now—why did I become a porn star and how did I know that I'd like it? I didn't know that I'd like it, but I have a strong work ethic and I'm good at giving people what they want. I like anything that's simple, quick and easy."

"What do you spend all your money on?"

"I save it," Levi said as he swirled the last fry on his plate around in ketchup.

"For what?"

"Retirement—looks don't last forever, Pi."

I laughed at his practical answer even though I believed him.

"We're even now for my early shenanigans. Will you answer my unanswered question now?

"My plan was—at least at first—for me to sleep with different people."

"How did you select them?"

"Social media posts, asking them to fill out an online application."

"I hope it included proof of them being STD free."

"It did. There would have been condoms used, but sex wasn't a guarantee. It was more of an 'if the vibe was right' kind of understanding."

"That's still pretty dangerous. You have no idea who you'd be meeting with."

"Well, you're the last person I'm meeting with and like they mentioned at dinner, the whole thing was a flop. I never slept with anyone."

"What are you going to do now?"

"Well, I didn't really tell anyone the details of what I wanted to do, so I'll just evolve my piece to work with what I have. I still think it'll be interesting, it just won't be as interesting as if I'd actually pulled off what I'd wanted to."

"I know tons of people that you could have noncommittal sex with, but I'm not going to help you."

"Why not?" I stammered.

Levi watched me for a moment. He looked like he was trying to calculate the best answer and when he spoke, it certainly *was* the best answer I could have imagined him saying.

"I don't want to help you, because I like you."

6

I was speechless and a little flattered, but that was quickly diminished when I thought about what those words meant. Sex for money was good enough for him, but free sex with multiple partners wasn't something I should be doing? That was a ridiculous double standard.

"Are you really going to take the moral high road with me?"

"Not at all; I think it's an interesting topic but I'm not going to help you sleep with random men. I could offer myself up to you, but I don't want to do that either."

"I'm really pissed off by that last sentence," I said honestly. The night had been going so well, but now I wished we'd driven separately.

"I meant it as a compliment," Levi said in a very controlled voice.

I defensively crossed my arms over my chest.

"I'd love to hear you explain how being repulsed by the idea of fucking me is a compliment."

"I swear," Levi vowed solemnly, "I didn't mean to offend you. It was one of those inside monologues that should never have actually been said aloud, but now that I've put it out there, I can't just take it back so I might as well own what I said."

I squinted my eyes at him and his cheeks reddened. A blush? Really? That completely threw me. Was Levi acting? Playing vulnerable? Trying to get me to trust him? If so, this was the most impressive back-pedaling I'd ever seen, and for what? I had no idea.

"Seriously, Piper," Levi insisted. "I have meaningless sex every other day and it's just that—empty, void, unsatisfying. I do it for the money; it's a means to an end. I'm really *moved* by you and I don't want to cheapen what could grow between us by having emotionless sex with you. I guess it's hard to believe that someone in my line of work has any substance to them."

Now I was the one who blushed. He actually *had* meant it as a compliment. Abruptly my brain hit the brakes—wait, he *liked* me? He was *moved* by me?

Levi watched me silently. I'm sure he was wondering what I was thinking just about as much as I was wondering if this was real, that somehow we'd gotten too honest over burger and fries or maybe this was just an act.

Neither of us gave the other any clues.

"Ready for the bill?" Darby asked.

"Yes," we both said in unison.

I'd been so sure I hadn't judged him, but the truth was I'd had my ideas about what type of man he was from the moment I saw him on set—even if it wasn't all negative it was still preconceived and if I dared to believe him, wrong.

We reached for the bill at the same time but I got there first.

"I'll pay," I insisted.

He gave a very seriously agitated expression and I quickly relented.

"This has been the oddest day for me," I mumbled.

"Not just for you," Levi said as he pulled out his wallet.

We walked back to his car. I felt awful. I'd had so much fun up until that last little bit.

"Levi, I'm sorry I—"

"It's fine. I shouldn't have assumed you were feeling what I was feeling. You're just very refreshing to be around, Pi. I got carried away. I know my career choice changes things and the only people who seem to not be bothered by it are people I'm not interested in."

"To be honest, I'm not sure what we're talking about. I was upset with you because you made an allusion to not wanting to sleep with me."

"Well, I'm an ass and can't string words together fluently. I was trying to be charming and instead I ruined a perfectly good dinner."

"It wasn't ruined," I insisted. "I had a good time."

"You're not just being nice?"

"I was trying to pay the bill as a peace offering but that just seemed to piss you off even more."

"I find the thought of you *paying* to spend time with me repulsive."

"Well fuck, I hadn't meant it like *that*," I said.

"Truce?" Levi asked, leaning past me to open the car door.

"Fine by me," I agreed.

Levi turned the key and the classic muscle car roared to life.

"Are you tired?" he asked.

"Not at all."

"Come have a drink with me, there's this great little spot not far from your hotel. They've got live music."

"All right," I agreed far too quickly. I couldn't say no, not after our truce. I wanted more time with him even if we seemed to misunderstand every word that came out of each other's mouth.

We drove listening to an oldies station. The city was fantastic. The later it got, the more alive the town felt. It was thrilling to drive past all neon lights, beautiful buildings, but I couldn't imagine every night being like this. I wonder if nights in Vegas ever felt normal.

"That's the spot," Levi said, jabbing his thumb towards my window as he drove. "There's a parking garage a couple blocks down."

It was a quick, short walk and when we came through the front doors the music hit me like a warm summer breeze as soon as we entered Tippin' and Sippin'.

"They play a little bit of everything here. I love it!"

He reached behind me for my hand. I shyly gave it to him, letting him guide me through the crowded front to an empty booth in the back.

"I'll go get us something from the bar. What would you like?"

"Something super sweet."

He nodded and strode away.

I idly checked my phone. I had a couple of messages from Berea.

52

BEREA: Kendyl is so drunk and she is telling me everything. She wants Levi bad.

BEREA: You're okay, right? Not angry at me for leaving you at the hotel?

I quickly typed a message back to her.

ME: I went out with Levi. Got some food, now we're at a bar.

Almost instantly I received a text back.

BEREA: WHAT? OMG!
ME: IKR! He's so hot and so out of my league, yet here we are.
BEREA: HIT IT HARD.

A thick glass bottle appeared in front of me.

"Do you like ciders? They had a seasonal blueberry honey one that I thought you'd like," Levi said. "It sounded sickly sweet."

"That's fine. If you're ever in New York, I'll take you to this great beer garden where there's Karaoke and amazing cider—well, and of course beer."

"Yeah?"

I nodded. "It's Berea's favorite spot that she found in Little Italy."

"I'll have to make sure I visit New York then."

"Where in Michigan did you grow up?"

"On the east side of the state in a city called Flint."

"I've heard of Flint, it's notorious."

He grinned. "Just like me."

"Do you have siblings?" I asked.

"One blood brother and a couple of halves; I only know of two but I'm sure there's more. My father wasn't an honorable man."

"My dad left when I was a kid. Don't know him and I'd like to keep it that way."

53

"Do you have siblings?" Levi asked.

"No, but Berea is like a sister. I love this place!"

Levi nodded and I stretched back in the booth, placing my feet up beside him in the booth across from me. His hand curled around my ankle and I immediately went to move my feet back down, realizing maybe it was rude of me to be so informal.

He didn't move my feet; instead his thumb tapped against my skin in beat. His hand slipped up flirtatiously under the hem of my jeans. The band was playing slow jazz and the combination of his hand on my calf and the rich tones felt seductive.

"Do you want to dance?" Levi asked.

"Do *you* want to dance?" I asked, trying to be "cool" even though I was feeling pretty hot and bothered.

Levi smiled, nodding yes.

"This is feeling awfully like a date," I commented, scooting out of the booth.

"Good." Levi stretched his hand out to me and I followed to the dance floor.

He spun me in a slow single twirl that guided me right into his arms. I let him lead, following his movements easily.

"I thought this was going to be the part where you told me you didn't know how to dance," he said in my ear as we swayed.

"You smell good," I accidentally blurted out.

He pulled back and smirked at me.

"Do I?" he asked.

"I have no idea why I just told you that," I muttered.

"I have a rare genetic abnormality that allows my glands to secrete what humans would deem as 'good-smelling' pheromones."

"I take it back. I was lying to boost your self-esteem."

"I love the way you lie," Levi purred. "Keep going."

I laughed and relaxed a little more into him. He would have been easy to follow even if I hadn't known how to dance. Berea and I danced all the time. It was the best way to blow off steam. You didn't need drugs or drink, you just need to dance.

"People are starting to stare," Levi said, turning me slightly.

I pulled back abruptly and he was right.

"Neither of us realized the music wasn't slow anymore."

My ears snapped back, it was some upbeat fast song now. Levi gave me a final spin that ended with him kissing my hand.

"What a flirt," I said, even though I was gushing inside.

"We should probably call it a night. I have no idea what time it is, but it has to be late. We'll have to go dancing again sometime," he said as he took my hand.

"Right," I said with a laugh, "we'll do it all when you come to New York."

I wondered if he was being serious. I'd just assumed this was his normal flirty, charming, sexy self—it was just dawning on me that maybe he did really like me. My stomach flipped at the idea.

The drive back was quiet. I'm sure that part of it was that we were both tired, but it also felt more like the kind of silence where you're just drinking in everything. It had been an epic twelve hours that I wouldn't soon, if ever, forget.

When Levi parked in front of the hotel's door, I reached around into the back to retrieve my purse and jacket. He immediately moved to help me and our arms rubbed together as they crossed. I felt my skin prickle into little goose bumps. Neither of us moved away. I felt his fingers curl around my wrist and his thumb stroke softly against my palm. I wondered if he could feel my pulse quicken.

His body shifted, his free hand sweeping across my face to hook my hair behind my shoulder. I finally looked up at him. The lights from the hotel lit up his eyes; his dark features were raw. He wanted me. He leaned forward, resting his forehead against mine. I'd never felt so seduced in my life. I'd give myself to him, if only he'd ask. I knew these were dangerous emotions but I didn't care.

"I want to kiss you so badly," Levi said.

"Then why don't you?" I whispered.

Levi tipped my head back and lightly kissed the curve of my jaw line. I closed my eyes. I felt like putty and I'd never wanted to be molded so badly in my life.

"I like you more than you like me, Piper."

"You're making assumptions," I murmured.

"What are we doing?"

"Talking too much," I muttered.

He laughed and I opened my eyes.

"Let's sleep on it then," Levi said, pulling away. I felt the void as soon as he wasn't as near.

"What time do you want to meet tomorrow and where?" he asked.

The interview; I'd forgotten why I was even in Vegas. I thought for a moment, trying to determine where we should meet and at what time.

"We could get lunch and talk."

"Yeah, sure," I mumbled.

I felt confused. I thought Levi had been trying to let me know he wanted this force between us to stick to a strictly professional path.

The moment I moved to exit the car, his hands were on my face pulling me to him. Levi held me to his mouth as if he were afraid I'd run away—and oh, how contrary that was to my idea of what we should be doing. I'd never been kissed like that in my *life*. He oozed pure masculinity and that spoke to every part of my body. I bowed under him. If anything, I wanted more, to get closer, but I couldn't move. I was too enthralled with everything he was doing to me with just a kiss.

When he finally did pull back, his heavy breathing matched my own and we studied each other for second, as if we needed a moment to make sure *this* was really happening. Then he came back to me, giving me a second tender kiss. I simmered. I sparked. My soul sang. I realized then that my body wasn't broken, it had just never been woken up.

"Do you like pancakes?" Levi asked.

His words sounded weirdly sexy in my turned-on stupor.

"Yes," I answered slowly.

"Text me when you wake up tomorrow, okay?"

I nodded in agreement.

"Thank you for going to dinner with me, Piper."

"Thank you for asking me.   I'll see you tomorrow. Goodnight, Levi."

7

"You're finally back!" exclaimed an excited and drunk Berea before I could fully even open the hotel room door.

"Did you have fun with Kendyl?" I asked sweetly.

"Don't you *dare* change the subject! Where did you go with Levi?"

I shimmied out of my jacked, kicked my shoes off and began searching through the room for my earlier discarded sweat pants.

"Exactly where my text said we went: to dinner and then to a bar with live music."

"Are you and Levi going to...?"

"God, I hope so, but honestly when could that even happen?"

"Tomorrow?"

"He wants to 'talk' tomorrow."

"About what?" Berea asked eagerly.

"Don't know, maybe he just meant the interview."

"I bet that's not what he meant. Lucky, lucky!"

I laughed.

"One night in Vegas and you're a professional gambler, huh?"

"He probably wants to set up ground rules for your love affair."

The idea of having an affair with him made my mouth go dry. *Shit.* I had to stop thinking about him or I'd never be able to sleep again. I began to dig in my suitcase, looking for my tank top and sweats I'd packed.

"You should have rolled up your clothes when you packed. You can carry more and it's easier to find everything," Berea said.

"I'll pay you to pack for me next time," I promised sarcastically.

When I finally found some black loose-fitting sweats and a tank top, I sambaed to the bathroom.

"Did I mention we kissed?"

"NO!" Berea squealed. "Well, damn! My night was interesting too, but I would have preferred your scenario. Are you even slightly interested in hearing about Kendyl's and Levi's past?"

I poked my head back out the bathroom door.

"I'm assuming they've fucked?" I guessed.

"Nailed it," Berea giggled. "He was a boyfriend for hire basically. She needed a date to some porn event and then the next morning offered him a job."

I felt like the normal response should be shock or disgust, but the idea of how much *experience* he had was a turn on for me. Everything about Levi was hot and I wanted to get scalded.

"Now she *pines* for him," Berea continued, "and he refuses to sleep with her again. He's not interested. He won't date anyone he works with and if he thinks you like him, he's not even cordial offset. It's just business, making money, that's it. The man draws a hard line between work and pleasure."

"I'm not looking to date him," I reminded her.

Berea flashed me a devilishly daring grin. "I bet you a hundred dollars he can fix your problem."

I snorted and went back inside the bathroom. After I had gone through the normal nightly rituals, I turned off the lights as I headed back towards my bed. Checking my phone as I hooked it up to a charger, I noticed a few missed texts from Berea. They must've come through while I was dancing. God—Levi really had smelled good. I was a little embarrassed that even my nose was attracted to him.

I didn't have any texts from him though. I thought about sending him one, telling him I'd had a good time, thanking him for dinner—but, somehow that felt needy.

I flung myself down on the bed beside Berea. Right now I just needed sleep.

My phone buzzed on the night table and I silenced the alarm quickly.

I squinted at my phone; it was only a quarter to eight and I had a missed text from Levi. He'd sent it at the crack of dawn.

ADONIS: Last night was great. When are you going back to New York?

I grinned like an idiot as my thumbs blazed across the screen formulating a response.

ME: Heading back early on Sunday. Are we still getting pancakes?
ADONIS: Yes. I'll bring them to you.

"Levi is bringing us pancakes!"
What?" Berea mumbled incoherently.
"I don't want to like him," I groaned.
"What are you talking about?"
"Wake up!" I yelled, nudging her in the back.
Groggily, Berea finally sat up.
"What time is it?" Berea asked.
"Quarter to eight."
"Heifer, you better go back to sleep," Berea growled as she slumped back down into the comforter. She was asleep again in seconds.
There was no way I was going back to sleep. I sent Levi another message.

ME: Why are we having pancakes?
ADONIS: Because we like each other.
ME: Are you trying to court me?
ADONIS: Yes.
ME: Why?
ADONIS: You're the only person I've wanted to have pancakes with in years.

ME: You're very serious about your breakfast foods.

No response back. I hoped I hadn't teased him too much. I decided to send one more text so he knew I was only teasing.

ME: ;)
ADONIS: xo

"HOLY SHIT, BEREA! He just texted me a hug and kiss. You need to wake up right the fuck now."

Berea shot straight up like she'd just risen from the dead

"Let me see!" she screamed.

I watched her face as she read, wondering if I was reading too much into all of this.

"Well," Berea said with a smirk, "he's seriously flirting with you. Didn't you mention he was bringing breakfast?"

"Yeah, pancakes."

"I love pancakes! Since I'm up, give me the details!"

I filled her in with an overly detailed version of my night.

"He drinks diet?"

"No—but he does like olive burgers, and he drives my dream car. Is it weird that we're so much alike?"

"Clearly you're soulmates, because olives are disgusting."

"But it'll never work," I sighed.

"You don't know that," Berea insisted.

"We don't even live on the same side of the country," I reminded her.

"Isn't he loaded? Plus it's not like adult films are only shot here or he'll never have any down time."

"We're leaving tomorrow."

"So have a fling and leave tomorrow," Berea said with a shrug. "This is your perfect opportunity to actually prove your thesis *and* what a story this'll make. Your future grandkids will love it."

I hopped off the bed and straight for the shower.

"Ride him like a thoroughbred!" Berea shouted after me.

"You're ridiculous," I said, shaking my head.

Not even an hour later there was a knock on the hotel door. I pinched myself in a bizarre attempt to stop grinning. I didn't want to come on as some super-intense female. I could do casual. I could do fun. I took a deep breath and opened the door.

One look at him and that stupid grin was back.

Levi pressed a light kiss against my cheek and walked into the room.

"Hey, Pi. I brought enough breakfast for you too, Berea, if you're hungry."

Berea pranced over to the table he'd set the bags on.

"How sweet of you," she said approvingly.

Levi had gotten way more food than three people would ever need. I watched in awe as he unpacked, eggs, bacon, toast, pancakes and—best of all—pancake toppings: fruit, drizzles, whipped cream, chocolate-chip morsels.

"Levi, this is amazing! Thank you."

Levi shot a dazzling smile over his shoulder.

"You're welcome, Pi. Now, there are normal pancakes, but since you and I seem to be synced-up when it comes to food, I got us chocolate-chip pancakes."

"I'm impressed," Berea said, as she continued to fill her plate. "Those are her favorite. We practically lived off of them through college, especially that first year."

"What was Piper like in college?" Levi asked.

Berea shrugged and popped a chocolate chip in her mouth. "Neither of us has really changed. What you see is what you get."

A little while later, we'd cleared away the food containers and were sitting across from each other at the table. Berea had gotten a call from

Kendyl and they were off gallivanting somewhere. I think Berea genuinely liked her, even though with the information she'd given me last night about Kendyl's past with Levi, I imagine Berea was also keeping her preoccupied as an unspoken favor to me.

"Ready?" I asked.

"You're so serious," Levi said a soft, intimate smile.

I felt his long legs stretch and his shoes kick off. His socked foot began to rub methodically against my ankle. I could have just moved my foot but I liked this secret touching. I stretched a little closer and his foot worked its way up my calf.

"That shouldn't feel as good as it does," I said under my breath.

"I'm ready to start when you are, Pi."

"Describe the difference between sex on the clock and sex for fun?"

"Great question," Levi teased in a very formal, unlike-him tone. "There's really no difference between casual sex and getting-paid-for sex. Love makes all the difference.

"Do you have committed relationships?"

"If the shoe fits, yes, but it seems to rarely fit."

"Maybe you need to try a different brand of shoe," I suggested.

Levi laughed.

"That's exactly what I've been thinking," he agreed.

"What is your favorite type of shoe?" I asked.

He leaned forward trying to catch a glimpse of the questions and I quickly shifted away.

"Comfortable ones. Was that really on your list, Pi?"

"Mr. Gallant, which gender do you think is more likely to get attached in a frequent sexual relationship?"

"I think it depends on the person. I don't believe it can be defined by gender."

"What about for you?" I asked.

"I might fall first."

"Might?" I asked, pushing for a better answer.

"I'm not usually that affected by sex. I like it, but it's rarely magical."

"I completely understand what you mean."

Levi's face had become completely serious. He caught me with those green eyes and I felt compelled to answer him. Clyde's hurt words echoed in my mind. *Cold. Unfeeling.* I licked my lips, sucking on my bottom one as I tried to formulate the best answer that wouldn't make me sound—broken.

"Turn the recorder off for a moment, Pi."

I obeyed and with a few tabs on my laptop, everything we said would stay just between us.

"I assumed you weren't a virgin."

"I'm not," I answered quickly. My voice was oddly layered with emotion. I swallowed, stuffing whatever those *feelings* were back down before they couldn't be felt too much. I was just starting to think he was seriously interested in me and I would hate for this to be the moment that changed that.

"You've just never had *good* sex?"

"Something like that," I mumbled.

"You're holding something back. What is your thesis really about?"

"I want to prove that women are capable of having emotionless sex."

"Why?"

"Why not?" I said a little more defensively then I'd meant to.

He sat back more in his chair and studied me closely.

"I want you to trust me," Levi said quietly, "and I'm willing to earn that trust."

"Why does it matter if I trust you or not?"

"I'll give you a real answer if you give me one. What did you mean when you said 'magical' sex?"

Being honest with him could cause two reactions: either he'd be weirded out or he'd be determined to be the man to finally make me come. Admittedly, I'd like him to be the dream man who could, but if he

64

couldn't then I couldn't be in denial anymore. I'd finally have to face the fact that it's me and not the world. I'd have to accept the fact that my lady bits were *defective*.

As Levi watched me ponder his offer, a smile twitched at the corners of his mouth.

"You should gamble at least once while you're here, Pi."

"What happens in Vegas really does stay in Vegas?"

"I'll never tell anyone what you tell me," Levi promised.

"Fine, but I'm going first."

I twisted my hands in my lap as I calculated how I wanted to say it. In the end I defaulted to my comfort zone: direct.

"I've never had an orgasm."

Levi's eyes widened.

"Even when you masturbate?"

"That's two questions," I warned. "Do I get two real answers about your life?"

"You'll get three, because I have one more after you answer that one."

"Fine. No, not even when I—masturbate." I blushed as the words slipped out. What an insanely personal truth to tell someone you were attracted to and didn't know that well.

"Have you ever been in love?" I asked, desperate to turn the limelight back on him.

"No," Levi answered just as directly.

"Why? Are you against love? You said you weren't against committed relationships, so why would you have one without love?"

"My heart is defective. I'm broken."

I was stunned. Levi had everything: looks, women, money, fame. How could he think he was broken?

I reached forward across the table and took his hand in mine.

"You're not," I said affectionately.

Levi leaned in.

"Then neither are you."

I felt my face redden again. How had this stranger (who already didn't feel like a stranger) gotten me to tell him all my secrets? And he understood them. He was making my soul start to feel free.

There was a rapid knock on the hotel door.

"Housekeeping!"

"Let's go so she can clean," Levi suggested, getting up from the table.

"What about the interview?"

"This weekend isn't going to be the last time I see you, unless you want it to be.

"No—yes—no."

I paused for a moment then tried again. "I don't want it to be the last time. Where do you want to go?"

"Lots of places; I have the whole day planned."

8

"You didn't have other plans for today, did you?"

"No—at least, nothing set in stone."

Levi had just parked the car in front of the Nevada State Museum. I'd finally managed to get out of him that we'd be museum hopping all day. The museum almost blended into its dusty dry surroundings. We past a Nevada state-shaped sign and the heat felt like it was toasting my shoulders as we walked. My not-so-hidden inner nerd was very excited.

"It's not super fancy," Levi said.

"I don't museum discriminate."

I felt him reach for my hand as he laughed. His light touch felt so natural but was still so exhilarating. We walked in silence for a while, moving through the exhibit, stopping when I wanted to stop.

"How many times have you been here?" I asked as we neared a large skeleton of a mammoth.

"A few," Levi confessed.

"I read an article about scientists who wanted to try and bring them back."

"What would be the point?" Levi asked. "Did you know there's only one male white rhino left in the whole world? We poach for greed. We don't even deserve what we barely have left."

I bit my lip to keep back a smile. Obviously, this was no joking matter.

"Clearly you're not a fan of that idea and no, I did not know there was only one male white rhino left or that there were even white rhinos." I said.

"Sorry," Levi said, laughing, "I get a little worked up about animals."

"Perhaps you should give up your cozy life here in Vegas and join the Sea Shepherds," I teased.

"Ha! Now that is funny. Those people are ridiculous. If the whale is already dead, what good does it do to destroy the carcass? No there is really no value to the whale's life at all. I get their point, but sometimes a point is just a point. It's not worth killing humans over it and," Levi added with emphasis, "in certain parts of the world people actually eat whale."

"I love your blend of passion and practicality."

"Are you flirting with me?"

"I believe I am."

"That's a dangerous move, Pi."

Levi turned to me, the green of his eyes darkening to a mischievous shade of rich jade. The look he was giving me was so sizzling that it left me a little breathless and completely unable to articulate a response.

As we were driving to our next museum, I saw a sign for a custard shop and Levi asked me if I wanted to stop. Now we were seated in a little, cozy air-conditioned cafe and I was embarrassedly flustered watching him lick his cone. I, politely, had chosen to use a spoon.

"I hope you at least knew that cone's *name*," I muttered.

Levi's rich laugh saturated the air.

"No—but it's good practice."

I blushed, an image of him licking me like that cone filled my head.

"Always working, huh?" I teased.

Levi didn't look too amused.

"I have a personal life too, Pi. What kind of questions did you ask in your other interviews?"

"Sometimes they talked and I just listened," I said.

"Ask me something. I'm a fountain of sexual experience."

I leaned back in the booth, dug deep into my custard and asked the first cliché question that popped into my mind.

"Do you always start with oral, when you have sex?"

Levi's eyes widened a little.

"It's a great icebreaker."

"Some people say it's more intimate than sex."

"It can be," Levi agreed.

"How could it not be?" I tossed back.

"If there's no connection between the two people, it's just pleasure but when there's a real, deep-rooted attraction, mixed with emotional vulnerability, that's when oral sex is the most intimate and satisfying."

"What is your least favorite thing about sex?" I asked.

"When it's over."

I rolled my eyes at his response.

"You don't believe me?"

"Of course not."

"Fine." Levi thought for a moment and then said, "Is this in real-life sex or work-sex?"

"Either."

"My least favorite thing is when I want to make love to a women and she wants to fuck or vice versa. I like us to be on the same page with what we want and need."

That was an interesting response. He was okay with just fucking but only if that was what they both wanted. So what did I want? Were he and I on the same page? It felt too soon to know for sure.

"What are you thinking?" Levi asked.

I opened my mouth to quickly deny that any thinking had taken place but he wagged a finger at me.

"Be honest, Pi."

"I'm not sure that I want to be honest."

"Why? We've been pretty open with each other. Nothing horrible has happened."

"We just met last night," I reminded him.

"Yeah, but you've got to admit, it feels like we've known each other much longer."

69

That was true. We'd spent a lot of time together in the past thirty-six hours. I was very comfortable with him—possibly naively comfortable.

"Being this open isn't easy for me either," Levi confessed, "but I'm trying to be braver than I want to be."

That little omission gave me enough courage to say what I'd actually been thinking.

"I was wondering if I want to be fucked or romanced."

He reached past my almost empty custard cup and took my hand in his.

"You think I'm trying to just seduce you? I want to get to know you," Levi said.

I wanted that too.

My phone rang in my purse and our hands retreated back to their own sides of the table.

"Hello?"

"It's me," Berea chirped in my ear, "just calling to see if you and Levi have been married by Elvis yet."

"Very funny," I said.

"I think our friend is catching on that you've stolen her beau. She's been texting him nonstop and getting no response back."

"You didn't tell her that we've been together all day, did you?"

"Of course not, I'm no snitch!"

"I know, I know! I just don't want to cause any *drama.*"

"The pot has already been stirred, Piper! Kendyl's basic bitch senses are tingling. You might as well enjoy yourself. Kendyl invited me and you to a burlesque show tonight at some theater. You want to meet us there?"

"Sure!"

"She's been inviting Levi too, but you know, he's been too busy to text her back."

"God, if she's that awful we don't have to go tonight."

70

"No, she's actually really nice, she's just lonely. I'll text you the address."

We disconnected our call and I looked up to see Levi skimming through messages on his own phone.

"Kendyl has been trying to get a hold of me."

"Berea was just mentioning that. Is there something going on between you two?"

Levi immediately locked eyes with me and their expression was odd. He looked hopeful, as an inquiry about Kendyl meant that I was either interested, jealous or maybe a mix of both. I was surprised after the kiss we'd shared that he wasn't more confident.

"She's made her interest clear and I've made my lack of interest clearer."

Well, damn!

"I'll take any excuse to get to spend more time with you, Pi. Did you want to go to the show?"

I had to admit, I wanted to spend more time with him too.

"Yes, I'd like to go."

"Good, then we'll go. Kendyl said the show started at seven; it's only three now. Do you want to go to another museum?"

"What type?"

"Art."

"I'm down! Let's go!"

When we finally caught up with Berea, Kendyl's face crimsoned as soon as she saw us—bright, fire-hydrant red. *She knew instantly.* She snarled some angry words at Levi but I only caught his response back.

"We have some business to discuss on Monday," he said calmly.

I glanced at him curiously, wondering what *that* meant.

"Do we?" Kendyl retorted sharply. "Make an appointment then."

Berea winked at me, quickly linking arms with Kendyl and leading her away from us.

"What were you saying about the male acrobat that you know in the show tonight?"

"I like Berea," Levi said quietly beside me. "She's loyal."

"She likes you too."

"Was it the pancakes that won her over?"

"Probably," I said with a laugh.

"Good, I want her to approve."

Levi took my hand as he spoke, leading me the rest of the way down the steps. When we got to the row, he stepped back, ushering me down to sit next to Berea.

Kendyl's mood seemed to have improved with all the undivided attention Berea was giving her and I was glad. I hadn't meant to piss her off. In fact, I felt a little in debt to her. If she hadn't sought me out, I never would have met Levi and this whole weekend would never ever have happened.

The lights dimmed almost immediately the show was starting.

"Hey," Levi purred in my ear. "Let me come see you in New York."

"Are you serious?" I whispered back.

"I don't want the night to end without knowing if you'll let me see you again."

"Are you sure?"

"What kind of question is that?" Levi asked. His tone had a shocked edge to it and I realized I was being too stubborn and cautious. My brain was just wired to not accept a good thing. In my world, there was always a price for happiness. But I was willing to ignore my fears and acknowledge the mutual attraction that was growing between us.

"I'm sorry," I stammered, "I've just never met anyone like you."

"I've never met anyone like *you*," Levi said, with a small smirk.

The lights fully dimmed, and the show began.

Levi leaned in, close enough for his scruff to tickle the curve of my ear and his breath to warm my neck as he spoke.

"I have business in New York next week. Let me come visit you."

My mind was screaming no but the rest of me was chanting *yes*.

"Modeling," Levi said, answering my obvious next question. "My porn days are done."

I turned towards him, completely surprised. This was fast but it was real. If Levi would change for me, I'd change for him too. I'd take a chance. I'd have faith. I'd trust him.

"All right," I agreed.

"Yeah?"

"Yeah," I said, nodding excitedly.

"Don't waste my money," Kendyl snapped.

"Ignore her," Levi said to me.

Levi's curt response caused a flurry of angry sentences to fly down the row from Kendyl but my brain didn't process any of it. All I could think about was *him* and that I'd see him again in less than a week. Hell, forget throwing caution to the wind, launch it into space! I wanted Levi and I was willing to go as far as he was.

9

I heard a door slam and trotted excitedly to the window of my apartment that overlooked the front of our building. The six days had dragged on and on like an episode of *Just Shoot Me.* I'd tried to busy myself but I was far too excited to be able to distract myself. Still, there was that little part of my mind that told me it was only a matter of time before something bad happened. I didn't really know what, it was more like a gut feeling that I didn't deserve to be happy so things would ultimately turn to shit. What had I done to earn him? I couldn't come up with anything.

Berea excitedly slid down the hallway in socked feet.

"Is it him? Is he here?" Berea asked.

"Yes, and god he looks amazing."

"Scoot over—fuck," Berea cursed with a drawn-out whistle, "I forgot how pretty he is; lucky girl!"

I swallowed nervously. Berea was right. This was luck and only luck.

Levi bent down, leaning into the taxi to tip the driver and his ass looked amazing even from the fifth-floor window. I was lusting after him *bad,* but that was another thing I shamelessly didn't care about.

"There has to be something mentally wrong with him," I murmured.

"Shut-it!" Berea scolded. "None of this 'I'm not worthy' shit. Enjoy this gift from the gods."

Berea was right. I couldn't ruin this with overthinking *later.* Right now, I just wanted to be optimistically in the moment.

"Is that what you're wearing?" Berea asked.

"Yeah," I said.

She quickly scanned me up and down.

"You look cute. How long is Levi in town?"

"No idea."

Levi and I had talked a little. Just quick texts, normal "getting-to-know-you" chatter. Nothing too serious—it'd been nice. It was easy to talk to him and we were becoming real friends.

The door dinged and I jumped at the sound of the buzzer. Berea skipped down the hallway to her room, stopping at the door to buzz him in.

"I'm going to go hide now. Wouldn't want to be the weird drooling awkward roommate."

I laughed but got butterflies when I heard Levi knock. I walked as calmly as I could to the door, took a deep breath and opened it.

"Hey," Levi greeted me quickly, engulfing me in a hug that felt surprisingly natural considering we'd known each other a week. His hands lingered on my hips before dropping to grab his large suitcase.

I moved back so he could come inside.

"I hope you don't mind me stashing this here while we eat? I came straight from the airport," Levi explained.

"No, that's fine," I told him.

"Love your place," Levi said politely from the entrance way. "Don't you have a roommate? Berea lives with you, right? Does she want to eat with us?"

"I don't think so. She mentioned she had plans in a couple of hours. A blind date, I think."

"Mind if we head out then?" Levi asked.

"Not at all."

I slipped on some comfy walking ballet flats and slung my cross body over my light, loose-fitting navy sweater. I locked the door behind us, clinking the knob a few times left and right to make sure it was locked. OCD habits die hard.

"It just a few blocks from here, right?" Levi asked.

"Yes, and you'll love it! It's delicious."

As soon as we hit the sidewalk, I felt his long fingers link with mine. We fell into an easy stride. Being together felt so simple, casual even, but it still made me girlishly-giddy. I turned my face, giving the street traffic the smile I couldn't bite back.

"I love the city," Levi said.

"Me too," I agreed.

"Have you ever seen the Great Lakes? They're amazing. I used to think they were the ocean as a kid."

I smiled at the idea of him as a kid. He must have been ridiculously cute. We rounded the corner and arrived at the fantastic Puerto Rican style brunch restaurant I'd discovered by accident with Berea. It was like a catered styled buffet with *real* food, not that fake Ponderosa stuff. I'm taking about, eggs, steak, potatoes—and of course, mimosa.

We opened the door and were quickly seated at a table tucked in a corner. A pretty waitress took our drink order and we headed up to the catered styled buffet. This restaurant was self-serve.

We didn't waste any time. I'd always had a good appetite. I self-consciously filled my plate. I turned a little, glancing over my shoulder at Levi and caught him piling his own plate up twice as high as mine. I smiled and relaxed a little. I was in good company. I could trust him. I could be real. He wasn't going to judge me. I had to stop letting my brain force personality traits on him that he clearly didn't have.

We both made it back to the table at the same time, which was perfect because I hadn't really wanted to be polite and wait for him to start eating. I was starving.

"This doesn't count as my date-date, does it?" Levi asked between bites.

I looked at him curiously over my glass of water.

"I suppose you could take me to my mom's gala dinner as a date-date."

"When?"

"This Friday; how long did you say you'd be in town for?"

"At least a couple of weeks. Hopefully longer." He smiled and began eating again. "Is the gala for your magazine?"

"Yep, we've had some sort of party every year since conception. My mom thinks she's clever because 'gala' is the first four letters of 'galaxy.'"

He laughed, nodding appreciatively.

"It *is* clever."

"Are you being sarcastic?" I asked, with mock offense.

"Will you be wearing a devastatingly romantic dress?"

"Yes, and I can even swing a tux for you."

"I have a tux."

I felt like an idiot. Of course he had a tux.

"Come on," Levi said, getting up from the table, "I want seconds."

"How do you keep your girlish figure if you eat this much?" I teased.

"Extra cardio," Levi said with a wink.

With our full stomachs, it felt like it took us twice as long to make it back to the apartment and even longer to lug ourselves up the flights of stairs.

"What floor was it again?" Levi asked.

"Oh god—so full—shit, we passed it!"

Levi smirked.

"And how long have you lived here?" he asked.

I laughed, playfully nudging him as we shuffled back down a floor to my apartment. I kicked off my shoes and flew to the couch. Levi followed casually behind me.

"When do you have to work?"

"Agency wants me to come in early tomorrow. I won't normally work weekends, but they want to get the paperwork and all of that out of the way."

"What are your plans for the rest of the night?" I told myself I was just being polite but really I was hoping he'd stay. I awkwardly grabbed the remote and turned the TV on.

"Do you want to watch TV?"

"Sure," Levi agreed.

"Yes! *Cops* is on," I squeaked excitedly, forgetting Levi was there and that I should act—I don't know, maybe *suave.*

"I haven't watched this in ages," Levi said, sitting beside me on the couch.

"I'm going to change really quickly," I announced.

I bounced back off the couch and walked briskly to my room. I quickly slipped on a pair of yoga pants and a loose, soft-grey v-neck tee. I thought for a second as I saw myself walk past the full-length mirror that this outfit wasn't very impressive, but then I remembered that he was around beautiful woman all the time and he wouldn't easily be impressed. I shrugged off the self-hate and relabeled it in my mind as just being realistic. It wasn't like he didn't know what I looked like; dressing a pig up in silk didn't make it anymore less of a pig, did it?

Feeling empowered, defiant and oddly self-confident with my "this-is-what-you-get" attitude, I went back to the living room.

An episode was just ending. It was one I'd seen before: the police had been doing a standard pull-over questioning for odd driving behavior and the guy had tried to get away on foot but tripped—of course—and the cop tackled him. The police officer was on screen, recapping the whole scenario to one of his fellow cops. The theme song began to play and my eyes grew heavy. I felt Levi's arm roll around my shoulders and I let myself lean into his side.

The next thing I remember was jolting awake. I had no idea how long I'd been asleep, but Levi and I had ended up laying down on the couch with me cuddled into his chest.

My abrupt jerk woke him up.

I awkwardly tried to sit up. My face just a breath away from his.

Levi's fingertips traced the outline of my face as he yawned.

The husky scent of his cologne clouded my senses. He'd caught me again, the green-grey of his eyes peering into mine as if I were the only thing he'd ever seen worth seeing. It was impossible for me to look away. The tips of his fingers curled, guiding me to him. His tongue slipped gently into my mouth, while his hands cupped the side of my face as my heart raced.

"You're so good at that," I murmured in disbelief.

He hummed something that could have been a *thank you* before leaning back in. A sigh escaped my lips and I pulled back, startled and embarrassed by my reaction to him. I'd never been kissed like this. My body felt like it was thawing out, waking up, warming to him.

"It's okay," Levi said softly. He watched my face earnestly as he sat up.

I sat back on my knees. I felt the crackle of sexual energy between us as we watched each other. I ruffled my long curly hair with my hands before pulling it up into a messy bun. I could hear *Cops* still playing in the background and quickly searched the couch for my phone. I'd just found it jammed—along with the remote—in the cushion when I heard Levi's phone ring.

He swooped his cellphone off the table and glared at the screen.

"It's my agent. I'm sorry, I have to take this."

I nodded understandingly. I checked my own phone. I had a missed text from Berea.

BEREA: Our dates bailed. We're blind-dating each other. Hope your night's better than mine. #winning

I smiled at her hashtag. Berea had never really been a fan of Clyde. In her opinion—and I agreed—he had the "little man complex." Every time we all got Chinese food, we snatched his fortunes before he could read them and told him they said things like: The large truck in your future will make you feel better about yourself" or "a new exciting bro-mance will come your way." Clyde put up with us so we put up with his quirks. Deep down though, he was a good person.

79

ME: It's a hot bowl of cray-cray stew over here. I think he likes me. #delusional.

She responded back almost instantly.

BEREA: You twat, of course he likes you.

I had no response for that. *Of course* I wanted him to like me, who wouldn't, but I couldn't afford all the ice cream and time off from work I'd need when he got bored with me.

Levi smiled at me over his phone; the person on the other line was droning in his ear robotically. My stomach fluttered. He was making me feel like all the things I thought I knew about love, sex, men, *myself,* were wrong. I felt like I had just busted the angles for my piece. I'd have to start from scratch.

Levi's face became suddenly stern.

"I don't care. I didn't sign my soul to Kendyl. We signed a contract project by project because I wanted to make sure I could leave whenever I wanted. We had no signed contract."

As soon as he'd said Kendyl's name, my interest was piqued and I shamelessly listened to the rest of his call.

"She can use those scenes," Levi continued, "and whatever other work I did for her as she pleases. I have my money and that was all I wanted. Respond back to all my New York contacts, book me modeling gigs, advertisements, magazines, whatever—no more porn, no more escorting. You're on *my* payroll. Make it happen."

I pounced as soon as he hung up.

"You're really not doing porn anymore?"

"It was never permanent," he said as he strode back to me.

"She was so excited to introduce me to you. Kendyl called you her 'new star.'"

"There's always a new star. This means," Levi said as he moved towards me on the couch," that I'll be in New York for a while. You're

80

the only native I know so that makes you responsible for my well-being."

My breath quickened before we even started to kiss.

I followed Levi's lead, letting him sink me down into the sofa cushions. Our bodies aligned seamlessly, our lips blending with an earnest hunger I'd never known before. I wasn't even aware that my legs had spread until I felt his thick erection grinding against me. His hand latched into my hair, securing my mouth in the position he wanted. He had my body so preoccupied that I didn't correlate the building, aching pressure between my legs as the formula for an orgasm. It snuck up on me and I broke our kiss to let out a surprised gasp.

Levi stilled but he stayed close. I could feel his breath on my face and I knew he was watching me. I couldn't bear to open my eyes. I'd just come for the first time and we weren't even having sex. We weren't even naked. We were just *kissing*. Well, and he was grinding on me, but still he'd managed to do what all the other would-be lovers could not in just a few moments of foreplay. I was afraid of the depth which he could make me feel.

"Open your eyes," Levi commanded softly.

I shook my head no.

"Baby, I know what just happened and it was the sexiest thing I've ever witnessed."

His words melted me into a weird mix of arousal and self-consciousness.

"Don't hide from me. That wasn't a first just for you."

"Really?" at the sound of my voice he pulled back so he could see my face.

"Yes," Levi insisted.

I heard the door open and Berea's voice fill the apartment.

"I'm back! Tell me all about your date with Adonis!"

Berea was in the room before we could even manage to untangle ourselves. Levi stood up briskly and I got a full view of strained jeans harnessing his unforgettable erection to his thigh. I blushed and dragged my eyes away from the outline of his sizable arousal through his jeans and back to his face.

Levi gave me a wicked but somewhat slightly apologetic smile as he turned away and attempted to adjust himself.

"I should probably get going. Walk me out?" Levi asked.

I nodded, following wordlessly behind him as he made his way to the door.

We passed a dazzled Berea.

"Let me know what she really thinks of me, okay?"

Berea snorted at Levi but my death-star glare kept her silent.

"You're already coined a nickname for me?" Levi asked.

I groaned embarrassedly.

Levi laughed and pulled me close.

"I like the nickname and I like you more than anyone I've ever known."

I shifted uncomfortably under his gaze. When he was near me, I felt like I couldn't hide my feelings from him. I couldn't run, didn't really want to run, so that left me stuck trying to process everything new he'd awakened. It was overwhelming.

"Look at me," Levi commanded. His voice was so low and soft that if there had been anyone else around no one would have been able to hear him but me. His thumb hooked under my chin and tilted my head up. "Strip everything else away from me and I'm just a man; I'm yours, Piper."

My eyes widened. I was speechless.

"Can I see you again?"

"Yes," I whispered.

He pulled me into a hug, brushed a swift kiss on my check and left.

10

"Girl," Berea said with a mile-wide smile, "you are flushed from head to toe."

She had taken a seat on the couch and was casually flipping through the channels.

"He is amazing," I confessed.

"Does that mean you're going to take my advice and trust him?"

"You really think I should? He's got your seal of approval?"

"Yes!," Berea exclaimed. "The man flew here to see you; so romantic!"

"I'm just—it's just—" I sighed, completely exasperated in trying to articulate how I felt.

"Write it all down, even if you don't use it in your end piece," Berea instructed. "It'll help you understand what you're feeling."

"He gave up porn," I said.

"I'm telling you, this is one of those love-at-first-sight things."

"I'm taking him to the gala next weekend."

"Really?" Berea said excitedly. "There's something I want to run by you, promise you won't get weirded out."

"I promise," I said quickly. I hadn't seen her look that excited in a while, and for a minute I wondered if she'd met someone. But there was no way I wouldn't have known—we told each other everything.

"Clyde asked me to go to the gala with him."

"Really? That's crazy!"

"Piper," Berea said, as she brushed her hair back from her face nervously, "I—I think I have a little crush on Clyde."

"What?!"

"I think he feels the same way too."

I just stared at her, completely shocked and half sure she was teasing me.

"It happened at dinner. Usually you're with us, and he's liked you for a while I know, but something was different tonight. He didn't talk about you *once*. It felt real, you know?"

"Have you liked him for a while and just never said anything?"

"Of course not, well, not that I'm aware of, but something changed tonight. Don't say anything to him. I just want this to play out naturally. Who knows, maybe I'm just horny and desperate."

"You're *not* desperate," I corrected her sternly. "You're supportive of me and Levi; I'll be supportive of you and Clyde."

Berea stared at me, awestruck.

"What did you think I'd say?"

"I honestly didn't know, but I'm so relieved it doesn't bother you."

I got up and hugged her. "I just want you to be happy, okay?"

I felt her nod as we hugged. I was surprised, but if Clyde was serious and treated her right, I'd have no problem with him dating Berea.

He'd better not fuck this up.

I took Berea's advice twice that night. I decided to be brave and see where this romance between Levi and me might lead and I also wrote down all my anxieties, hopes and fears about the possibilities. It was mostly just random things; almost like a diary entry but it felt good. I fought the urge to edit what I'd written. This wasn't that kind of writing. Its only function was just to exist and maybe add some clarity to how I felt about things.

I'd just turned off my laptop and opened my e-reader when my phone buzzed. I snatched it from the nightstand excitedly, somehow knowing—or really just hoping—that it was Levi.

84

ADONIS: Nothing I do will make my boner go away. ☹ I think I have a medical condition. I've googled it and it says it'll be relieved if it's jammed into some pie.

ME: Do you need the number to Sara Lee?

ADONIS: I'm in a committed relationship. Haven't you seen my Facebook profile?

ME: We're not friends on Facebook.

ADONIS: We have to fix that. I need us to be official.

ME: Have your balls turned blue yet?

ADONIS: I'm afraid to look.

ME: I'll look, send me a picture.

ADONIS: You can check them next time we meet.

ME: I won't have time then. We'll be too busy watching *Cops*.

My phone was silent for a few minutes and then it dinged with a new message. I was scared to look but I had to look all at the same time. He'd sent me a video and I had to tap it for it to load. I cursed my slow internet. It played immediately once it had fully downloaded.

The background was full of neon lights and I heard the knocking of pins in the back. Glow bowl. I recognized Levi as the camera rolled over to him. He looked younger and exuberant. He was suggestively swinging his hips as he held two large bowling balls.

"You'll never need a couch with those big nuts!" a male voice said in the background. I assumed he was the one filming.

"Real original," a female voice rang out. "Come on, Levi, it's your turn."

"I'm saving this!" the recorder said with a laugh.

"Post that shit online, Liam! It's pure gold!" another male shouted.

"Maybe it'll go viral and we'll be rich!" Levi teased.

Don't post it," the girl insisted, "dad will freak!"

"Who gives a fuck?" the recorder said.

"That's right!" cheered Liam. "We do what we want!"

"Rebels for life, right, Mariah?!"

The clip ended with more bad jokes and Levi's rumbling laughter. I laughed too, loving this side of Levi he'd let me see in this video. I quickly typed him back a final text.

ME: I love your balls!

ADONIS: I knew you would. I'm so glad we met. 'Night, Lemon Meringue.

ME: Funny how that worked out, huh?

ADONIS: Not funny, perfect.

Fuck. He was so romantic. He was so genuine and not in the least afraid to tell me how he felt. Was he always this open with his lovers or was he just evolving for me? It made me want to evolve for him. To get past my fears and just trust that sometimes good things happened for no reason. I hooked my phone up to its charger and smiled broadly. I was giddy with the idea that perhaps I'd been wrong about myself and the cosmos for once.

11

The rest of the weekend was fantastic. Berea and I binge-watched television and I texted with Levi practically nonstop. I noticed Berea was also messaging someone. I assumed it was Clyde, and considering the frequent soft giggles coming from her direction, they were really hitting it off. I took the time and wrote a lot. It helped. I wrote what I felt too, and by the time Monday came around, I was feeling energetic and fresh.

But my cheery mood wasn't meant to last. I'd been at my desk for barely a half hour when Evette flew by on her broomstick ushering me angrily into her office for a "talk."

"A birdie told me that you flew to Las Vegas Friday afternoon and met with a porn star director—explain!"

Clyde, that fucking traitor. I was going to skin him alive next time I saw him. I knew it was him, Berea would never betray me like that.

"Am I explaining as an employee or as your daughter, because as an employee since it costs the company nothing I shouldn't have to—"

"EXPLAIN!"

I crossed my arms over my chest and the glaring standoff between us began. I *hated* when she raised her voice like that—especially at work. I refused to enable her to treat me like a child. I'd be silent until she addressed me with respect. I wasn't even remotely intimidated by her antics. I wouldn't let her bully me. We were both adults.

Evette gave a disapproving shake of her head before finally relenting. She took a seat at her desk and asked in a much more appropriate tone to verify whether what she had heard was true.

"Perhaps we need to *discuss* your thesis, Piper. You gave me the impression that this was about couples and their sex lives, not gigolos and their clients."

I gave nothing away, but inwardly I was cringing at her implication that I had paid Levi for sex.

"Levi is just a man."

87

"Nothing happened?"

"I don't report to you, Evette, not when it comes to my personal life."

Evette hated it when I didn't call her Mom. She clenched her jaw, a vein twitching on the side of her neck.

I went in for the kill.

"Don't worry! Levi is my date to the gala so you will get to meet him."

"Brilliant," Evette muttered, tapping her ballpoint violently on her desk.

"Don't ask Clyde things about me."

"I don't, not really," Evette lied horribly. I glared intensely at her and she caved.

"He's worried about you," she insisted.

"He has no *right* to be worried."

"He's such a nice boy," Evette continued. "Why won't you date him?"

"Berea is dating him," I snapped. I got up. If I wanted to be able to finish the work day, I had to get out of this office.

"When did that happen? Look, Piper," my mother called from her desk. "I didn't mean to blow up at you. Just—honey—try to be safe, okay? Multiple partners can be dangerous for your health. This is your mother talking, not your boss, all right? I just want what's best for you."

I almost let her know that I hadn't actually slept with any of them and that the only one I'd planned on sleeping with was Levi. But I didn't say anything. I was done talking to her. I was so livid about her and Clyde *talking* about me behind my back that I wasn't going to give her or him any more personal information. I was officially emotionally cutting them both off.

I was almost back to my desk when Clyde strode up.

"Hey, do you want to go get—"

"Fuck off, Clyde!" I snarled.

"Whoa! Why are you upset?"

"If we were really friends, you wouldn't tattle on me to Evette."

"I ran into her and it just came up," Clyde insisted. He'd never been able to lie to me. He'd totally snitched on me to my mother.

I pushed past him, crossing the office space quickly. I really hated him. If he was really concerned, why didn't he go to Berea or, hell, why didn't he just talk to me about it? I sat at my desk, cursing the open-space concept and the lack of privacy.

Clyde came up to my desk just a few moments after I'd sat down, but I acted like he wasn't there and began reading emails and going over corresponding paperwork.

"You're not going to talk to me now? Real mature, Piper."

Oh, I'd show him mature.

I put on headphones and started listening to music and typing furiously. Eventually he sulked away.

I wrote on and off the rest of the morning, sometimes stopping to answer emails or do some editorial work. I was just considering taking a break and head out for lunch when my phone vibrated on my desk.

ADONIS: We still on for tonight?
ME: Of course, any time after six.
ADONIS: Want to order in?
ME: I'll cook. How about breakfast for dinner?
ADONIS: Sounds perfect. See you soon.

Just like that, my day was better.

"Clyde told me you're mad at him," Berea said. She came around the corner of my desk and leaned against the edge..

"I thought you guys didn't talk about me," I snapped.

"Look—I'm not here to defend him. I just wanted to make sure you were all right."

I sighed and then apologized. "He told Evette everything and now she's riding my ass like a shiny new bike."

"Your mom is just being a mom. You can't fault her for that. At least she cares."

"I thought you said you weren't coming over here to defend anyone?"

Berea laughed. "I meant I wasn't going to defend Clyde's actions, but he is sorry—for what it's worth."

"It'd be worth more if he'd just kept his mouth shut," I sneered.

"Clyde's offering to take us all out for an apology dinner tonight."

"I have plans with Levi," I said with a sorry-not-sorry shrug.

"He could come too. We could—dare I say—double date?"

"Not sure it's safe. I wouldn't want Clyde reporting back to Evette with juicy tidbits."

"You're going to introduce him to your mom before the gala, though, right?"

"Nope; she can meet him there. It'll be public and she'll be nicer to him."

"Good plan," Berea said with a smile. "Let me know if you change your mind about dinner, okay?"

"I won't, but thanks."

Berea sighed as she walked away. I'm pretty sure I heard her mutter something about me being unnecessarily stubborn.

I hurried home after work and took a quick shower. I was still working on my curly hair when I heard a knock. I'd expected the buzzer to go off first, but someone must have let Levi in from downstairs.

I opened the door and gasped. Levi was holding up a beautiful bouquet of flowers. It was so unique, mostly purple irises and some other soft flowers I'd never seen before.

"You look shocked," Levi teased. "Were you expecting someone else?"

"Of course not," I said quickly. "It's just, the flowers are gorgeous."

Levi came in, walking through the kitchen to set my flowers on the island. I dug around in the cabinets until I found the only vase Berea and I owned. When the flowers were settled in, I turned to thank him but Levi pulled me into his arms instead. He dipped his head, and I rose up on my toes to collect my kiss. It was a slow and almost lazy kiss, as if we had all the time in the world to just enjoy and draw out the moments when we were alone.

"I'm glad you like them," Levi told me. "Are we hanging out alone tonight?"

"Just us. Clyde and I fought earlier. Berea defended him, which made me even angrier. I was meaner than I should have been even though I have a right to be upset."

Levi took my hand in his.

"What was the fight about?" he quietly asked.

"You," I said with a sigh. "Want some coffee?"

He nodded yes, then asked, "They don't approve of us?"

"It's not just that. Clyde told my mother about my project. Of course, she flipped out, called me into her office for a nice round of boss-mom. He's such a little snitch. Do you like French vanilla?"

"I do," Levi said, smiling. He pulled out one of the backless barstools tucked beside the kitchen island and sat down. "I take it you didn't tell Clyde or your mother that you didn't sleep with any of the applicants?"

"No, I left that part out."

Levi laughed. "He's probably insanely jealous. I would be."

"It's not his place to be *anything*," I said sternly. "He's out on a second date with Berea tonight."

"He might like you more than you think."

"You think it's a ploy to try and make *me* jealous."

"Could be, but it doesn't matter, though, does it?"

He gave me such a confident, seductive smile that I almost dropped the coffee pot I was filling with water in the sink.

"I don't care what people think."

91

Levi hadn't suggested that I did care, but I felt like I had to say it out loud so he would know how I felt.

"Everyone does sometimes," Levi said.

"Fine, I don't want to care what people think."

"I want to ask you a couple questions, if that's all right?"

"Should I be nervous?"

"Not at all," Levi insisted, "and you don't have to answer if you don't want to."

I took a deep breath. "All right, ask me."

"On the couch a couple days ago, was that really your first orgasm?"

"Yes," I answered cautiously.

"Now that you know you can, do you think you know why you haven't in the past?"

"Not a clue," I said quickly.

"If it was someone else in your situation, what would you say?"

I paused from scooping coffee. I could fluff my answers or I could be honest. Being honest felt terrifying but somehow freeing. I could have sex with someone who knew all my secrets—it might change everything.

"We don't have to talk about this," Levi said. "I just want to know you—it's the only reason I'm asking."

I bit my lip. *Trust him,* my mind yelled at me, *don't get defensive, he is the one person who isn't judging you.*

"I think it stems from intimacy, trust and control issues. Maybe it's a line of defense. If I don't give anyone that kind of power over my body, they can't hurt me; they'll never mean anything to me. Letting someone make me come feels like I'm giving them a lot of myself and I'm not sure I want anyone to have that kind of power."

"That's the same reason why I *like* meaningless sex. You're controlling how much people have of you. It's physical and it's enjoyable, but touches nothing that's real."

92

I flicked on the coffee pot and turned to face him. The noise of the machine brewing was the only sound in the room. Levi and I just kept looking at each other, undoubtedly wondering what the other one was thinking.

"Everyone in my industry isn't like me," Levi said, breaking the silence. "I'm not saying you have to have some weird love hang-up to do porn or escorting, but I definitely have my reasons for why I did it and why I hadn't stopped."

"Why are you stopping now?" I asked.

"I'm not sure, but the decision feels right."

"I wouldn't have asked you to stop. I accept you as you are."

"Maybe," Levi started, "I wanted to come here, be close to you, get to know you, get to know myself; forget everything I was and just start fresh."

We stared at each other; ironically, both of us blushing. It reminded me of the first time our eyes locked on set, I'd sworn I'd seem him blush but it seemed so improbable that he could be intimidated by anything. He was everything.

The coffee pot stopped brewing. I turned and got the mugs out of the cupboard behind me.

"You'd take that big of a risk on someone you've just met?" I asked quietly.

"Yes," Levi said. "Be brave with me, Pi. Let's see where this goes."

I nodded and we smiled at each other like two love-struck idiots. I felt jittery from the emotional intensity of our conversation, and I realized in a half stupor that I was pretty sure I'd just agreed to an exclusive monogamous relationship with a beautiful, gorgeous model, *ex*-porn star.

"I'm hungry," Levi announced.

"Was that whole conversation just a ploy to get me to cook dinner for you?"

"Did it work?" he asked, grinning.

I winked at him.

"How about—" I said, stretching the sentence as I dug through my fridge, "a fancy grilled sandwich? I have deli turkey and monterey jack cheese. I think we have some Doritos too. Or we could always order in?"

"No, that's fine. I accept your offer for a fancy grilled cheese."

"Since our relationship is so accelerated, why aren't you making *me* dinner?" I teased.

"I'll bargain with you. If you make me dinner, I'll give you a foot rub while we watch *Cops*."

I tossed the ingredients on the island bar and went to work.

"I take it you accept my offer?" he asked, watching me sprinkle cheese onto the turkey I'd placed down on his bread."

"How could I refuse? Do you want more turkey than this?"

"Double turkey, double cheese," Levi informed me.

"Are you one of those beautiful people who can't cook?"

Levi grinned. "I make up for it with other talents."

I grabbed the butter and put a generous amount in the frying pan.

"Such as?" I asked innocently.

"Foot rubs."

"You've got to have more to offer than that."

"Back rubs, leg rubs, butt rubs," Levi listed.

"Anything that's not 'rub' related?"

"Did I mention I'm good at back scratches?"

I laughed.

"Now you're talking," I said.

"You could always teach me how to cook," Levi suggested.

"You really are planning on sticking around for a while."

I felt his arms curve around my hips from behind me. I almost flipped the grilled cheese out of the skillet.

The door slammed open from the hallway.

"Is she here?" I heard a breathless Clyde ask.

"Does it matter?" Berea asked quietly.

"No, Berea, it doesn't."

I turned away from the stove and put a finger to Levi's lips. He nodded, understanding that I wanted to eavesdrop.

They passed through the kitchen, completely oblivious to our presence. Clyde was carrying her awkwardly, bumping Berea into the wall, end tables, edge of the couch, but Berea didn't mind; each minor collision making her giggle and increase the urgency of their feverish kisses.

"I'm going to have to set you down, okay?"

Berea laughed lightheartedly.

"It was your idea to pick me up in the first place!" Berea insisted.

"I thought you'd appreciate the showmanship," Clyde answered back.

I heard Berea's bedroom door open, close and the rest of their conversation or lack became muffled.

"Don't burn my sandwich," Levi warned playfully.

"Why not? Since you can't cook, wouldn't it be the kind of sandwich you're used to?"

Levi's answer was to lightly pinch my ass. The small, flirtatious action made me tingle from head to toe. I had a feeling I was really going to like *us*.

12

There was a loud honk and I scrambled excitedly out of the apartment lobby. I'd already come down, too excited to wait in my apartment. I'd asked him to wait, rather than come up. Clyde and Berea had left earlier to get dinner before going to the gala. It was a sweet prom-like gesture that I knew Berea would be wooed by. Ironically, things had not been awkward at all since they'd started seeing each other. We'd even made plans the following week to go out on a double date. I'd find out then if this would be permanently okay or perpetually weird.

I'd seen Levi every night this week. We'd fallen into a routine of getting dinner together and then making out on my couch until he reluctantly went to his hotel room. The chemistry between us was insatiable but he seemed to be cautious, almost careful even, with me. He didn't grind on me again which was *very* disappointing. Mostly he just wanted to snuggle and kiss. Last night, I'd tried to have things progress to *more*. I was ready but Levi wasn't.

He'd insisted we wait, his breath heavy and hot as his words drizzled against the skin of my neck.

"I don't want to rush with you," Levi explained.

It was chivalrous but more frustrating than sweet. He was the first man I'd known who could give me what I physically needed and he was holding back. I knew he wanted me, but a part of me worried that he might just like the idea of us and that once we had sex the allure, the mystic aspect of it, would no longer be enticing.

I was having a lot of feelings with this man and it was something I wasn't prepared to deal with.

During the week, Levi was apartment hunting and he was even having his car shipped rather than sell it or fly back and drive it here. When Levi made up his mind, he was all in.

Tonight, Levi was picking me up. I'd expected a cab, but as I strode down the steps of my apartment complex I saw that he had *his car*. I'd figured it would be a while before his belongings were shipped here, especially his Trans-Am.

"I swear I didn't mean to honk," Levi explained as I got in the car. "Darla adjusted the seats and I was trying to get it back to the sweet spot and I slipped."

"It's all right. I told you to honk, remember?"

"Yeah, but I wouldn't actually have honked. You look amazing, Pi."

I smiled shyly at his compliment.

I'd been hoping he'd like the dress I'd chosen months ago for tonight. I loved it. It was loaned to me by an upcoming designer we were featuring in the debut of *Galaxy's* print edition. It was a sleek, midnight blue, with a bateau neckline that allowed the back to cascade dramatically down, exposing my smooth caramel skin almost all the way to my tailbone.

It was the kind of dress that made a person.

"You're free tonight, afterwards, I mean?" Levi asked.

I nodded yes. I didn't want to be self-conscious but my thoughts were so brazen—he'd be an idiot not to know that I *wanted him,* almost unbearably so.

"Darla's here?" I asked trying to gain some composure and change the subject. The more I thought about him and the things I wanted from him the more flushed and obvious I was. I took a breath and tried to think non-sex thoughts.

"Yes! I paid her to drive my car out here. I want her to stay and work for me. Darla has been a good friend to me, my only friend until recently."

I smiled, glad Levi had someone like Darla in his life. Darla was his Berea and we all needed a Berea in our lives, someone who sincerely had your best interest at heart and would always tell the truth. Those types of people were few and far between. You had to keep them close when you could. It mattered to me that he showed loyalty to those who mattered to him and I had a feeling Darla hadn't had an easy life.

"You think she'll move here and work for you?"

"I hope so, I really hope so."

We drove the rest of the way chitchatting nervously; the weather, the TV show we'd watched last night, a couple flirty innuendos. Both of us anxious for the same reason: my mother. He wanted to impress her and I just wanted to minimize their interaction. I wasn't really afraid that she'd be rude to him; my mother wasn't that type of person, but I was concerned that the longer they were around each other the more she'd have to use later on. The most I could hope for was damage control and perhaps the rare miracle that she'd actually *like him.*

The Galaxy Gala was hosted at the Bronson House. It was an old historical mansion often used for different high- end events. As we walked through the foyer towards the ballroom, the voices of sponsors, coworkers, and some of New York's most influential people tingled like fine jewelry. Evette and I had started doing this about six years ago while I was still in college. Every year, we rented the same building. It was another world up here, north of the city in the historic district. I felt transported to the pages of *Gatsby.* The elegance of the building alone was enough to forget the honking sounds of the city.

I stole a long glance at Levi, admiring him as we walked. With his hair combed back, sleekly in waves, his strong frame filling out his tux perfectly, he oozed dapper manliness. He was beautiful. Levi belonged anywhere that there was air. I was bashfully proud to be on his arm.

"Are you ready to meet *Evette?*" I asked.

I was more surprised that he'd admitted it than the fact that he was nervous.

"That's my mother," I said, nodding in her direction, "the blonde in the blush-colored gown."

Levi unconsciously adjusted his tie as he gazed around the room.

"You don't look like her at all," Levi said, clearly surprised.

"That's because my father is black."

Levi looked at me, a crooked half-smile

"I guess I never mentioned that."

"I never mentioned I had a mixed-race heritage too; except for me, both of my parents are interracial."

"Is this the young man you've told me close to nothing about?"

Fuck. I was hoping to introduce them after Evette had a few cocktails and wasn't so much herself. I took his hand firmly in mine. We were a united front. My mom could suck it.

"Yes," I said smiling as sweetly as I could, "this is Levi Gallant."

"Charmed," Levi said, taking her outstretched gloved hand in his.

"How'd you meet my daughter?"

Double fuck. My mother hated me. That had to be it. Why else would she be such a raving bitch?

"In Las Vegas," Levi answered smoothly.

My breath sucked in sharply. There was no way to *like* where this conversation was headed.

"I'm *familiar* with your line of work. What brings you to New York?"

"Your daughter," Levi said. He hadn't missed a beat. If he was nervous he definitely hid it way better than I did.

Evette arched a single eyebrow critically.

"Evette! Is that you?"

My mother's attention diverted away from us and towards the male voice greeting her. She recognized him and to our surprisingly good luck, forgot about us completely.

"Phillip?"

"God, I thought it was you! You look stunning."

I grasped Levi's hand firmly.

"Now's our change to flee," I whispered through gritted teeth.

Levi smiled and led me through the clusters of socialites onto the ballroom floor. The big band we'd hired had just started an instrumental rendition of "Fly Me to the Moon." He gave me a smooth, elegant twirl, guiding me right into his arms. I could see Evette through the crowd giggling at whatever Phillip was saying. My existence to her was for once oblivious. God bless that man, whoever he was. Just knowing she wasn't paying attention unraveled some of my nerves.

Levi held me close, his hand following a path between the nape of my neck and the small of my back. Between his simple touch and the slow drone of the music, I was entranced. I curved my head against his neck and my lips rested just barely on his skin. I could feel his pulse quicken beneath my lips. I wanted to kiss him there, but the tiny part of me that cared about decorum kept my lips shut and a public display of affection at bay.

We danced to a few more slow songs, my body following him easily through the ballroom. I was enjoying this, savoring it even, but the longer we danced the more I ached. I couldn't just be this close to him, not with all the pent-up sexual energy that we'd accumulated all week. For me, there'd never been a reason to wait. It was time.

"Take me outside and make love to me," I whispered, my lips pressed below his ear.

Levi's whole body reacted to me. His breath quickened, catching in his throat as he heard me. His arms loosened around me as he pulled back.

"Are you sure?"

I moved closer again, this time giving in to the urges to kiss his neck. The lights were dim, no one was watching and if they did, well, I hoped they enjoyed the show. I closed my eyes, nuzzling his neck before giving it a slow kiss.

"Don't make me beg," I teased.

Levi groaned something incoherent and quickly led me off the dance floor.

The air felt warm or maybe I was just drunk with romance. I laughed with anxious anticipation as we ran through the little courtyard and into a grassy park area.

"I think we're far enough away so no one will see us," Levi stated.

"Or hear us," I added with a light giggle.

He shrugged out of his tux coat and laid it in front of him on the grass. Then he turned to me, his eyes dark and eager.

I licked my lips anxiously. *I was in trouble.*

Levi moved towards me, his fingers dancing along the side of my face as he pulled me in. We got close, taking each other in. His fingertips found the small zipper hidden within a fold of fabric of my dress easily. I stood still, enjoying the expression on his face was he unwrapped me like a present. He slipped each strap off. My gown fluttered down around me, pilling silently onto the garden grass.

Levi devoured the space between us, his mouth clamping onto mine. He was an engulfing flame, warming me straight through. The kiss left no exit strategy for either of us. We tumbled down onto the grass, not even on the jacket. I kicked off my heels. He shrugged out of his shirt and his pants. I wiggled out of my lacy panties. We couldn't get the contact we needed fast enough and when we were finally free, skin to skin, the momentum between us became an all-consuming madness.

"I promise to take my time when I get you to a bed," Levi moaned as he kissed my neck.

I heard the rip of a foil condom wrapper and Levi shifted his weight to his side. A few seconds later (record time) his hand moved between my legs and then I felt *him.* A hard, thick rock of certainty. He eased himself in slowly, the most controlled, restrained motion that we'd had so far on this dreamy midsummer night. I'd never realized that the act of being taken, the slow first thrust, could be almost as delicious as an orgasm itself.

Magic, my brain clamored, *it does exist.*

"Are you okay? You're so quiet," Levi said.

"Just taking it all in," I sighed and then, embarrassed, covered my face with my hands.

He laughed and pulled my hand away.

"I love everything about you, Piper."

Levi began to move, rocking me into the lush lawn with each roll of his hips. I closed my eyes in blissful surrender.

"Tell me what you need," Levi panted above me.

"More," I moaned.

Wrapping his arms firmly around my waist to keep us together, he rolled to his back. It was exactly what I had *meant*. Levi was still guiding me, his hands controlling my hips over him, giving me the perfect rhythm. I'd never felt anything compared to this. All that sloppy sex with past lovers was nothing to this. I felt like I couldn't even breathe, I couldn't think—but I could feel and I felt every inch, every push, every puff of his breath against my chest and it was all taking me there. Levi's hand curled around my neck cradling me to him and he shifted his pace beneath me. That was it. I shattered, crying out deliriously as I came. Levi shook beneath me too, our hearts thumping in rhythm like two clanging cathedral bells.

"I can't even think," I sighed.

Levi laughed. "Good."

He sat up, holding my thighs to keep me from rolling off him. I wrapped my arms around his neck, curling his head between my fingers.

"You are the best thing that has ever happened to me," Levi said earnestly.

I knew he wasn't talking about the sex.

"What's that buzzing? Is that your phone?" I asked.

"Don't care," he sighed.

He kissed my neck and I responded immediately. I could feel myself swooning, my body eager to come again. But my brain held me back.

"What if it's important?" I insisted.

"What's more important than us?"

It didn't take much to convince me.

"Let's skip the gala," I suggested, "and go somewhere with a bed or at least a carpeted floor."

"Mmm," Levi purred in agreement. We untangled ourselves and stood up. I wobbled, my legs mushy from the euphoria and he protectively wrapped his arms around my waist to steady me.

"We should have done that in a bed, but I think you wanted it this way."

I smiled, then turned to retrieve my dress, which I'd probably have to dry clean. Levi helped me get dressed and then the hunt began for my discarded underwear. Levi was tucking his shirt back into his pants when his phone began to ring again.

I took over, tucking and buttoning.

"Just answer it," I said, smiling.

"Gallant," Levi said in a very all-business voice.

"Slow down, Liam," Levi said quickly. "I can't understand—what? When?"

Even in the moonlight, I could see all the color drain from his face.

"For how long?" he snapped into the phone. "Is she stable? I'll be there as soon as I can. I'll let you know when I'm on my way."

"What's going on?"

"My mother is in the hospital. They don't think she's going to make it through the night."

13

"We've got to get you to her," I said quickly, grabbing his hand.

We ran across the grass around the outside of the mansion back to the valet. Levi fumbled for his ticket.

"I'll drive," I offered.

Levi didn't respond and I wasn't even sure he'd heard me. He mechanically got in and I had to scramble to get fully in the car before he pulled off. We drove in silence; the only sound that cut through the black night was the purr of the engine and the faded voices of the radio. Levi's face was void of any emotion. He was shutting down and locking me out. I was worried. The change had been so quick and harsh. He was stone now and I already felt alone even with him siting less than a foot away from me.

Desperate to be helpful, I began searching for flights.

"There aren't any flights to Michigan for hours," I told him.

Levi remained silent.

"We'll just drive, okay?"

He nodded yes.

"We'll need to stop and buy some food, water, cheap travel clothes. It'll be quick, I promise."

"You don't have to come," Levi said.

"I do have to, I *want* to. How long of a drive is it?"

"About thirteen hours," Levi deadpanned.

"We'll make good time if we drive straight through and we can switch out a few times."

Levi took my hand in his and I felt a little bit better, a little less distant. I didn't know what I should do or say, or if I should even do or say anything. I honestly wasn't even sure what was happening but I felt the urgency, the near hysteria in his voice, and knew I had to get him to his mother.

I fidgeted nervously as I watched Levi quickly pick some clothes from the Super Center twenty-four-hour store. He was undoubtedly terrified and I wanted to comfort him, to be reassuring, but he wasn't giving me the chance and I didn't know how to get past the wall that was quickly separating us. His mouth was pressed into a hard line. His eyes were sharp and agitated.

"This'll work for me," Levi said, absently waving the clothes he'd picked out. "Are you all set?"

I nodded, clutching the pair of Keds, black yoga pants, loose-fit tee and plain dark hooded sweatshirt to my heart like a shield.

We passed the chip aisle on our way up to the front and I nabbed a couple bags. Levi grabbed waters from a glass-doored fridge and I tossed some mints onto the belt.

"You look so nice! Prom?" the cashier chirped.

We both stared at her blankly. She awkwardly looked away and continued scanning in silence.

I reached for my purse out of habit, but Levi placed a firm hand on my wrist.

"Credit, fine?" the cashier asked.

"Sure," Levi said, his tone laced with forced politeness.

He scribbled his name with a plastic pen and we left.

"Levi, are you all right?"

"I'm—fine."

The pause before "fine" had me hopeful for a split second that he was going to tell me the truth. I knew it was a dumb question to ask him. Of course he wasn't *fine*. I just didn't know how else to ease into the conversation. How did you get someone to open up to you? I'd tried to give him space, but the silence was already beginning to gnaw at me.

"Who's at the hospital?"

Levi looked over at me and I wasn't sure he'd answer me at all.

"Liam."

"No other family?"

"There isn't any other family, just us."

"I'm sorry."

"Don't be," Levi said with a sigh. "I hate going home—it's my fault, I'm never there and when I do go I get anxiety about it. Almost like being in the city itself makes me feel, I don't know, suffocated? Now, my mom is really sick. Liam could barely explain what had happened and I just have a whirlwind of shit swirling around in my head."

I reached over and took his hand in mine.

"What happened?" I asked quietly.

"My mom had an asthma attack so bad she went into cardiac arrest."

"We'll get there soon," I said, trying my best to be reassuring.

"I haven't even talked to her in months. I just kept sending checks. She never even wanted the money."

Levi's hand quivered in mine. It was torture to see him like this. I felt saturated by him. His fear my fear; his anxieties my anxieties. I just wanted to soothe him. I closed my eyes and said a quick silent prayer that she was better by the time we got there.

It felt like days had passed by the time we got to the hospital, but in reality we made remarkable time. We'd made it in 10 hours instead of a legal 13.

"Dammit!" Levi cursed. "Liam isn't answering his fucking phone."

Levi broke into a brisk jog. I had to sprint to keep up.

"What room is Stella Gallant in?" Levi roared at front-desk nurse.

Her eyes widened and she nervously fumbled on her keyboard. Her eyes darted back and forth across the screen frantically until she found the information. She froze, the color dissipating instantly from her cheeks.

106

"Levi?"

A young man had come up. He looked similar to Levi. Same tone, same hair; their faces were different but it was easy to tell they were related. This had to be Liam. Levi whirled around at the sound of his voice.

"Why aren't you with mom?"

"Where were *you*?" Liam spat back. "Whoring around? I was right here. She needed you!"

"Where is she?" Levi repeated. His tone was cold but controlled. Whereas Liam's volume was steadily increasing. He didn't contain his emotions like Levi did. They were a drastic contrast to each other.

"She's dead," Liam yelled. "What the fuck is wrong with you? Even *he* was here but you—you were off doing whatever the fuck it is you do."

"What?" Levi asked confused

"Levi?" another male voice called.

Levi's body stiffened but he didn't turn around. He glared angrily at Liam.

"Why is he here?"

"How would I know?" Liam yelled back.

"I came because I loved your mother," the man answered back.

My eyes darted between the three of them and suddenly it hit me. This man was their *father.*

Levi whirled around.

"Shut, your, fucking, mouth!" he roared.

"Whether you like it or not, it's the truth. I'm still your father, son."

That did it. Levi lunged at him, slamming his father in the waiting chairs. Magazine, cheap plastic flowers, cold coffee in Styrofoam cups— all of it went flying.

Liam yelled for them to stop, immediately throwing himself between them. I just watched, feeling frozen. I'd never seen this side of him, but I recognized it. A thousand years ago, I'd done the same thing when my father said he was leaving and not coming back.

107

I had to get out of here.

They'd stopped physically fighting. A nurse must have called security because I could see a few of them coming down in every direction. I moved away, quickly sidestepping the knocked-over furniture, and sprinted to the exit.

"Piper," Levi called after me.

I heard him, but I couldn't stop; not until I had fresh air.

We'd been sitting on a bench outside the hospital for a long while. I hadn't spoken because I wasn't sure what to say, how to console him or how to even explain my own behavior. I'd felt like I'd had a panic attack back in the hospital waiting area. It was just suddenly all too much and I'd run. Not far of course, just to a bench outside, but still, that wasn't the best way to help someone deal with their own loss. I was adding to the chaos when all I really wanted to do was erase it.

"I'm sorry," Levi said

I turned to him, but before I could say anything his lips were on mine, desperate, begging for an escape. Was this what he needed from me? Was this the manifestation of comfort he wanted?. I wanted him to talk, but he needed to feel. When he pulled back, finally looking at me, his eyes were gleaming with tears but he still wasn't crying, still hadn't cried. My heart ached for him and I knew I'd do anything to make him feel better. Even for just a moment.

"Let's go," Levi said quietly

"You don't want to..." I was going to say "see your mom," but it just didn't feel right.

"Let's go," he repeated in a low, hoarse, strained voice.

We traveled in silence, from the hospital, to the car, down the street and finally checking into a hotel not too far away. He didn't want to talk and I didn't know what to say. All I could do was follow him.

As soon as the hotel door closed, he was back on me, scooping me up into his arms and tumbling us roughly on to the bed.

We didn't talk. We just breathed, sighed, moaned, both of us rushing to get to skin. It was like he needed something tangible to hold on to, words felt so fleeting but touching was the kind of intimacy you could smell and taste. It felt like the only real good thing left. He took me hard, and I gasped, relishing in the sweet mixture of pain and pleasure. I'd never given myself like this to someone, putting their physical needs before my own. It was a kind of empowering surrender that left me reeling.

I felt like I could heal him by giving him everything he needed and after he'd worn himself out, I held him to me and his shoulders as he finally shook, soaking my skin with his tears.

I slept hard, but as soon as I was awake, somehow I knew he was gone.

I jumped out of the bed and grabbed my phone; no messages. I looked around the room frantically trying to see if there was any resemblance of him but there was nothing.

On the bedside table, there was a note written on the back of a Do-Not-Disturb door-handle sign.

My chest tightened with a toxic combination of panic and anxiety. I felt dizzy as I frantically snatched it up.

I know you deserve better than this, but right now this is all I can manage to do. I've never loved anyone the way I love you but I have to end this. I can't stay with you now, only to lose you later. It's too much. I know I'm a coward but I hope in time you'll forgive me. I paid for the hotel and for a ticket back to New York. Please don't hate me, I just want you to have everything you deserve and that's more than what I can give you.

Screaming out in frustration, I crumpled the letter and threw it.

I felt devastated, completely wrecked. I wanted to call him, to tell him he was being an idiot, force him to let me in, to help him grieve, to let me love him, but his rejection was so final. He'd left me and I didn't have the strength to fight against his decision, so I did what he wanted and left.

PART TWO:

14

"Are you sure you don't want to go out with us tonight?" Berea asked.

"No," I insisted firmly. "I'm going to go to the Bitter End, get a chai latte and plow through some work."

"I could cancel with Clyde. We can hang out, catch up, like old times."

"Not tonight, sorry, Berea," I said, turning her down a second time.

"Call me later, okay?"

"I'm fine," I insisted, but the look Berea gave me suggested she knew I was lying.

Galaxy launched its print edition today and my writing wasn't anywhere in it. I ended up having to concede to my mother that I wasn't going to be able to finish and Berea's secondary pieces became primary. The loss stung but Berea's work was fantastic. I was an odd mixture of proud and jealous.

It has been over six months since I last saw Levi. Finding his note in the hotel room had left me completely devastated, completely shattered. There'd been no attempt at contact either. He'd never called, he'd never texted, he'd never shown up. He'd never tried to get me back. It was as if we'd never happened. I'm not sure which truth stung more, the fact that he left me or the fact that he didn't want me back.

To make it worse, Evette was waiting for me when I returned to work that following Monday morning with plenty of ammunition. Clyde had told her everything he knew—which thankfully wasn't anything more than his own assumptions. Clyde didn't know about our romp at the gala, going to Michigan or that Levi had ditched me there with just a prepaid ticket and a half-assed apology letter. Berea knew, of course, out she'd never tell a soul. For what little consolation it offered me, I was thankful that everything I was most ashamed of was safe.

I'd never tell Evette either. She would label me a slut. She would vehemently deny that any real intimacy could exist within the first month of knowing someone.

I knew I wasn't and when I looked past my anger, I knew that what we'd shared was real.

Just because Evette hadn't experienced an intense connection with someone didn't mean it wasn't possible or that it was only surface deep. We'd had something; what had Levi called it? *A recognition.* We'd shared a moment where we'd truly seen each other and it'd been real and that was why my heart was having trouble rectifying that it was over. When you let someone in even if they burn you, it's not easy to let go. I wanted to be over him, over being dumped, over being in love with someone who could just cut me off like that even when they claimed they loved me too. That kind of love wasn't sustainable but it was *real.*

I watched Berea leave and began gathering up my belongings on my desk. I should have been nicer. I'd really been awful to her these past few months, even though she'd been completely amazing to me.

Everything was falling in place for her. Berea was doing impressive photography and editorial work for *Galaxy*; she and Clyde had really hit it off. I imagined they'd be married in a couple of years, at least that's where it felt like they were headed, especially now that they were living together. He'd moved in a few months after my dramatic road trip to Michigan. As soon as he was in, I moved out. It was against Berea's wishes, of course; Clyde's too, if I choose to believe he was being honest, but I knew it was best for me. It was just time for me to have my own place. I just couldn't do it. It felt like they'd won at life and I just kept losing.

I knew I was being completely illogical and bitchy but it was just how I felt. I never said anything to Berea, of course, I had that much decency, plus, what would she have done? Dumped Clyde so *I felt better*? That would be ridiculous and wasn't what I wanted. I didn't

113

want her not to have happiness; I just wanted to have it too. I wasn't jealous, but I was definitely envious. It seemed like as soon as one of us had it good, a shit-storm rolled in on the other. I was starting to very dramatically think we both couldn't be happy at the same time. I knew that was ridiculous too, but I'll admit it feels good to wallow and feel sorry for yourself sometimes.

Today was a bad day and I was feeling pretty sorry for myself, but all my days weren't bad. In fact, most of them were fine, I just hadn't been able to quite shake off those lingering "what ifs." Perhaps it was because my relationship with Levi had ended so abruptly or maybe I was scared I'd never find another guy like him.

The Bitter End really was the name of my favorite coffee shop, and to my credit it had been so, long before I'd known Levi. It was open twenty-four hours, had wi-fi, broccoli cheddar quiche and occasionally creative genius Thelonious Monk playing on their speakers. It wasn't far from my job either, which was another plus; just a handful of blocks between me, a chai and burning the midnight oil.

I got there, ordered my drink, nabbed a nice table-chair duo and nestled in.

I was doing more editing than writing these days, but *Galaxy* had grown and that was where Evette needed my skills most. She told me to consider it as a form of "leadership training." I didn't have the confidence or the audacity to argue but I was skeptical. I found it hard to believe that this change meant Evette trusted me *more*. She was just in boss mode trying to reel me.

Even with failing at my expose idea, I still longed to make a mark of my own, to create something that was really mine. I deviously toyed with the idea of starting a small publishing company. Berea had always thought I should, but it had always seemed too much of an endeavor. I was chewing on the idea more and more. If I did it, I could do e-books at first, publishing a couple promising writers to get my feet wet. I still didn't have the nerve to spring the idea to Evette. I needed to make sure I had a solid plan first.

"Hey, don't I know you?"

I looked up to see a guy around my age, laptop bag swung over his shoulder, standing beside my table. He was a plethora of races; brown skin, full lips, luscious curly hair and sexy horn-rimmed glasses. He was art modeling as a man. His eyes were the best, a swirling golden-green hazel. The man was stunning and I immediately wanted to run the other way. Another beautiful chaos? No thanks. I turned back to my work, tossing him back a one-word response.

"No."

"Seriously, don't you remember me? Mathais? SmittenMitten? We met about a year ago, I think. You were writing a piece about how sex can be fulfilling even if it's emotionless."

I looked back up, stunned. To my embarrassment and horror, his detailed description jogged my memory completely. I *did* remember him.

"I knew you'd remembered me!" Mathais said cheerfully, watching my eyes. "How'd the writing turn out?"

"I never finished it," I confessed.

I internally scolded myself, why hadn't I just lied? Then this conversation would have been over with.

"Do you mind if I sit?"

He took a seat before I could say no.

"Why didn't you finish?" Mathais asked eagerly. "You were going to meet with twenty-nine applicants, right?"

"Right," I said. "I didn't think it through. In the end it was just guys wanting to sleep with me. There was not going to be any real discussion. It's just—I guess my idea was way grander than the reality could ever have been."

"Were you intimate with each applicant?"

115

I cringed at the question but when our eyes met, I didn't see any judgment there. It was literally just a question he was asking out of curiosity; nothing more nor less.

"No, only one and that didn't work out too great either."

Mathias nodded and took a sip of his coffee and I cursed myself again with the honesty. Why the hell would I tell *him* that I'd slept with Levi? I had to stop telling him random factoids about my sexual life. It was weirding me out how easy it was for me to open up to him.

"The concept was really intriguing, though," Mathais insisted. "I had some ideas I wanted to share with you when we met, but I didn't want to be the egotistical know-it-all ass telling you how to do your own idea.

I scoffed.

"But you're fine telling me how I should have done it now that I've failed."

His hearty deep laugh warmed the coffee house.

"Pretty much," Mathais confessed.

I smiled back. It felt good to make someone laugh and for myself to be more lighthearted.

I studied him, sizing him up. He certainly looked smart and he articulated his opinions well.

"Let me hear what you would have done," I challenged.

Mathais' eyes lit up. He was immediately engaged and leaned towards me excitedly.

"For starters, twenty-nine applicants is far too many. You wouldn't be able to really prove anything except that you can have random hook-ups without actually falling for any of them. Anyone can do that. It's consistent sexual experiences with someone you're physically and emotionally compatible with that would be the most beneficial to your hypothesis and, of course, create the most interesting psychological data for you to analyze."

Mathais was more than just book-smart, he was clever, and if I'd been working with him on the project—from a professional standpoint—I probably would have had the kind of piece I'd wanted.

I tipped my chai towards him in a salute.

"You have my creative permission to take over and bring the project back to life."

"I did want to participate, remember?"

I blushed at the word *participate.*

"I remember," I said quietly, "but it's far too late now."

"It's never too late."

"It is when you don't even believe in your own thesis anymore."

"Now that makes it even *more* interesting. I think you should give the project another try but do it differently."

"Was that an attempt at a pick-up line?"

Mathais winked.

"Not at all," he insisted. "I just think it's interesting. It doesn't have to be with me, but if we were compatible I'd be fine moving forward."

"How would we determine if we were compatible?"

"Through a kiss," Mathais said simply.

Although Mathais was very friendly towards me, he wasn't being overtly flirtatious. Which gave me the impression that he was genuinely interested in my thesis; which made him even *more* interesting to me.

"And if I was willing to try it again?"

"Then we'd do my version and not yours," Mathais said firmly.

"But it was my idea."

"But it was a flawed idea," Mathais countered.

"You're awfully confident."

The playfulness in his eyes dimmed and was replaced with true concern.

"I'm sorry if I've offended you," he said.

I bit back a smile.

"I'm not sure that you have offended me," I said.

117

"I know it probably seems strange that I'd want to help, but I've always been intrigued by the mixture of social and cultural standards compared to sexual desire. The world has put sexuality on a moral pedestal and it has shaped what we deem as acceptable. Sex without emotion is thought crass, lustful, even wasteful, but there's an undercurrent of passion in us that can never be fully tamed. Your piece explores that undercurrent and I think it's an interesting and socially pertinent discussion that is long overdue. Why can't we please the flesh?"

I'd forgotten how attractive someone's mind could be. Mathais was intelligent but he wasn't pompous. He had ideas but he wasn't closed off to other people's. Teaming up with him could be fruitful. I could learn from him. Honestly, just sitting across from him was making me feel stimulated."

"You sound like a professor," I said.

He smirked.

"I am. I teach English at Hayes University; Let me co-author this paper with you. We can combine our resources and make sure our work makes it to print form. I have a few academia connections and really believe with the right journal it could be published."

"I'm impressed," I said, honestly. He'd just told me he worked for one of the best colleges, not only in the city but on the East Coast. I was pretty sure that Hayes University was where our internship program was based.

"I'm also well-read," Mathais continued as if this were an interview, "have excellent social skills and plenty of field experience."

Field experience. He was funny and charming but it was his enthusiasm that won me over. I'd never met anyone who was this supportive of my writing. We didn't even know each other; Mathais was just that kind of person. There was something admirable about another person who could throw themselves head-first into someone else's dream. My eyes flickered to Mathais' lips. Even if it was practical, his compatibility test, a kiss, was a flirtatious dare and *why not*? If he was

118

confident enough to tell me he could fix my broken expose, well then, why not let the man prove it to me—on a Monday night, in a half-empty coffee house.

"You've won me over. If we're compatible then we'll work together, but we have to do the test right now, otherwise my piece stays dead."

"Do you write full time?" Mathais asked.

"My mother is the editor-in-chief of *Galaxy.*"

Mathais' eyes widened.

"Right here?" Mathais asked.

His surprise dimmed my confidence. *Don't wimp out,* I scolded myself. *It's just a kiss.*

I nodded yes.

"Go ahead, big guy; lay it on me."

"All right, but Piper, promise you'll be honest. You don't have to be attracted to me just because I find you so," Mathais paused, his eyes twinkling mischievously, "stimulating."

I laughed.

Mathais smirked as he took off his glasses and pulled a complete Clark Kent on me. He was attractive, but without the glasses he was mesmerizingly good looking. His hand stroked up the side of my neck into my hair. It'd been a long time since I'd gotten any affection, and even though we didn't know each other, his light caress was genuine. There was such a warmth in his touch. My stomach tightened nervously and I was reminded of just how lonely I felt sometimes.

I closed my eyes just as our lips touched. His kiss was slow and unexpectedly gentle. The energy between us sizzled. Mathais shifted, coming closer and his fingertips grazed lightly across my cheeks. My lips parted and his tongue slipped and our kiss went from a simple smooch to a hot romance-book-cover embrace. My body felt like it was humming back awake after a long sleep. I have no idea how long we kissed, but I did know that my hands shouldn't be on his thighs, nor should I be feeling quiet so—breathless.

119

Lord have mercy, that nerd could kiss.

A distinct throat-clearing cough snapped me back to reality and I remembered where I was and what exactly I was doing. I felt my face flash in heat and knew I was red. I opened one eye cautiously and saw that Mathais was grinning broadly.

"Is everyone staring?" I whispered.

"Oh, yes," Mathais confirmed, smugly smirking.

He'd enjoyed our kiss and he was proud that I'd enjoyed it too. He didn't inflate or assume or blow anything out of proportion. We'd kissed and we'd clicked. There was such a sincerity about Mathais that made me want to naturally trust him, despite the better judgment or caution I knew I should have after my experience with Levi. I was on the edge of taking a chance and accepting his help.

He continued to smirk at me. Waiting for me to tell him yay or nay.

"Dammit," I cursed quietly, "I'm in."

Mathais let out a whoop of success and I marveled at how he could be so enthusiastic about an experiment that had already failed once.

"I was thinking," Mathais said quickly, "that we could meet every Friday night for the next twenty-nine weeks."

"Sounds good. When do you want to start?"

"This Friday? Or is that too soon?"

"No, that'll be fine." I agreed. "My place or yours?"

"Mine," Mathais said, "I'll chrip or text you the address."

I scribbled my number on an unused coaster napkin.

"Not sure why I just agreed to this," I said with a nervous giggle, "but I'm excited."

Mathais smiled.

"You're agreeing because you're a literary pioneer; just like me."

That sounded way cooler than it should have.

15

I took a deep breath and then before I could change my mind buzzed unit twenty-nine. The door clicked unlocked and I hurried into the complex. Mathais lived in an older building that had been refurbished into posh apartment flats. It was way out of my price range. I moved up the stairs quickly and Mathais was waiting for me.

We greeted each other warmly with a light hug; he gave me a quick kiss on the cheek. His comfortable ease with me was charming and utterly disarming. I swallowed nervously and tried to look cooler than I felt as I followed him inside his apartment.

He took my coat and hung it in a small closet adjacent to the door.

"Want anything to drink?" Mathais asked.

"Water, please."

I studied Mathais as he moved around the kitchen, getting my drink and then motioning for me to sit down on the couch. He had on dark-washed jeans and a simple black v-neck t-shirt. His hair was a little extra wild, reminding me of a short version of my own curly mane. He looked *good;* too good.

"Are you still comfortable with the idea of making out with a stranger?"

"I'm here, aren't I?" I said cheekily.

Mathais laughed at that and took each of my hands into one of his own. I felt my cheeks warm at the sweet gesture. Hand-holding was awfully tender for our common goal.

"Did you want talk first?" Mathais asked in a soft tone.

Talk? Hell no. I shook my head. Mathais grinned, daring me to make the first move and in total disregard to any nervous apprehensions I might have had, I leaned forward and accepted his dare.

I must have been moving too fast because his hand caught my face as if he needed to brace our abrupt impact. Our chemistry crackled ferociously between us. His hands wrapped around mine and I couldn't even remember a single word that started with "L." He kissed with such velvety precision that a moan dripped out of my mouth that made us both lean back in surprise.

"Best decision ever," Mathais purred as his hands stroked up and down my spine, "and to think you wanted to pretend like you didn't even recognize me."

I smiled, laughing as I shook my head.

"I really didn't recognize you," I insisted.

Mathais set his glasses on the table and pulled me into a straddle on his lap. He pulled my cowl-neck sweater and bra strap to the side so he could kiss my bare shoulder.

He hummed approvingly, the deep, baritone sound making me clench.

His lips traveled north along the curve of my neck.

"You like shoulders?" I asked as my eyes closed and my head tilted.

"I like yours," Mathias murmured. "We should slow down."

I wordlessly began to move away, trying in vain to control the involuntary blush that I knew was reddening my cheeks. I didn't want to slow down; if anything I wanted to speed up, but his declaration of self-control pulled me a little out of my own sex-haze and back to reality.

"Wait," Mathais said softly.

I froze, still partially on his lap and he pulled me back for another kiss. He caught my pony tail, untangling the holder and setting my wild hair free. His hands kneaded gently against my scalp in a light massage that made me feel like putty.

His phone rang and he pulled away to answer. I ruffled his mussed-up curly hair far more affectionately then I'd intended to. Catching my hand, he kissed my wrist and then spoke again into the phone.

"Yep, I'll buzz you in when you get here."

"I should go," I said as I stood up.

122

"Here's your pony-tail holder back," Mathais said.

We smiled at each other while I redid my hair into a quick messy bun.

"You don't have to go," Mathais said. "A few friends are coming over tonight. We play board games, cards, a little nerdbox, eat pizza, drink; you should join us."

I surprised myself by wanting to agree to stay but I hesitated; could we really be friends and do the project? That hadn't worked *at all* with Levi.

"I want to be friends with you," Mathais said resolutely, "and although I think your thesis is fascinating I would gladly toss that aside to have you as a friend. Hell, we can forget the project right now and just be *friends.*"

"Friends who make out occasionally?"

Mathais licked his lips and grinned. "You are one hell of a kisser."

I did a little bow and we both laughed.

"All right, I'll stay for games and pizza and I'll think about whether I want to be friends who fuck or co-authors of a paper who fuck."

He looked at me squarely, dead on, as if his direct gaze was to let me know he was serious and how much he meant his next words.

"You will define what *friends* mean. I'd just like to get to know you better—period."

I was stunned, but if I was honest I wanted to get to know him better too and not just because we were compatible. I watched him move into the kitchen and wondered how I'd decide just how far I wanted things to go with him. It couldn't hurt to have just a friend for once.

"Is there anything you don't like on a pizza?"

I shrugged.

"Not really."

"Don't get weirded out when you meet my friends," he warned. "They'll adore you and seek to claim you as their own through their cunning dick-ness and horrible drunken college antidotes."

I listened to him order the pizza and gave myself a much-needed pep talk.

You deserve to have fun. You don't always have to be a lone wolf. It's healthy to make new friends.

"I'm pretty sure you're leaning towards us being friends but in case you're on the edge still, I thought up some nicknames that we could call each other."

I arched an eyebrow in a combination of wonderment and amusement.

"You can call me Mat, like a kitchen mat, and I can call you Pipe like a brass pipe I might find in my wall."

"You're jokes are horrible," I teased.

"But I'm a fantastic kisser."

He'd get no argument from me about that. My lips tingled just at the mention of kissing.

"Your friends come over every Friday night?" I asked.

"For the most part."

"Where'd you meet them?"

"College mostly; I never seem to like my co-workers or at least not enough to want to spend time with them."

"I work for my mom and I'm seriously starting to feel like a loser."

"I know how that feels, but if you love it don't worry about feeling like a loser. My parents have a business too but I'd go crazy if I worked for them. What kind of business does your family own?"

"An online magazine; the largest online magazine actually."

"You're the daughter-mom duo who founded *Galaxy?*"

I nodded. Mathais looked surprised and I wondered if he was thinking maybe I thought all of his literary advice had been bullshit. Of course I didn't. If I only took one thing away from working in the editorial industry, it was that every opinion had value even if it was minute.

"What about your family?"

"We own a grocery store," Mathais said.

His eyes trailed to my lips and like a moon in orbit I moved towards him.

"Want another seven minutes in heaven?" I asked.

I curled my hands in his shirt, guiding him to me, and soon we were tangled up on the couch again. We kissed, each kiss blending into the next until our breathing and bodies had melded together and I wasn't sure where I started and he began.

Mathais pulled back. His eyes were already filled with affection. I marveled at how unfiltered he was with his emotions. Mathais was so giving and unintimidated. He dipped his mouth down into the curve of my neck, sucking and kissing between the sections of his sentence as he spoke.

"We really need to figure out these parameters," he cooed.

"Yeah?" I stuttered. I could barely formulate words, and my physical reactions to the way his lips felt against my skin and the pressure of his weight pushing me deep into the couch cushions had the words I could manage to say come out unintentionally airy and breathless.

"I vote that we forgo all academic pursuits and have lots of sex."

"Tell your friends to come an hour later," I whispered in his ear.

Mathais pulled back, leaning on one arm to the side and countered my offer.

"Stick around after they leave tonight."

The knock at the front door startled us both so much that we smacked foreheads together.

Groaning, Mathais kissed my ringing forehead and hopped off the couch. I noticed immediately that he had to adjust himself a few times before opening up the door. I assumed it'd been to pay the pizza guy but I realized quickly his friends had arrived.

"About time you answered, bitch! What were you doing?"

"Our damn dinner would have been cold, if we hadn't snagged it from the delivery boy and *paid*."

"This smug rich bastard never changes, Henry!"

125

Henry made a very dramatic sigh. "Believe me, Orlando, I know."

"We have someone new joining us tonight," Mathias announced.

"What? WHO?" they all said in a chorused unison.

"Piper," Mathais called out.

I knew I was red and I took quick breaths to calm myself. For a minute, I considered making some excuse about why I couldn't stay and leave, but when I got up from the couch he had his pizza-free hand reaching out towards me and I told my pride to fuck off.

I walked over to Mathais and took his hand in mine. I was going to stay.

Mathais pointed to his two friends. "The hobbit is Henry and the elfishly tall one is Orlando."

I laughed and then quickly apologized.

"No need," Orlando said, smiling warmly, "Mathias has to embarrass people about their names because he is hurting unbearably on the inside; it's a defense mechanism."

"You'd make new friends too if you weren't such a Neanderthal," Mathais assessed.

"I've been telling Orlando to get his protruding brow shaved down," Henry said to me solemnly. "If he did, people would be able to see what beautiful eyes he has."

"See," Mathais said, turning to me, "aren't you glad you stayed?"

I made it through a game of Monopoly and four games of Euchre—which I'd never played before but was now addicted to—before I started feeling tired and realized how late it was getting. I'd come over around seven and it was now well after midnight.

"Nice to meet you!" I heard Henry howl as Mathais and I stepped into the apartment building's hallway.

I gave Mathais a playful nudge with my shoulder.

"You're going to walk me down *and* hail a cab for me?"

Mathais smirked.

"Your friends are really great," I added, and that made him laugh.

"You're only saying that because they so obviously like you."

"Maybe," I confessed.

As soon as we were outside, the cool air woke me right up.

Mathais turned to me.

"I'm glad you had a good time."

"Do you really think my flopped expose was a good idea?"

"I do, but I'm nervous about our twenty-nine encounters," Mathais said.

"Why?"

"There's just something about—us," he finished awkwardly.

"There isn't really an *us*," I reminded him as gently as I could. Even as I said it, I knew that wasn't what he meant. I thought he'd be insulted but he gave me this confident smirk, hooked a finger gently under my chin and pulled me to him. He stopped with just inches before our lips would have touched.

"There is an *us*, Piper, and I think we should consider the probability of one of us or both becoming attached if we aren't careful."

"I don't want a relationship," I said quickly.

"Neither, do I," Mathais said.

"Why don't you?" I asked curiously.

I wondered if he'd had a similar experience to my own. I wasn't even sure exactly why I didn't want one. It was a mix of still feeling like Levi might come back to me and not wanting to make myself that vulnerable with anyone else ever again.

"They take up too much time, they always end badly, women never say what they really want—"

"Neither do men!" I exclaimed defensively, interrupting his list.

"Do you want my professional assessment of our situation?"

He had a hand tangled into the hair at the nape of my neck, his fingertips touching me in a quickly growing familiar way. It was an intimate touch, but not offensive. In fact, it was relaxing me and making me want to get closer to him so he could touch me more. If he did this every time we "argued" I'd never win a single fight, let alone stay mad at him.

"Sure," I mumbled.

"We're more than just compatible. We have an easy way with each other that is rare. Why not scrap the thesis and just see where *us* goes?"

Mathais was looking at me so earnestly, but I couldn't make this kind of non-commitment commitment. I was only comfortable doing what we were doing because I had the assurance that it would *not* lead to anything more. It was physical. It was controlled. It was *safe*. I realized then that I'd just disproved my theory. There'd always be an unbalance. One person would always want more. I backed away from him, out of the reach of his touch, suddenly feeling so angry, irritated, hurt, out of balance, out of control and far, far too vulnerable.

"You can decide," I said. "How about that? Let me know when you figure it out."

I walked away but Mathais caught my hand.

"Hey," he said quietly. "I didn't mean to upset you."

Unable to look at him, I studied every detail of the sidewalk.

"I'm not mad, I'm just—tired," I said.

Mathais pulled me back to him and I surprised myself by letting him take me into his arms again. It felt like more than just a hug. *Be careful,* my mind snarled.

"You're afraid of intimacy?" Mathais asked softly.

I chewed on my lip. He'd said it so simply and he was right. That was exactly my problem and it was only exacerbated with Levi abandoning me. Perhaps it had been my problem all along.

"I never thought of it *that* way," Mathais continued, "I was thinking more of you not wanting to commit, which I can completely relate to. Society projects an idea, primarily in regards to women, that you can only have a healthy sexual relationship if it ends in marriage, or a committed long-term relationship, but I don't believe it. I've never felt compelled to be with one person forever. Maybe I'm too focused on living my life, maybe I'm too self-centered. I figured I'd love *eventually* and that just hasn't happened yet, but what you're saying is completely different. You're saying you don't want to feel anything as if it's some kind of proof that you're stronger than emotions, that you don't need them to be whole, but you're wrong. Now that I understand more of what you mean, I have this overwhelming urge to take you back inside and show you that there are so many good things to take from intimacy."

My eyes had been increasingly widening through his speech. Mathais was so passionate and I admired his ability to care about someone—me—that he barely knew. He had an ability to become an insta-friend and not in a phony way. He was being completely authentic. He'd admitted something about himself in that speech that some people would have frowned on, but all I could see was how natural it was for him to be honest and that in itself was a rare trait.

He held his hand out to me.

Fuck—I wanted to trust him, I really did, and the fact *that I wanted to trust him* made me back away from him. It was too raw, too soon.

I shook my head, but leaned forward and kissed him.

"Let's hang out again. Next Friday?" I asked softly.

Mathais nodded silently and then we both left.

The next morning, I stayed in my bed for a long time, just thinking. Mainly about everything I could remember that I thought was wrong with me.

I didn't trust anyone.

I had an unquenchable urge to control as much of my life as possible.

I had a need to be loved, but wasn't willing to risk loving.

Those were the top three that everything else seemed to feed back to. I didn't want to feel *pathetic* anymore.

Then make a change, my brain chided at me sarcastically.

Was it really just that easy?

Maybe.

I thought about Mathais and the way he seemed to get me before I even got me. He'd asked me why I was afraid to feel. I couldn't have been able to formulate an answer but he'd made a logical suggestion that my real motive behind wanting to prove that women could have flippant, non-attachment sex was because I wanted to validate something about myself. I'd chewed on that and I knew he was right. Just in my mind, when I'd mulled it over it hadn't felt like something I might want to change. Or maybe, I just was hoping to prove there wasn't anything that I needed to change; that the world was the one that needed fixing.

Mathais was right and I couldn't wrap my head around how he could be so spot-on with just having met me. Maybe it was time to just let go of how I'd once identified myself and just be whatever I was going to be. I was tired of analyzing and overthinking every little thing.

I just wanted to breathe easy for once.

My cellphone rang on my night stand. I rolled to my side, watching an image of Berea flash across my screen. I answered it immediately.

"Hi."

"Hey!" Berea chirped. "You never called last night so I figured I'd check on you. What'd you end up doing? Not more work, I hope."

"I went out last night," I said quickly.

"Did you meet someone?" she asked eagerly and I felt a guilty twinge at just how excited she sounded by the prospect of me having met someone. I realized how worried she really must have been for me these past few months.

"I ran into one of the old applicants from my failed experiment at the Bitter End Monday night and we decided to meet up Friday."

Berea gasped. "Which one?"

"Mathais. Did I tell you about him? I can't remember. He was the most normal. Maybe the fifth or sixth person I met way back in the beginning."

130

"I don't remember either, but tell me about him! Did you guys go out on a date?"

"Not exactly, he offered to co-write the piece with me and exclusively work together."

"No—Piper, don't you dare. You're just starting to recover from Levi."

"God, have I been that pathetic?"

"Of course not, but as your best friend I have to tell you when to bow out."

"This is one of those times, eh?"

"Yes."

"I'm really attracted to him," I confessed.

"Can't you just have a normal relationship with him?"

"Isn't that what failed so horribly last time?"

"Levi was more like a fling with relationship potential," Berea categorized.

I sighed. Of course, she was right.

"Nothing feels safe," I admitted.

"Nothing *is* ever safe. The point is to just see where things take you."

"How's Clyde?" I asked.

"Boring," Berea said.

"Fizzling?"

"There's no fizzle left, it's just flat now. We have barely seen each other the past few weeks and when we do—well, it's complicated. In fact, that was kind of why I wanted to talk to you."

"You're leaving Clyde!?"

"God, you don't have to be such a know-it-all-bitch," Berea said, laughing awkwardly.

She was right.

"I'm sorry. I don't know what's wrong with me."

"You're just in a funk. You need to have some fun."

"You sound like Mathais."

131

"If he's like me, then I *like him* already. I think you should have fun with him. Forget your thesis. Forget Levi. Just enjoy having someone who enjoys having you. Does that make sense or am I rambling?"

I laughed. I'd forgotten how much I loved Berea. She could always perk up my darkest mood.

"You are rambling, but it does make sense," I said.

"Next weekend, let's get together, okay? Just us, no third wheels."

"I interrupted you a while back and got you sidetracked. What'd you want to talk to me about?"

"Are you mad about me and Clyde?"

"I'm not upset that you guys are together, I'm just mad about life—everything, the air, the trees; you get the general idea."

"You won't always feel this way," Berea assured me.

"I did have a nice time last night."

"Let yourself move on, Piper."

We ended the call on an up note, making plans to get brunch sometime in the next few days. If it didn't happen, it would be because I canceled or didn't commit to a day, not Berea. Groaning, I rolled over and punched my pillow.

Berea was right and of course she was. Someone looking in on a situation was always going to give you a clearer image than the close-up one you had. I couldn't keep on like this. I had to let myself move on. I couldn't waste any more time secluding myself.

All right, I decided bravely. I rolled back over and grabbed my phone and dialed.

Mathais answered on the second ring, his voice rich, sexy and groggy.

"Good morning," he said.

"It's almost eleven," I teased.

Mathais laughed drowsily.

"On a Saturday," he reminded me. "Any plans for today?"

"Nothing that doesn't make me feel like an old woman."

"Come spend the day with me then," he offered. "Orlando has a concert tonight we might all go to—it's all pretty much up in the air, but you should join us."

Just like that? Mathais was willing to slip into an easy friendship. No questions asked, no apologies needed for my bratty-fit I'd thrown outside his apartment last night; no explanations on why I hadn't gone back upstairs with him; no decision on if I wanted to keep going forward with that expose. I knew right then that Mathais was a much better person than I was.

I wanted to address all of the things he was letting go, but I was frozen by an inability to decide whether to begin with an explanation or apology.

"You still there? Everything all right?" Mathais asked worriedly.

"Yes, sorry—phone must have cut out. What time should I come over?"

His one-word response stretched out like audible taffy as he yawned.

"Whenever."

"I have some work I should really do," I said slowly, teetering with the direction of my decision.

"I have work too, bring yours with you. I'll make us lunch."

Mathais, I—"

"Remember how you said you'd let me decide whether we were friends or we do the expose?" he asked, cutting me off but continuing without waiting for a response. "I choose friends. I want to get to know you, Piper, and you don't owe me anything; not an apology or an explanation. If more grows between us then it will, but what I really want is to get to know you and be friends."

I surprised myself by letting out a large sigh of relief.

"Were you worried? That was one large exhale."

"A little, I'm a little bit..." What? Shit, I didn't even have it labeled in my own mind, I didn't know how to explain it to him.

"Complicated?" Mathais offered. "We all are, but you called me and I get the feeling that you could use a friend or two. Why not let me and my crazy gang take you under our wings?"

I chewed on my lip. Berea had already given me a green light and she hadn't even met him, and I genuinely had fun hanging out with him. I liked his friends a lot and he was offering lunch. What the hell, I'd been thrust into this six-month funk and I was thrusting myself out.

"All right, I'll come over."

16

Mathais greeted me with a quick peck on the cheek when he opened the door. It felt friendly and natural, like something he would do for any close female friend that came over for lunch. He ushered me in, motioning for me to sit at the bar that overlooked the kitchen. I set my laptop on the table and threw my coat on one of the three high barstools.

Mathais went back into the kitchen and I deduced that he must have been in the middle of cleaning up from last night. There were dishes everywhere, crumbs, half-eaten bags of chips; it didn't look like he'd made much progress.

"You host a party, your friends wreck your place and then make you clean?"

Mathais smiled broadly.

"I told you they were pricks."

"Guess that makes me a prick because I didn't offer to clean either before I left."

"I can think of many 'p' words to describe you but none of them are *that*."

I fell in line beside him and began gathering up the beer cans to dump them in the sink.

"Let's hear some of those *preposterous* words you think describe me so *perfectly*."

He shot me a dazzling knee-weakening smile over his shoulder.

"Productive."

"Pragmatic," I shot back.

"Are you correcting me?"

"No, just playing along."

Mathais turned to face me, leaning against the stove he'd been cleaning and placing the wet rag on the counter.

"Every p-word I say that describes you, you're going to toss one back at me?"

"Probably." I said, grinning.

"The person with the last word wins, loser fixes lunch?"

"Deal."

"Ladies first, " Mathais insisted as he went back to cleaning.

"Promiscuous."

That had him dropping the rag and turning right back around to face me.

"Provoking."

"Profound," I tossed back.

"Patient?" I hadn't meant to inflect my voice at the end, turning the word into a question but the word had just come out that way.

"Pretty," Mathais said with steady eyes on mine.

I wasn't sure now if we were describing ourselves or each other. Was Mathais saying I was pretty or that he could be pretty patient? Puzzling; this childish game had an addictive, honest quality. I didn't want to stop and not because I didn't want to lose.

"Pretender," I said quietly.

Mathais' face darkened a little.

"Presumptuous problematic profiling."

"Overachiever," I said, laughing and raising my hands in defeat. "I think you won. How about we order in? My treat, of course, since I lost."

"Sounds good, I'll keep cleaning."

I retreated back to the living-room side of the bar and dug my computer out of the bag.

"Mind if I connect to your wireless?"

"Of course not, it's the connection called 'Welcome Mat' and the password is: YOURMAMA, all one word, no spaces. I've just never changed it from college—don't judge."

136

I grinned, but did manage to not verbally *judge* him.

There was this online site I loved called *Just Eat.* It hosted, organized by zip code, all the takeout delivery places nearby. I scrolled through the texts between Mathais and me until I found where he'd sent me his address. He was elbow deep in the sink, working furiously on the dishes.

"Even though I won that impromptu game," he said over his shoulder to me, "I'll let you pick what we eat."

"Any food you *don't* like?"

Sometimes it was easier to start with the no and then get to the yes.

"Not really. I'm kind of a pig when it comes to food."

I chewed on my lip—that was the first time that tactic hadn't really worked. I guess I would just choose a place I liked to eat and hopefully he'd like it too.

"There's a Mexican restaurant that I've had before. Want to come take a peek at the menu?"

"Sure," Mathais agreed.

He moved to stand behind me, leaning over my shoulder to peer at the screen. I could smell his cologne and I had to fight the urge to do anything embarrassing like drool or sniff him.

"Yeah, order me that quesadilla with extra sour cream and salsa on the side."

I ordered a large steak nacho with extra everything.

"I've never used this site before. It looks amazing," Mathais commented before strolling back into the kitchen.

"Need any help? Our food will be here in about thirty."

"No, I'm fine. You said you had work you needed to do?"

I sighed dramatically. "Yes, editorial work haunts me year round."

"Sounds as bad as my job. Now, I'm feeling like we should both rebel and not work at all today."

My mind wantonly flashed back to memories of when I'd discovered just how comfortable Mathais' couch was earlier the night before.

"Do you really get that sultry expression on your face when you order takeout or are you having promiscuous thoughts?"

I made a non-committal humming sound and pretended to be extremely interested in the work I hadn't even pulled up yet on my computer. I was pretty sure I caught him smirking at me out of my peripheral vision but I continued to stare at my screen and he went back to cleaning.

We stayed like that while we waited and although I opened up a couple of documents I couldn't stop sneaking peeks at him moving through the kitchen. My eyes constantly trailing over him from head to toe, I was interested in everything from his bare feet to the way his jeans were just a tad more fitted than the average man wore them. I liked his mannerisms too. I could tell he hadn't worked a crappy food job because he was the slowest cleaner I'd ever seen, but it was cute and oddly methodical even if it wasn't efficient. I was contemplating showing some domestic initiative and helping him clean when his apartment door buzzed and the food arrived.

Mathais bounded to the door, turning the knob simultaneously as he took his wallet out of his back pocket.

The delivery girl—a very cute one, I might add—let out a flirty, confused giggle.

"You paid online all ready. All of our orders are prepaid."

Mathais gave me quick, questioning glance before putting his wallet away and accepting the parcel of food. He turned towards me, balancing our food on one hand and locking his door with the other.

"I said I would pay, remember?"

"Chivalry thief," Mat said, accusingly.

"That's not a real thing."

"Sure it is," Mathais insisted, "I'm looking right at one."

"No, you're looking at a feminist and believer in true equality between the sexes. That means everyone gets an opportunity to be chivalrous."

"Hard to see any fault in that; it would be nice to have someone else snag the door when my arms are full."

"*Exactly.*"

"Do you want something to drink? I have beer, hard cider, pop, water?"

"Water would be fine. Thanks."

Once the containers were open it was deathly quiet between us. The food was delicious and as I shoveled improper bites into my mouth of cheesy nacho chips, I forgot where I was. I cautiously glanced over at Mathias but he was deep into his own food. He looked over at me and gave me a puffy food-filled-cheek smile.

"This is fantastic," he groaned after he'd swallowed enough to be able to speak.

I smiled and went back to gorging.

I snagged a mint from my purse and popped it—I hoped very casually—into my mouth.

"Do you have another?"

I nodded and tossed Mathais one.

The food carnage had finally ended leaving the kitchen bar a messy casualty.

I began to clear everything away. Mathais followed behind me with cleaner and paper towel. When we'd finished, I turned to him, planning on offering to help clean the kitchen. Mathais had been closer than I'd realized and I smacked right into him. I wobbled on my feet, but his arms were around my waist steadying me before I could really lose my balance. Nevertheless, I was still breathless like I'd fallen.

I could smell the sweet wintergreen on his breath. His eyes flared with specks of amber as he looked at me. I was just a little more than a head's length shorter than him. I stretched up, grazing his jaw lightly with my lips. I wanted to kiss him but after all the confusing signals and conversations we'd had, I wasn't sure if that was agreeable to him anymore. Maybe being friends meant *just friends* for him now. This feathery kiss on his jawline was an offer; he could choose to take it or walk away from it.

17

Mathais didn't hesitate; his strong arms pulled me up onto my toes and straight to his mouth. His lips were so smooth and soft. I had to have more. I enriched our kiss with my tongue and gripped his shirt tightly.

Mathais stopped.

I opened my eyes and he took a step back, tugging at his collar as if it were suddenly too tight.

"What's wrong?" I asked hesitantly.

Mathais stared at me, his expression confused and unsure.

"Nothing," Mathais insisted quietly.

"Should I not have kissed you?"

"Did you want to kiss me or did you think you had to?"

"Didn't you want me to?" I asked.

Mathais gave me a surprisingly worried look.

"Only if you wanted to because you actually *wanted* to. Does that make sense? We're starting fresh. No baggage, no labels, no expose— just us, as we are."

"Kiss me again, Mathais"

He came back to me and the second kiss was just as slow and soft as the first but twice as good. I was thawing again; it was spring and every part of my body, from my hair to my toes, was tingling awake.

"Put your hands on me, touch me," I pleaded.

Mathais curled his arms around my waist, his lips skimming down against my neck as he held me. His hands grazed my hips before ascending underneath my shirt and up my back. The physical contact had me humming. His touch had me simultaneously relaxing and revving up.

"Bedroom," I whispered.

His head shook against the curve of my shoulder.

141

"There's no rush," he said quietly as his lips explored my skin.

I sighed half in joy, half in frustration.

"No reason to wait," I said back.

"Aren't we hanging out for a while?"

I blushed, feeling like a hussy for practically jumping him in his kitchen. What was wrong with me? I took a deep breath and tried to still my racing heart and overly sexual mind.

"I—I didn't mean to be so eager," I choked out awkwardly.

"Don't apologize," Mathais said. "I love kissing you, Piper. God, it makes me feel like a wild, uncontrollable teenager which is something I never felt as an actual teenager, ironically."

"Then why pull away?"

Mathais' eyes were earnest. "I didn't want to rush you."

Looking away to hide the mix of emotions I was feeling, I nodded.

"I understand."

"I'm not sure that you do," Mathais said quietly.

Mathais wrapped his arms around my waist. He pulled me close and I couldn't fight the urge to close my eyes and breathe him in. He smelled good and he felt even better.

"You make me nervous," Mathais said quietly. He pulled back, taking my hand in his, and led me out of the kitchen down the hallway to what could only lead to his bedroom. I had wanted this and I swear I hadn't been nervous until the moment I realized I was about to get exactly what I'd been pushing him for. Mathais halted us in the doorway of his bedroom, bending to give me a light kiss before effortlessly swooping me up into his arms. I gasped, both delighted and surprised. He nuzzled the side of my face as he walked through the doorway.

"What were you planning on doing once you got me in here?" Mathais asked.

My skin prickled as Mathais spoke. The words were heated, packed with the tension that had been bubbling between us since the unexpected success of our first kiss at the Bitter End. I tilted my head and sucked on the first bit of skin I could reach. I could feel his pulse quicken beneath my lips, and his response to me gave me courage to respond to him.

"Anything you want."

Mathais sat down on the bed, still holding me in his arms. I shifted to straddle him, sucking in a quick breath as I felt him hard beneath me. He groaned, deep in his throat as his hands swept up my back, catching my shirt as they went. I lifted my arms, silently following his wordless command. I had no idea where my tee went. His gripped lips curved into a smile against my neck; his fingers dug into my hips.

"Anything I want?" Mathais repeated back.

"Anything," I promised.

Mathais came back to my mouth and the way he kissed me made it impossible not to rock on. Mathais groaned.

"Why am I the only one who's topless?" I asked.

He gave me a dashing smile, quickly pulling his own shirt off. I sucked in a sharp breath. I'd known he wasn't out of shape but I hadn't thought he was in this great of shape. I wantonly stroked my hands across his arms, shoulders, chest and down his rippled torso.

"What, smart people are supposed to be fat?" he asked, laughing as I touched him.

I laughed too. *Shit.* I hoped I wasn't drooling.

"I wasn't thinking that," I assured him.

He caught one of my hands and kissed my palm.

"What were you thinking then?"

"About how beautiful your body is."

"You're breathtaking, Piper."

He tumbled us backwards, down onto the mattress.

"Let's make a deal," Mathais said.

I arched an eyebrow.

"Whatever I do to you, you have to do *to me.*"

"Deal," I agreed far too quickly. I knew exactly where I wanted those pretty, pouty, full lips of his. I beelined to his fly.

143

"Not so fast," Mathais said, wriggling away from me. "You don't get to go first. Shimmy out of those pants and socks."

I shrugged, feigning coolness I didn't feel at all. I took a breath and undressed. Mathais watched me hungrily. I unhooked my bra, watching his face closely as it dropped to the floor. I loved how honest he was, how he didn't even try to hide his admiration. It was sexy, a major turn-on, and I absorbed the attention hungrily.

"Lay down on your stomach."

I rolled on my belly, glad my face was hidden. I was a bit of an emotional-sexual mess right now. I was nervous, but more excited and completely riled up. I was ready for him to touch me. I wanted him to touch me, and when I felt his weight shift the mattress, I quivered in anticipation.

Mathais swept my hair to the side, kissing my neck briefly before he began to massage. He started at my scalp, gently kneading it slowly. I melted. It wasn't just his touch relaxing me but the energy, the warmth of affection, behind it. It was as if he took pleasure, pleasuring me. I was mentally purring when his hands moved over my shoulders, working my skin in smooth, firm lines. I moaned appreciatively.

"Good?"

"I feel powerless," I muttered, turning my head as I sighed.

"I was afraid I might have lost my touch."

"Popular with the ladies?"

"In my massage therapy undergraduate general education course—yes."

"I can't talk—"I mumbled. I could barely think too; it was fantastic.

I heard him chuckle and then felt him lean forward, kiss my shoulder and then begin massaging my arms, even each individual hand, stretching my palm in a way I hadn't even known could be relaxing. He worked back up my arms and then down my torso all the way down to my hips. His hands paused there, his fingertips curling under my boy-shorts lacy panties.

"May I?"

144

I hummed a sound that meant yes and raised my hips so he could roll my underwear down my legs. He kissed a cheek before giving the same spot a playful nip that evoked a muffled squeal from me. I felt his lips curve against my ass and then his attention went to each individual thigh, calf, ankle and foot.

"Roll over," Mathais instructed.

I did and his hands went back up each leg simultaneously until they met at my breasts. He kneaded them and my eyes closed as I arched. I was so aroused I felt like I couldn't breathe. I'd been relaxed on my stomach and now I was aching. I reached for him and he lowered his lips to mine.

"Ready?" he asked quietly.

I nodded, surprised myself with how easy it was to trust him and to let him have control. He had me in a good place where I wanted to explore and just let things *happen.* I wasn't even thinking really about what he was going to do, I was just letting it come, and when his lips went south of my navel my body opened for him.

I heard him curse under his breath in admiration—which I unexpectedly loved hearing—and then I felt the pressure of his lips and the soft curls of his head brushing against my thighs. He kissed, licked, sucked and by the time his tongue finally slipped in I was hurtling down that wonderfully slippery slope of pleasure.

Fuck, I came quickly with an intangible combination of conflicting, delicious sensations so different from the limited orgasms I'd known. I was out of breath, my hand knotted in his hair, and my legs—somehow—transported over his shoulders.

"One more, baby," Mathais said, his face still nestled into my core.

I was barely processing his words before I felt his mouth sucking on my clit and two fingers slowly slipping inside of me.

"I don't know if I—" I gasped, unable to even finish my sentence. I was building up again, the twisting motion of his hand catching me off guard. He was teaming up with my body against me and as far as I was

145

concerned it was a beautiful partnership. I let go and I shook under the weight of a heavy, fast second orgasm.

Mathais quickly moved up the bed, kissing my mouth—the taste of myself on his lips and tongue. I was in the best sexual haze of my life and his hand lingered behind as he held me, caressing me in gentle strokes that spread the after-warmth from my core to my limbs. I sighed—feeling completely satiated and curled into him and this small paradise he had created.

When I woke, I was still nestled in the nook of Mathais' arm. He was still asleep too, lying on his back with the sheet low on his boxer-brief-lined hips. I trailed the outline of his taut abs with a finger. Mathais gave me a small semi-asleep smile.

I studied him while he slept, thinking about the long massage he'd given me, followed by some fantastic special attention to my lady bits. God, it had been so good that I'd fallen into an orgasm coma almost immediately after we'd finished. My mouth went dry just thinking about how easily I'd melted for him. All my fears felt like yesterday's problems. I was floored by how relaxed and smooth a transition it had been from friends to lovers. I liked that he wasn't interested in labeling our relationship right now; maybe that's why it was working so well—it wasn't complicated. We just were and it was enough. For now though, the only thing I had in mind was making good on my promise to do onto him as he had done onto me.

In one confident motion, I pulled him out of his boxers and slipped my lips over his tip and down his shaft as far as I could take. His eyes opened wide but quickly drooped, lustfully heavy, as he watched me suck. He'd been semi-hard when I'd started but he quickly grew tauter as I enthusiastically worked him over with my mouth and hands. I felt him tremble beneath me and I loved the power of making him shake. I was doing this to him. I was filling his body with pleasure, hopefully, that was just as good as what he'd given me. I'd never known how intoxicating it could be to make someone fall apart.

"Baby," Mathais moaned earnestly, "I'm not going to be able to—"

His sentence was finished with a throaty groan that only made me more determined to achieve my goal. I didn't want him to just come either; I wanted him to empty. Cursing, he knotted a fist into my hair but didn't stop me. I felt him tense as he came. I took everything he spilled, sucking slowly until he was spent and stilled.

"Come here," Mathais beckoned softly a few minutes later.

I did, curling immediately back in the crook of his arm. He kissed my forehead as I nuzzled him before falling right back to sleep.

18

I heard the slow music of a piano and opened my eyes.

"Where am I?"

"In my bed," Mathais answered from beside me.

"Is that music playing?"

"Yeah, Chopin. Want me to turn it off?"

"No," I murmured, still half asleep. It was dark, my body felt amazing and, most importantly, I was comfortable.

"Only briefly waking up for a location check?"

I sighed, half trying to formulate an answer, but really, I was more interested in going back to sleep.

"It's almost eight o'clock."

That jolted my mind awake and our little oral romp flooded back to me in quick waves.

"At night?" I attempted to clarify as I rolled towards him.

"Yeah, we both kind of passed out. Then you gave me sleepy-head and then we both zonked out again."

I stretched, smiling at him shyly as I woke up the rest of the way and remembered in detail the day's activities.

"We missed the concert."

"I'm sorry."

"Don't be. I'm glad we missed it," Mathais added with a smug smirk.

He reached over to me and idly twirled a piece of my hair between his fingers.

I sat up, realizing that my hair probably looked insane and wanted to get it tied down and under control immediately. As soon as I shifted, so did the comforter. It slid down to my waist and I remembered that I was still naked.

Mat hummed appreciatively. I realized that I wasn't self-conscious when I didn't stop watching him looking at my body. I'd never had a chance to see someone's reaction to my form, to observe their expression as they took me in. I didn't think I was beautiful by any means, but he clearly liked what he saw. What did he see when he looked at me? Could he see all the things that had damaged me, or was I just what he imagined me to be? Maybe that was how people were born again and given second chances, through someone else's interpretation of what they think they see in you.

Mathais' eyes lingered a second longer before he turned, reaching for something on the nightstand behind him. I noticed he'd had time to find all his clothes.

"Did you watch me sleep?"

He turned back in my direction and handed me my hairband, followed by my underwear, bra, shirt and pants.

"No, but I did dream of you."

"Oh? What was I doing?"

"It wasn't a good dream, not at first at least."

"That's a bit creepy," I said as I pulled my shirt on.

Mathais smiled.

"No one can control their dreams."

"So, what was I doing?" I asked again.

"Afraid I'll discover your secrets through my magical dream powers?"

"Maybe..."

"You were sitting on a bed, crying," Mathais said.

"Now I know it was a dream. I rarely cry."

"You were holding a letter," he added.

I gulped, immediately thinking of the night Levi dumped me—what an odd coincidence. I thought about fessing up and letting him know he really did have creepy dream powers but instead I stayed silent and he continued.

"I came in, read the letter, and then we kissed."

149

"What'd the letter say?"

"I have no idea, but when I kissed you, you crumpled the letter and threw it away."

"And then?" I asked as I stood to put on my jeans.

"Magic," Mathais said, grinning.

I laughed.

"What was that music again?"

"Chopin, the only one I can play because it's super slow."

"You play the piano?"

"Yeah—the pack texted me to see if we wanted to join them for dinner. Concert will be ending soon, we'd have to leave now but we can still meet up with them."

On cue my stomach gurgled.

"Is that a yes?" Mat asked.

"Should I?" I asked myself aloud.

"Probably, I mean you love my company and you're hungry."

"Will they think it's weird that we're together so much?"

"It's none of their business," Mathais said resolutely. "Besides, why would it be weird?"

"I'd have to have a firm grasp on normality to be able to answer that, that's why I was asking you."

Mathais grinned at that.

"You think I'm normal? You don't have to flatter me. I'll gladly let you use my body, Piper."

I laughed again—it was so easy to laugh when I was with him. It felt good.

"Are you driving?" I asked.

"Sure, Pi."

I froze and he read my mood immediately.

"I didn't just ruin the evening, did I?"

Yes—No.

"No," my mind settled on quickly.

"I didn't mean to call you that, not really, it's just—well—we just click, you know? I forget that we really don't know each other. It feels like we've been friends our whole lives."

"I know," I agreed honestly. "My mom used to call me that and then an ex did—and since him it's kind of lost its charm."

"Ah—you're not against nicknames, just *that* nickname."

"Exactly."

"Then I can make up something sickeningly sweet to call you by when we're alone?"

I raised an eyebrow.

"We're going to have pet names for each other now?"

"Well, you do owe me a back rub. In exchange, I'll take lifetime rights to calling you the nickname of my choice. It's a fair trade."

His offer plus the wiggling of his eyebrows while he said it had me almost rolling with laughter.

"God—I've laughed more times this weekend then I have in a long time."

Mathais took my hands and pulled me into a quick hug.

"Good," Mathais said as he released me. "I'm going to text Henry back and let him know we're on our way."

"She's back!" Henry crooned delightedly when he saw us walk in. We'd come to a popular spot called Corkscrew Pub. I'd passed it a million times but never gone in. The atmosphere was peppy, light and fun.

"Yes, I am," I said, smiling warmly as I sat down at the table. "Mathais feels sorry for me because I only have two friends and they're now dating each other."

"Permanent third wheel; that is harsh," Orlando said, nodding in agreement.

"Mathais doesn't feel sorry for you, he feels empathy," Henry corrected.

"Remember Nate and Cordelia from last night? Mathais and she were an item until Nate stole nerdie-zues's thunder."

"Is that right?" I asked, turning to Mathais. I wanted to see his reaction to Henry teasing him so brutally. I was assuming it wasn't true but when I saw Mat's face it was *totally true* and not only that, Mathais was frowning; he practically had a scowl on his face. That was definitely the first time I'd seen that expression.

"Lovely time to bring that up," Mathais grumbled from beside me.

"I just wanted to fill her in—she can't be in our pack and not know all of our secrets," Orlando insisted.

"Douche," Mathais cursed under his breath. He began flipping through the menu and Henry began telling equally embarrassing anecdotes about Orlando and his lack of game in pre-college, during college, after college and, according to Henry, in the future.

I leaned towards Mat and placed my hand just above his knee.

"Perhaps that was really you on the bed crying in your dream," I whispered in his ear.

Mathais looked at me, a challenge brewing in his eyes. I realized then, a bit too late, that I probably shouldn't have teased him. Clearly, this was a touchy topic.

"Do you know what you want to eat, love?" Mathais asked loudly.

"Wait—," Henry said, stopping his story mid-sentence, "are you two *dating*?"

"How long have you been fucking?" Orlando piped in.

"Just since this afternoon," Mathais said coyly.

"Bullshit," Henry called out. "Pet names are awfully advanced— they might be past the fucking stage and to the *lovemaking* stage which is only two stages away from the baby-making frenzy stage."

I blushed and withdrew my hand from Mathais's thigh. I might have bit off more than I could chew with him. He was quick, smart, and loved to tease as much as I did. I wasn't intimidated; in fact, it was invigorating that he could actually keep up with me and wasn't offended by my crass, almost tormenting, sense of humor. Mathais blew me a kiss

152

before turning back to his menu. He did not answer a single one of their questions. *Well played, Mathias,* I thought, smirking down at my own menu.

"That was dirty," I said under my breath.

"But fun," he whispered back.

"You didn't even try to come to the concert, did you?"

I looked up and saw Nate and Cordelia headed to our group.

"Of course he didn't," Cordelia teased, and then her eyes saw me and she froze. She looked back between the two of us—quickly making assumptions. I didn't like her—just like my first impression she was too perfect, but at least now I knew she had a flaw. If she really did choose Nate over Mathais she was an idiot and didn't deserve him. All right—maybe I was being a bit judgy—I didn't know what the real story was, but I was betting it was close to what his friends had said. All jokes are made of a small percentage of truth, after all.

"You're back!" Nate greeted us, with a good-natured smile.

"Nice to see you again," Cordelia added politely.

"Mathais wants to adopted her into the pack," Henry added.

"When's her initiation?" Nate asked.

"Initiation?" I said

"It's a pack, not a girl scout club! There's initiation for every membership."

"You're not really going to go through an initiation," Mathais assured me. "It was just something we did in college."

"You shut your filthy mouth!" Orlando said in a completely all-business tone.

Mathais sighed.

"I told you they were pricks."

"You told her we were *pricks?*" Henry questioned, in an honestly offended tone.

"Piper can hang with us without being *initiated.* We're intellectuals, not frat boys," Mathais said.

"It's just a little fun," Cordelia chimed in, with a sweet smile that didn't quite reach her eyes. "She looks tough. I'm sure she can handle it."

"Ready to order?"

I had no idea when the waitress appeared and I quickly ordered something off the menu.

I chewed over my decision while the others ordered. Half of me thought it was childish that I wanted to agree to be initiated, the other half was ecstatic at the opportunity to prove myself. My mind was racing with excitement. God, it was so stupid but I kind of wanted to be in the *pack*. It couldn't be that bad. Besides, they couldn't make me do anything I didn't want to. It was ridiculous, I knew, but ultimately felt daring and exciting; so unlike the very controlled existence I'd had. Even the idea of the expose was still heavily organized and planned on my part. I never gave up control. I'd never really been spontaneous, and the more I thought about it the more resolved I became to doing it.

"I'm in," I declared excitedly.

Mathais looked surprised.

Cordelia looked irritated.

Orlando had a slightly intimidating, conniving smirk.

Henry looked like he was in love.

Mathais broke the haze first. "As the alpha of the pack, I have to approve of her initiation challenge and for fuck sake, don't embarrass me anymore or I won't share her and Cordelia will be the only female— besides your mothers—that you have access to."

Henry scoffed and fixed his horn-rimmed glasses.

"Not true, I'm a professor, I see plenty of women," Henry corrected.

Orlando, Nate and Mathais ruthlessly stared at him—and Henry, well, he didn't even make it a minute before he cracked.

"Being a bit socially awkward around the opposite sex is *common* for someone of my intellectual fortitude."

"Right," Nate said with a smug smile before turning to Mathais. "I vote for the Dunes."

"I wholeheartedly concur," Henry agreed quickly.

"I second!" Orlando chimed in.

"Pigs," Mathais muttered under his breath, but I caught the little amused glint in his eyes. He was enjoying this, at least a little.

"What are the Dunes?" I asked, with a nervous giggle. "Like sand dunes or some weird sci-fi themed bar?"

"If you're serious about getting initiated, you don't get to ask questions," Orlando said matter-of-factly.

"It's an hour and half drive from here," Mathais reminded them.

It was out of the city? Now I was really intrigued.

"I'm up for anything," I vowed.

Mathais smiled; the turn of his lips was just a touch wicked.

"Do I finally get initiated in tonight too?" Cordelia asked. She'd been so quiet I'd forgotten she was even there.

"Didn't you go through this already?"

"When I met them, it was an all-male pack," Cordelia said.

"What do you say, Alpha-Matthias, can she assimilate?" Nate said, wrapping an arm around his girlfriend's shoulders.

"Hold up—" Henry said, adjusting his glasses as he raised his hand. "She's not exactly trustworthy."

Oh snap, I thought. They sure were open with their feelings. I snuck a peek at Cordelia. She couldn't make eye contact with anyone.

"Low blow," Nate muttered.

"It's not a lie though, is it?," Orlando retorted.

The tension at the table shifting dramatically. Everyone seemed to be waiting for Mathais to speak.

"It's fine," Mathais said. "Eventually we'll all have girlfriends and since you all won't let the whole 'pack' thing die, I suppose they'll all have to get initiated in, right?"

"Let it die? What the fuck, man?" Orlando said with pure disgust.

"He doesn't mean it," Henry soothed.

155

"Once Cordelia is in, we're going to stop bringing that old shit up, right?" Nate asked.

"I didn't bring it up," Mathais said coolly, reaching for his drink.

"You didn't have to. You're not over it, so *they're* not over it either," Nate insisted.

Mathais shrugged.

Cordelia scowled.

"So fucking childish," she muttered.

"Kind of a rough second introduction," Nate joked, "Piper won't even want to hang out with us if we keep bickering like eighty-year-olds."

Mathais took a deep breath.

"Next time, we're going out to dinner just the two of us," Mat said to me.

"It's fine," I insisted. I wasn't really offended, just surprised. His friends were an odd bunch—not that I could talk—but all the same, I liked them and even though it made me feel a little juvenile, I couldn't wait to find out what was in store for me at the Dunes.

19

"You know, none of this is really necessary," Mathias told me as we got in his car.

"I'm actually excited about it," I confessed.

"Really? *Why?* My friends are completely idiotic."

"They're sweet and loyal; they're the kind of friends that are *family*."

Mathais snorted.

"How many people actually like their family?" he asked.

"That's why friend-family is way better than family-family," I insisted.

"Want me to tell you what the Dunes is?" he asked as pulled out of the paid parking ramp.

"I should wait, but I hate waiting. Tell me."

"It's a private beach. The call it the Dunes to make fun of me because they found some pictures online—that my mother posted—of me on a beach in Michigan."

"Going to the beach is a lame initiation."

"You're going to skinny dip. Actually, you're going to streak from the parking lot to the water and then skinny dip."

I gasped.

"I tried to warn you."

"I'm doing it!"

"Why?" Mathais asked.

"I'm too serious," I said. It was the best word I could think of to articulate how I felt and it was true. I was *way* too serious. I took life too literally. I never did spontaneous things or anything just to do it. All my decisions had some figurative or physical motive. I wanted to just do something, for no reason other than wanting to. Mathais gave me a half-smile but didn't say anything else. His focus went back to driving and I grew silent too, watching the city lights glaze the dark sky as we drove. Soon, the highway turned to state road and that twisted into a lakeside community. Even in the dark, I could see the outlines of manicured lawns and beautiful cottages. An hour latter we turned down a paved driveway and my stomach tightened nervously.

"Is this private property?" I asked.

"Yes, but you can't really own a lake, can you?"

My stomach flipped. I was going to be a skinny-dipping, trespassing rebel.

"I bet the owners will make a pretty strong argument against that statement."

"It'll be fine. It's a private, public beach for the neighborhood. My family owns a house here, so even if we got caught it would be by people I know."

Mathais parked his car and we got out. The others hadn't arrived yet, so we leaned against the car, gazing out across the dark water. We were in a small, ten-car cemented parking area. There were a couple of iron lanterns posted throughout the small space enclosed by trees, and then directly in front of us was the black water lapping across the private beach. I could hear the waves washing rhythmically across the beach; the sound lulled me. I took a deep breath. The air smelled wonderful.

Our fingers interlocked as we waited for the others to arrive. It was a simple touch but so sweet and so sincere. It felt like it could lead to anything, that one day we could be anything. I marveled at the mixture of emotions Mathais stirred in me. How was he able to make me feel like that? Had Levi made me so raw that now I was ultra-emotional and romantic, desperate for a happy ending? I swallowed nervously and tried to keep how vulnerable I was feeling under wraps. I was starting to wonder if orgasms could be mind-altering. I had to get a grip.

As if on cue, the rest of the pack arrived.

"Thank God for GPS!" Orlando exclaimed as he stepped out of a dark-colored Jeep Laredo.

"If I didn't know better," Henry piped in, "I'd swear you were trying to lose us."

Cordelia and Nate also got out of the car but Cordelia didn't look excited.

"I can't believe I'm doing this," she muttered.

Nathan wrapped an arm around her shoulders encouragingly. "Don't worry, you two will do great."

"Enough talk! Get to it!" Orlando boomed.

Mathais shook his head and gave the back of my hand a light kiss before retreating to where the other guys were standing and hooting.

I took my shoes off and set them behind me. The small paved parking lot was scratchy and warm on my soles. It was maybe fifty feet or less between me and the water's edge. I might as well strip here and then streak to the water. It wasn't that far and at least my back was to them.

"I don't want them seeing me naked," Cordelia complained next to me.

"Well," I said, as I shimmied out of my pants, "all they'll really see is our bare asses fading away into the night."

"Until it's time to get back out—then it's full frontal."

I cursed under my breath. I hadn't thought of that. Well, maybe Mathais would come down to the edge of the water with my clothes. If he didn't, well, I'd just deal. I ate my fear, swallowing hard and shoved my self-consciousness deep down.

"I'm not doing it. If we both refuse, they'll have to give us some other type of dare," Cordelia said. The words blew out of her mouth quickly as if she was stating something that had already been agreed upon between us.

There was no way I was backing out.

"It won't be that bad," I insisted. I started undressing quickly and soon I was down to my underwear. We heard a woot from the parking

159

lot. I giggled nervously. I didn't turn around. Instead, I focused on the onyx-crystal water in front of me and finished stripping. I couldn't chicken out; I'd regret that more than having them seeing my apple-shaped rear, wide hips and mini-melon boobs.

"Mathais is such an ass," Cordelia grumbled. "As long as he's not over it, *they'll* never be either."

A quick shrug was the only response I gave her. I didn't like the sense of entitlement I got from her. She had cheated on Mathais with his best friend; why shouldn't she have to eat a little bit of shit over that? If she wanted pity, she wasn't getting it from me.

"Shit or get off the pot!" I heard one of the guys yell.

They were right, time to fly! I took a deep breath and ran.

I don't know why I shrieked as I sprinted but it was a gleeful war cry that felt wonderful, and when my toes broke the edge of the water, I jogged even faster. The waves lapped against my bare thighs and up my stomach. When I was deep enough, I dived down and rose back up new. The water was warm, but that might have just been my adrenaline—didn't matter, I was in heaven. As stupid as that might sound, I really felt that way. I was weightless, limitless, regretless.

I heard cheering on the chore and stretched out, floating on my back, just watching the punched-out star-holes in the black night sky.

"You look breathtaking."

I repositioned myself upright. Mathais was in the water too now just a few feet away. I thought of a few clever things to say but all I could do was watch him get closer. He thought I looked breathtaking. I wished he could see himself —wading towards me in the night like some sexy sea god —his brown hair wet and dark and extra curly on his forehead, his eyes completely focused on me.

"Hi," I said.

Mathais smiled and I felt his hands hook beneath my thighs guiding my legs around his naked hips. He held me tight, humming a hello against my throat. His skin radiated heat, even in the water, and I could feel every inch of him against me —abs, thighs, pelvic bones, and that

160

magnificent *rod.* Mathais hooked a finger under my chin and I rose up on my toes for a kiss that was sweet but over far too quickly.

"They're fucking!" someone yelled.

"God-dammit," Mathais cursed and then we both laughed.

I slid off him. I gritted my feet into the sand and stood. The water rose up to my collar bone.

"Ready to go back?" he asked.

"You want me to be your shield, so they don't see your magnificent rod?" I asked sweetly.

"Trying to seal chivalrous thunder again?" Mathais accused in a soft tone. "I was planning on shielding you from them."

I laughed and began to move back towards the shore.

"I'm fine," I insisted.

"Well, so am I," Mathais said as he followed.

"Then let's walk back to our clothes hand-in-hand," I bargained.

"Or, I'll give you a piggyback ride up the beach?" Mathais countered.

"Sold!"

We hadn't gone too far out, and by the time our terms were set, the water was barely covering my chest. Mathais moved in front of me and knelt into the water. I awkwardly got behind him and wrapped my arms around his waist. He stood and the water sunk low on my back. Then, with surprising gracefulness, he ran through the water and up the beach. I totally forgot to be cool and squealed the whole way.

20

"Hawthorne and his scarlet letter left us," Orlando announced as we neared them, fully clothed again. I squinted in the night and, sure enough, only one car was left. "

Why did they leave?" I asked.

"She had a bitch-fit, like always," Henry answered.

"I'm glad," Orlando added. "She's never been pack material."

"Were you really doing the nasty in public?" Henry asked with a smirk.

"We should have hidden both of your clothes," Orlando teased.

Ignoring Orlando completely, Mathais took my hand and led the way back to our car. Ironically, whatever good his silence might have done my cheeky grin ruined. I wasn't trying to intentionally make them think they were right, it was just that the idea of sex on the beach with Mathais sounded downright magical and definitely something—if we'd been alone—I would have let happen.

"We're crashing at your place, right?" Henry asked.

"Of course we are!" Orlando answered excitedly.

"I hadn't been planning on driving back but I also hadn't planned on *all* of us staying either."

"Don't you Judas us! There's plenty of room in your swanky cottage," Orlando scolded.

"If my memory is correct, isn't it just a block or two from here, right?" Henry asked.

"Yeah, it's near. We can all crash there tonight," Mathais consented.

"Mathais may seem like an open book, but he is a dungeon of secrets," Henry told me.

" For starters, he's filthy rich," Orlando added.

163

"No—I'm normal non-rich," Mathais interjected. "It's my parents' property and lucky for us they aren't using it right now so we can spontaneously crash there."

"Your parents' store must be very successful then," I said, as I climbed into the passenger side of his car.

"*Stores.* They own a *chain* of them," Orlando corrected.

"If Mathais wasn't already such an outstanding person, the endless supply of food delivered to our dorm room during college would have bonded me to him like a greedy symbiont for life," Henry said.

I looked over to Mathais, curious to see what his reaction was to his friends telling me about how well-off and generous his parents were, but he seemed to only be half-listening and only offered a shrug in response, as if all parents would be that kind if they could. Of course, that was a sunny, optimistic view of the world that most people never experienced.

"I'm hungry again," Henry whined as we pulled up to a lightly painted perfect dream house cottage. I couldn't see much more detail in the dark, but I knew it would be picturesque in daylight.

"We can always order a pizza," Orlando suggested.

We got out of the car and Mathais was quickly at my side. He wrapped an arm around my shoulder and I leaned into him, thankful for the warmth. It was getting late and the night air was chilly so close to the water.

"Are you hungry?" Mathais asked me quietly.

"Not really."

"All right, we can just go to bed, but if you get hungry let me know."

I nodded in agreement. My stomach had flipped when he said *we can just go to bed*. After my little taste from earlier, I wouldn't turn down another round of sexual activities. Although, I suppose it was rather soon. Maybe not for my history, but for the general history of appropriate relationship progression, it was kind of soon to be getting intimate. Then again, we weren't in a relationship —we were just friends who were exploring their extremely powerful and unable- to-be-ignored sexual attraction. That made things different—normal rules or any rules didn't apply.

"Don't be loud," Orlando warned.

"Goodnight," Mathais said, with dismissive but good humor. His arm fell from my shoulder and he unlocked the door. He strode to a nearby wall, punched a code into the alarm system and then took my hand.

Mathais turned on lights as he led me through the house. I heard Orlando and Henry whoop as they found something edible in the kitchen, but the sounds of their triumph faded quickly as Mathais took me up the stairs, down a short hallway and to the master bedroom.

"There's so much I don't know about you," I said.

"Finding out my parents are loaded didn't make you think differently about me, did it?"

"No, not really, but I can see their generosity and openness in you. They're lovely, rare traits to have."

"Thank you for saying that."

I was going to stay something else deep and intelligent but he started undressing and I couldn't stop staring at him, and his goofy grin told me that he loved every minute of it. I hypnotically began to shed my own clothes, dropping them sporadically piece by piece on the floor.

I couldn't even stop looking at the parts of his body that weren't what you'd normally stare at. His thighs, his shoulders, his neck, his chin, even the way he moved was sexy. He held his hand out towards me, motioning for me to come to him. I let him lead me into the small bathroom just big enough for a standing shower, small sink and toilet.

"My parents haven't rented this house in a while. They like to stay here when they visit. There should be some toiletries so we can shower. I'll toss our clothes in the washer so we'll have something clean to wear tomorrow."

I nodded and wrapped my arms around myself in a hug.

"Cold?"

"A little," I admitted.

Mathais turned on the shower, waited a minute and then motioned for me to get in.

The spray felt amazing and I closed my eyes, leaning into the stream. After a moment, I opened them and poked my head out of the shower. Mathais had gone back into the room. After a moment, he appeared again with towels and soap.

"Will you be joining me?" I asked innocently.

I scooted back in the shower to make room for him and he grinned as he peeled off his boxer briefs and climbed in.

It was really made for one person and two had us practically on top of each other. Mathais set the soap and shampoo into a shower niche and posted an arm against the wall behind my head.

I immediately closed the space between us. The softness of my wet skin slicked against the firmness of his body. I never wanted to be this close to him and unable to touch him, and the way his breath quickened as I leaned into him, I knew he felt the same. Not touching each other was quickly becoming an unnecessary torture; why should we resist then? We shouldn't. We should always indulge.

Mathais leaned forward to kiss and I met him halfway. His hands were all over me—up my back, down my sides, in my hair, gripping my hips, before finally returning to cup my face.

"You shouldn't taste so good," he said, pulling back to smile at me. "Turn around."

"I'm ashamed about how much I like it when you're bossy," I retorted as I obeyed.

I heard him pop open a bottle and the light-scented soap blossomed around us. Expectantly, I swooped my damp hair over to one side. The lathered cloth swept over my shoulders, across my back, down my spine. I felt him kneel behind me and kiss my hip before sweeping the washcloth over where his mouth had just been.

"You like it when I touch you like this?" Mathais asked softly, the bass of his voice riveting against the back of my thigh. It was all incredibly erotic, but that wasn't what he meant. I knew he was asking if I liked the affection he was giving me, the tenderness. I swallowed hard, fearing the answer. He stood, swooping his hand up round my waist as he lightly kissed the rim of my ear.

I turned to face him and was surprised by how unsure he looked. Had he always wanted more even when he'd been willing to agree to the expose? I was starting to think, just maybe, yes. I grabbed another clean washcloth and made a spinning motion with my finger. Mathais grinned and obediently turned around.

He held his palm out and I put a dollop in each of our hands. Smiling childishly at each other, we suds up our scalps. If I hadn't been so transfixed on his warm eyes, I would have taken the time to gaze at his soap-covered, gleaming body, but I couldn't look away from the face that was becoming so pleasantly familiar to me.

"Yes," I confessed. "I do like it."

"Good, I do too."

We finished showering and I was instantly drained. It was after three in the morning and my body was done. Half asleep, I crawled into the bed naked and with heavy eyelids watched Mathais scoop up our clothes we'd left on the bedroom floor before disappearing out of my line of vision. I was asleep long before he came back.

I felt someone move beside me and my eyes flickered open. It was early, the room still pitch black. I knew my hair had to be a dry, wildly curly lioness mane and I immediately wanted to pull it up and off my neck. Mathais was asleep beside me and I moved slowly so I wouldn't disturb him. When I slipped out of the bed, the cool air prickled my skin and I remembered I was naked.

"Are you all right?" Mat mumbled almost incoherently.

I found my purse in the dusky light and dug out a ponytail holder.

167

"Do you want to leave? I'll take you home if you do."

I knotted my hair and slipped back beneath the covers.

"It's really early."

"I know," Mathais said with a loud yawn, "but I'll still drive you home if you're ready to leave."

As he spoke, his foot moved through the blankets until he found mine. His feet were large and I wasn't an incredibly touchy-feely person, but the way he did it made me want to *reciprocate*? I just went with it. Scooting closer to him, I entangled my leg in his. I snuggled closer. His hands stroked my cheeks, which led to kissing and then petting and in an instant we were both wide awake and kissing. I rolled onto my back and he towered over me. His hand trailed down the bare skin of my stomach to my waist and I quivered. I was aching for more.

"I'm not ready to leave yet," I said quietly.

"I don't want you to leave," Mathais purred against my neck.

"Kiss me."

Mathais gave me a mischievously sexy smile and disappeared beneath the light sheet that had been covering us. His face slipped between my already spread thighs and he kissed me. I moaned, unable to stop myself from arching against him as he licked and sucked. I fisted the sheets and my thighs began to tremble with pleasure.

"So good," I murmured.

I felt his wet lips curl into a smile; pleased, that I was *pleased,* but I couldn't be anything else. I'd never had anyone touch me like he did, not even Levi. What we had was different than anything I'd ever imagined.

He switched to his hand, sliding two fingers in while his thumb circled my clit and I didn't even know I was coming until I was already encompassed by the rich ecstasy of it. A heavy sigh ripped through my throat as I pulsed against him. He kept stroking me, caressing my body, drawing the orgasm out longer than I knew was even possible. I could do nothing but feel.

Mathais pulled me into his arms.

"You're so beautiful," he purred into my ear.

I grinned. "I would have returned the favor without flattery."

"That wasn't what I meant," Mathais said softly. I turned my head towards him. He looked like he wanted to say something else but his eyes closed, and he licked his lips as he felt my hand glide over his thick erection between my lips. I needed him, wanted to touch him, feel him, please him. Another first—I'd never cared for this particular act. With other lovers it had been a means to an end, the end being my excuse to leave, but for Mathias, it meant something entirely else to me. It was intoxicating to see him fall apart and know I was the sole cause. It was becoming as satisfying as getting me off.

He groaned and I sucked harder. I wanted him to come just as frantically hard as he'd made me.

"Baby, come here," he said, his voice thick and deep.

I moved up his body until I was straddling his hips. He hooked a finger under my chin and guided me forward until I was leaning just inches above his mouth.

"I want more but I want it to be right. I want you to be ready."

I swallowed hard as I processed what he was saying. Of course I wanted to have sex with him but something in the way his eyes looked into mine when he said it meant that wasn't all he meant. This *more* could be anything and that was frightening.

Mathais watched me for what felt like a long moment, waiting for my response, but I didn't have one. He leaned up, kissed my forehead and then brought me down into his arms.

"When you're ready," he repeated softly in my ear.

I nodded, not knowing what to say but wanting to at least acknowledge him. He sat up and I slid off him and onto my side on the mattress. I was worried that I'd offended him, but he just leaned up to grab the comforter and then he snugged me back into the nook of his arm. His hand trailed up and down my back soothingly and before I knew it, I'd fallen back to sleep.

21

Monday morning came and I felt like a phoenix rising from the ashes of a shitty love life—fresh, confident and up making hash browns patties in my toaster oven like a boss. I was early to work and even had time to dip into the Bitter End to grab a chai—all soy, no water—latte. Everything felt fresh, like the storm Levi had left in my heart was finally clearing up. It was only a matter of time until I dried out, until the ground forgot it had ever rained.

I felt good—no, better than good, I felt superb.

"You're here early," Berea commented. I looked up from my desk and smiled. "We still on for dinner tonight?"

"Sure, where do you want to go?"

"How about Muchachos?" Berea suggested.

"God, we haven't been there since—"

"Right before our trip to Vegas," Berea said, finishing my sentence.

I took a nervous sip of my chai. I dreaded confrontation or discussing feelings but I had to get over myself. Now that the rain was gone, I could see clearly now and Berea had stuck by me through my emotional shit-storm and would continue to do so for the rest of my life. My best friend deserved her long overdue apology.

"Look—I'm sorry. I've been such a shitty friend. That whole thing was a horrible idea and although I didn't deserve what happened to me, I kind of set myself up for it. You know?"

"I don't think that's fair at all, Pi. Love happens and sometimes isn't everlasting, or even nice; but I like to think it's always worth it. Maybe your expose was bit wild, but it wasn't horrible. I understand why you wanted to do it and I've always envied your tenacity and, well, you've inspired me to do something I've wanted to do for a long while but I'll need your help."

Berea took a deep breath and then told me.

"I'd like to start a publishing company. We could both still work here, but I'd like to branch out, try something new and I want you to do it with me."

"Have you pitched it to my mom yet?"

"No—why would I? This is for us; it doesn't have to involve your mom."

"Galaxy Publishing sounds nice. It could be partially owned by the magazine, which would give us some advantages."

"Like funding?" Berea suggested.

"Exactly," I agreed.

"Ten percent to your mom, the rest we can split between us?"

I smiled, nodding excitedly. I was completely enthralled by the idea of having a small publishing company. I was sure the *Galaxy* readers would make submissions and it felt extremely adventurous to go out and find new talent. It was Berea's idea, but it felt like it embodied everything I'd always wanted: creative freedom.

"Are you sure you're all right with your mom having an interest in this? I know how frustrated you get with always being in her shadow."

"I'm sure. Besides, she doesn't have the energy or the time to control everything and as long as we don't split the equity three ways with her, we'll always have the final say. She's basically just an investor who can sit back and get paid."

Berea nodded in agreement.

"All right, let's figure out the details at dinner. We'll start off small, see how it goes, but getting submissions shouldn't be a problem."

"I know, I was thinking the same thing."

"Hell, you could even write, Piper, maybe you could turn your whole Levi adventure into a literal literary work of fiction."

I laughed but it was true, the whole experience was just that absurd to actually make a good, but heart-wrenching, novel.

"Or you could write something new," Berea said encouragingly, "or edit or whatever you want."

"I've never thought about writing a novel. I'll definitely chew on the idea, but we'll have enough work to keep us busy. She might let you go, but my mom is definitely not letting me stray too far from the kingdom."

Berea grinned and gave me a quick hug.

"That's what happens when you're the next brilliant heir to an editorial throne. I'd better get back to my desk. I'll see you tonight, okay?"

"Thank you," I said quietly.

Berea smiled, a little teary eyed, and I knew things between us were finally back on track.

Dinner that night went well, and Berea even came back over to my place afterwards to hang out. I'd missed my best friend more than I'd realized and I was thankful that she'd forgiven all of my bitchy-weird-emotional behavior from the past few months. It felt like old times, no, it felt better than old times.

"There's something else I wanted to talk to you about," Berea said as we sat down on my couch. "It's about Clyde."

"I'm sorry about that too—anything I said before that was mean or bitchy, just disregard it. I was just jealous. Everything went so smoothly for you and then things ended so horribly with Levi. You deserved a better friend than me, but I'm grateful you stuck it out."

"You really mean that? You're okay with us?"

"Don't break up with him," I said taking her hand. "You never needed my approval, Berea, and I'm sorry I made you feel like you did."

She wiped a little tear away from her cheek and pulled me into a hard hug.

"I really love him," she whispered.

"Good, because I'm a bitter jerk and I've made everything ridiculously uncomfortable for far too long. I'm so sorry. I'll smooth things out with him, okay?"

172

She nodded, looking immensely relieved.

"Seriously? You'd do that?"

"Yes, of course! I promise, Berea. I'll do what I can to make it right."
There was a knock at the door.

"I'm scared to see who it is," I said with a nervous laugh.

I looked through the keyhole, but no one was there. I opened the
door and found a large box with my name on the delivery tag.

"What is it?" Berea asked from the couch.

"Don't know," I said, pulling off the card stuck to the top. "There's a
card, I'll open that first."

"Hurry up already!" Berea squealed excitedly.

I ripped the card open ungraciously and quickly skimmed the letter.

Congratulations on joining the pack. If you can successfully set up
this Nerd-Box console, a party invite will be waiting for you at 10:05 PM
tonight.

Mathais

I smiled excitedly and opened up the box. It was a gaming console
with about ten games in it, an extra rechargeable controller, a very
expensive looking headset and a prepaid membership for online access.

"What is it?" squealed Berea. "You're just standing there smiling."

"It's a Nerd-Box!"

"Oh, one of those gaming things?"

"Yes! Mathais got me games and accessories too," I added
excitedly.

"You always did love accessories," Berea said laughing. "Mathais is
the new guy, right?"

"Yes, he's amazing. You'd love him."

"Careful, you're just showing signs of recovery," Berea said softly.

I looked over at her. Her brow was furrowed with concern. She pulled her knees up to her chin, a worried expression crinkling the skin around her eyes.

"He's not like Levi and we're just friends who—do stuff."

"Just don't rush," Berea advised, "and always be honest with what you want and how you feel."

"You can meet him, if you want, and tell me what you think, but I'm telling you—he's different and we're really becoming good friends. He's so kind and his friends are hilarious. It just nice to have people to hang out with you know? You'll like him, I promise."

Berea nodded and then pulled me into a hug again.

"I didn't mean to lecture you; I've just missed you and I'd hate to see you hurting again."

"I promise I won't cut you out again like that, Berea. I'm so sorry."

I heard a little sniff from Berea as she got up from the couch.

"I'd better get going. Let's get lunch tomorrow, okay?"

"Sure! Just tell me when and where."

After Berea had left, I examined the contents of the box.

I was excited. I'd never had money for things like this as a kid, and then as an adult I'd kept myself so busy with school and work, there hadn't been much down time. I was ready for some fun. I checked the time and it was just after nine. Exactly an hour later, a feat that my ego assured me meant that I was a natural born gamer, everything was set up.

My headset dinged, and a box blinked onto the screen asking me if I wanted to accept SmittenMitten's friend request and party invite.

I did, and I heard Mathais' voice ringing in my ears through the headset's speakers.

"Hope my package found you in good health," he greeted in an overly formal manner.

"If you had gifted me this before I knew you were rich, I probably would have not accepted it, but now that I know, I'll just tell you thank you."

"Knowledge is power, plus, since you're part of the pack and a writer, Henry expects you to help him with his gaming reviews. All the games in the boxes are classics, but you should be getting some betas games emailed to you for you to try out in the next month or so—if you want."

"So this is one of those gifts that's really more beneficial to the pack than to me?"

"Basically," Mathais conceded with a chuckle. His laugh was rich, deep, and as I listened to him bellow, I realized how much I enjoyed the sound.

Next, Mathais explained the simple controls, picked a game for us to start with and guided me through the first few levels. It was relaxing, and I could see why people easily fell in love with video games.

"Damn—when did it get to midnight?"

"I'm going to be tired tomorrow," I sang giddily into the microphone.

"After we fight through this swarm, we'll be able to save and quit."

"There's so many of them!" I squealed as our avatars pressed forward into a temple.

"Fuck, stay close. Don't panic."

I did just that and we forged our way through killing these odd little dwarf-sized monsters by the dozens. I felt giddy and accomplished—and okay, a little bit like a bad ass.

"That's what I'm talkin' about, suck it, bitches!" Mathais cheered as our checkpoint saved.

"I can't believe I've lived my life up until now without this magical box."

"You're welcome," Mathais sing-songed into the headset.

"What are the other games about?"

"Everything amazing you could imagine. We can play this one again tomorrow night, if you want?"

"Yeah, sure," I said. I flicked onto a different screen and began customizing my character's outfit, hair, physical features—every aspect of this game was addictive.

"Have I earned some alone time yet?"

I snorted. "You could've just asked."

"I did just ask—but I was trying to be *romantic*."

"When?"

"When was I trying to be romantic?"

"No," I said laughing again, "when do you want to meet up?"

"Friday night, I'll pick you up around seven."

I stayed up for another hour—which was dumb, but hey, I was an adult and besides, wasn't that what coffee was for?

22

The week went by so fast and by Friday morning I was really looking forward to my scheduled "alone" time with Mathais. If I hadn't liked him before, a week of texting, quick chats on the phone and playing various Nerd-Box games was enough to bump Mathais up from friend to top three friends of all time. Granted, there wasn't a long list. When you worked as much as I did, you didn't really make a lot of new friends. Even so, I was thankful for my new friend and curious about what he had planned for our alone time tonight. I was a tad bit feverish with my assumption that tonight would be *the night*. We'd fooled around, gotten to know each other's bodies, but there'd been no penis-to-vagina contact and I was eager for the experience. Sexy time was coming and I couldn't wait.

Evette hadn't come in yet and Berea was perched on the edge of my desk picking at a cinnamon roll while I passionately tried to convince her to get her own Nerd-Box. I was just on the cusp of getting her to agree when Clyde joined us.

"Hey, Piper," Clyde greeted uneasily.

I nodded hello.

"Are we okay now?" Clyde asked.

I realized then—between his tone and his earnest, honest expression—how badly I'd messed up. Despite the fact that sleeping with him had been a mistake, we were good friends and he only wanted what was best for me, hadn't he? His advice would have probably kept me from getting so caught up in Levi, and the expose, but I'd been too proud and too stubborn to consider anyone else's point of view. I felt sorry for him for having to put up with me and my dark mood. Since the Levi breakup I'd either sent him the death stare, given him short, one-word responses or just ignored him altogether. I knew it wasn't his fault that he'd been right about Levi, but I just hadn't been able to get over the fact that he'd fed information to my mom. It'd felt he'd betrayed our friendship by siding with her against me and that wasn't something I could easily forgive; but that was then and I had to let it go.

"I've been meaning to apologize," I confessed. "I've just—well—I'm not exactly that great of a friend."

Clyde nodded and just like that I was forgiven. I really *really* didn't deserve the friends I had. I thought he was going to say something else but then Evette came barreling around the corner and interrupted us.

Berea and Clyde immediately tried to disperse, but she called them back to my desk.

Fuck, I thought in annoyance. It was never good when she wanted to talk to *all* of us together.

"Girls! I'm glad you're all here; you too, Clyde. Are you all free for dinner tonight?"

I opened my mouth to say no but she excitedly cut me off.

"I've met someone. Actually, I've been seeing him for a few months now. It's getting serious and I'd like you all to meet him."

We all blankly stared at her.

"You've been dating someone for months and have never mentioned it?" I finally manage to blurt out.

"Don't be mad, Piper, but you have been a bit squawky lately. You weren't exactly *approachable.*"

I crossed my arms and tapped my foot in annoyance.

Berea stifled a laugh and I shot her a death glare. My mom and I bumped heads normally and she had not been kind with the little information she had known about Levi. If anything, she and I weren't closer because she was unapproachable. Our relationship had been broken for years and we could never seem to mend it because she was always saying or doing things that chapped my ass and put me right back into my perpetual status of almost hating her.

"I have a date on Friday too, so no—I can't go to dinner," I said.

178

"Really? That's fantastic," Evette said, giving my arm an affectionate pat.

"Who are you?" I muttered in disbelief.

"Squawky, was me being *nice*. You need to adjust your attitude pronto."

"Right," I muttered in annoyance. "I'm the problem."

"Is this the same guy from—"

"No," I said quickly, cutting Evette off.

"So, I'm not the only one then who's been seeing someone without mentioning him."

"Berea knew," I said quickly.

Berea shot me a look that told me she wasn't pleased at being brought into this feud.

"Clyde and I will try to make it," Berea told my mom. "Thanks for inviting us and congratulations on the new man! I'd better get back to work."

I glared at her, livid that she was abandoning me.

"Piper," Evette said, drawing my attention back to her. "We haven't had that good of a relationship for a while now and I know it is my fault."

I was stunned. Evette had never admitted fault especially when it was about our relationship or lack thereof. It was somehow always solely my attitude that caused any rifts between us.

"It's hard balancing work and family," Evette continued, "even when you work with your family. I'm sorry, sweetie, okay? Please consider coming to the dinner—I'd really like you to meet the man I've been seeing. He's—special to me and he's made me realize I have a few changes I can make that'll better our family. Bring your date. I'd love to meet your new friend."

I had no idea who this women was. It was as if Evette had transformed back into *my mother* from long, long ago.

"I'll come," I said quietly. "I don't know if Mathais will, but I'll be there."

179

Evette was ecstatic.

"Thank you," she said, pulling me into a hug. The embrace was long and sincere, as if this hug was an apology for both of us for every catty thing we'd done to the other. When she let me go, I caught her quickly wiping a tear away. I stared at her as she went back to her office in awe. I wondered if this was a serious change or just a moment of guilt. There was no way to know for sure.

I sat back down at my desk and rifled through my new emails but I couldn't focus on anything work-related. My mind was spinning in bewilderment. I couldn't remember seeing my mother so emotional. I mean, granted, for a normal person an invitation to diner, a single tear, and a hug wasn't really emotional, but for me and her it was huge. We'd never really done the whole *feelings* thing. Maybe that was why I'd had problems letting people in and I suppose it was all tied into why I hadn't been able to orgasm. You have to let yourself feel a multitude of things, you have to be willing to trust someone, and above all, you have to want to. That was the problem before: I never wanted to let anyone see that much of me. I didn't want to be vulnerable because that had been just another form of weakness in my mind.

Then Levi had come along. He'd been just the right potion of lust, charisma, openness—and a host of other things that I'd found irresistible. He thawed right through my frozen defenses and got down to *me,* the real me but he had his own demons and at the moment that should have bonded us together he abandoned me. You couldn't undo abandonment. Neither of us would look back. Neither of us would give the other a second chance—and what we both didn't do was even more profound than what we had done.

I had to stop scratching at all my old wounds. I wasn't just thinking about any resentment towards Levi, I was looking at the whole picture. I had to let myself get over things. My mom included. Hell, I didn't even think of her as my mom most of time, she was just Evette. Fuck. I was such a shitty daughter. At least no one could hear my inner monologue.

I let out a grandiose exhale. Maybe everything wasn't all her fault. I could try to be more *approachable*. I chewed on the inside of my cheek as I tried to decide what to do about my plans with Mathais. I could cancel on him or I could invite him to meet my mother. I thought about the dinner with him and then the experience of going through it without him and realized my choice was already made. I picked up my phone and sent him a message.

ME: Can you be my plus-one to the most awkward dinner ever?

I set my phone down on my desk and tried not to wait for it to ding with a response. Luckily, I didn't have to wait long. My phone started buzzing a few minutes later and I realized nervously that Mathais was calling instead of texting me back.

"Should you really be using your phone during class?"

"All the cool kids are doing it," Mathais said. Then he added, "I don't have classes on Friday, just open office hours for students."

"Oh—," I bit my lip not sure how to segue back into the topic of my text message.

"I was just calling, because I'd rather talk to you than text you."

That was sweet. I smiled and swiveled my chair from side to side.

"So, you got my text then?"

"Yeah—I'll go with you. Can we just move my date to Saturday?"

"We can't just have *alone* time after dinner?"

He made a little naughty-sounding hum on the other line.

"I could figure something out. Anyone else going to this dinner or will it just be the three of us?"

"Berea, Clyde, my mom and the man she's been secretly dating for months."

"Does she know about me?"

"I tried to get out of going by saying I had a date."

"Sounds like it didn't work," Mathais said, and I just knew he was smiling on the other end of the phone.

"No, not at all."

"I don't mind, Piper. In fact, I'm flattered."

"You won't be after you meet her. You'll feel very ill-used."

"Well, I promise I'll let you make it up to me."

"I love the way your voice deepens when you start insinuating, Mathais."

"I love the way you say my name when you're thinking about me insinuating."

"I'll text you the address in a bit and we'll meet there at seven-thirty tonight?"

"I'll be there," he promised.

"Thank you. I couldn't imagine going to this dinner without you as backup."

There was a pause and for a moment I wondered if that had been too friendly, to intimate of a statement, but when he spoke his voice sounded pleased and I relaxed.

"Of course, I'll see you in a bit," Mathais said.

I'm glad Mathais ended the call first because I never would have hung up. Friendship with him was definitely interesting. I might just have to give him a spot at the top of my bestie list and never admit it to Berea. I felt so much relief that he was coming I was almost excited to go to this dinner tonight. I pinched myself, but I was still here and the excitement hadn't left either. I was introducing my best kept secret to my mother and her boyfriend tonight. I had no idea who I was anymore.

23

After work I changed into a dark, flowy, long-sleeved top; slim, ankle-fit dark-wash jeans; and flat leather sandals. I hailed a cab not far from my apartment and headed to the restaurant. My mother had offered to pick me up, but I'd quickly declined. Tonight was already going to be awkward enough. I didn't want us to get into it before dinner even started.

We were just minutes away and my anxiety was already threatening to get the best of me. I fidgeted with my phone. There were so many reasons to be nervous tonight: Evette, her new boyfriend, Berea, Clyde and *Mathais* all in the same room. I wasn't worried about Mathais embarrassing me—it was the other way around. Evette could be overprotective and rude. Clyde could stir up some shit. I took a deep breath, mentally coaxing myself to stay calm. That wasn't going to happen. Clyde wouldn't do that, even if he was still mad at me, and I know my mother had tact. As long as I didn't say something dumb or pick a fight, the night would go just fine.

"Miss?"

I blushed, realizing that the cab had stopped and the driver was waiting on me and handed him a twenty.

"Sorry—no change, please. Thank you."

I got out and adjusted my outfit quickly, smoothing, pulling, tucking; basically all the things nervous people do that really have zero effect. I could see Mathais standing outside with some flowers. He was wearing a dark purple, almost black, v-neck shirt and grey jeans with tan loafers; so simple, yet timelessly sexy.

It wasn't long before Mathais saw me; his face lit and his lips curved into his signature gorgeous and very endearing smile.

"You look amazing," Mathais said first.

I gave him a shy kiss on the cheek.

Mathais opened his palm, revealing a plum-sized, creamy-vanilla-colored silk origami flower.

"The flowers are for your mom," Mathais explained, "but I did make you this."

"You made this?"

"Just another nerd talent I picked up in college," Mathais said.

"It's beautiful," I said, smiling as I rose up on my toes and gave him a quick light kiss.

He shrugged, his cheeks reddening.

"Mathais, are you being bashful?"

He laughed and I hit him with a second wave of wit. I motioned to the bouquet.

"Buttering up my mother?" I asked.

"I can't hurt."

I slipped my hand in his and we started walking in.

"Well," I said, "if you get on her good side, maybe you can negotiate a peace treaty for me. With you here, this dinner might actually be bearable."

"What do we know about *the enemy*?"

I snorted and quickly covered my mouth with my hand. Yes, Mathais was my ally and I loved it. Everyone deserved to have someone like him in their life.

"Nothing—but he must be crazy since he's into my *mother*."

"Do you have a reservation?" the greeter asked politely.

"Yes, should be under Ezrah."

"Of course, right this way."

"I love how they say 'of course' like they knew who we were when we walked in," Mathais joked in a low voice.

"It's all part of the *ambiance*," I whispered. I tried to do a snobby, high-society accent but I was pretty sure I just sounded like I had serious sinus congestion.

It was still a few minutes before everyone was supposed to arrive but Evette was already seated.

184

As we neared the round table, Mathais' hand tightened unconsciously in mine. I squeezed his hand encouragingly. We'd be fine as long as we stuck together.

"Mom, I'd like you to meet my Mathais," I introduced, swiftly.

Very suavely, Mathais handed Evette the bouquet of flowers, and to my horror and slight amazement my mother *blushed.* I knew right then that she liked him and I was officially in the twilight zone. This dinner was going to be fine—no, better than fine—marvelous.

"How sweet," Evette cooed as she inspected the mixed bundle of flowers, "so thoughtful! Thank you!"

"I'm glad you like them. It's a pleasure to meet you," Mathais said.

Mathais and I sat down, our legs brushing as we both scooted our chairs forward. Mathais' hand found my knee and slid slightly up my thigh before retreating back to his own lap. Out of the corner of my eye, I caught the quick flash of a confident smirk.

"Would it be too forward to ask how you met my daughter and what you do for a living? She tells me *nothing.*"

Now I blushed.

"Mom," I warned.

Mathais took my hand in his under the table.

"Not at all," he said, smiling warmly at me and then at my mother. "We met in a coffee shop, not far from *Galaxy*. She was working on some writing, I was grading papers; I'm a professor at Hayes University. I struck up a conversation and we've been friends ever since."

"Just friends?" Evette asked with a raised eyebrow.

"Where is your *date*?" I asked. "Matter of fact, where are Berea and Clyde?"

"How did you meet—" I paused, realizing I didn't know his name.

"Phil," Evette said, finishing my sentence.

"Right, where is *Phil* anyway? In fact, where are Berea and Clyde?"

"They canceled, and Phil is just in the bathroom. What department do you work in at Hayes, Mathais?"

"English."

My mother's face became completely animated.

"Phil is the dean of that department. Would that make him your—"

Mathais' eyes darted past the table, locking on a tall, broad, stately man walking towards us. I covered my mouth to stifle the involuntary giggle-hiccup that bubbled out of my mouth. I was having dinner with Mathais, my mother and his boss—who was dating my mother. This was even more bizarre than any daytime television show.

"Mathais!" Phil boomed.

Mathais stood up and the men firmly clamped paws.

"I didn't know you were dating anyone! It's so good to see you, Mathais."

"It's a pleasure to meet you, my dear," Phil said, reaching for my hand as well. "Evette has nothing but wonderful things to say about you."

I raised an eyebrow at my mom—which she didn't see because she was too busy puckering up. I cringed awkwardly while they kissed, not knowing where to look or what to do. I'd never seen this side of my mom. She's never dated, not once, for my entire childhood. After my father left, it was like she'd sworn off love. I wasn't prepared to see my mother as a *woman*.

Mathais' gaze caught mine and he mouthed: What the fuck?

I tried to choke back a laugh but the giggle bubbled up like a squeaky hiccup.

"Mathais' family is one of the school's biggest donors," Phil continued when he was done slobbering on my mother, "Now, I love to tease young Mathais about how his family is paying me to keep him, but honestly he's one of the best English professors Hayes has ever had. If the board would allow it, I'd pay *his* family for allowing us to employ him!"

Mathais smiled politely and whispered, "He makes that same goddamn joke every chance he gets."

"Are you from this area?" Evette asked Mathais.

186

"No—my family is actually from Michigan."

"They're from a charming little town on one of the lakes, right?" Phil asked.

"Yes, that's right," Mathais confirmed.

"Erie?" Phil guessed.

"Lake Michigan, "Mathais corrected politely.

The waiter came by and the conversation paused for a moment while we ordered. I'd gone last, quickly skimming my menu and ordering the first thing that sounded edible. Of course as soon as he was gone my mother had another question locked and loaded.

"Are your parents retired now?"

"No, they still work. Mainly, they oversee that our family businesses are being run and maintained properly," Mathais answered calmly.

I was horrified but he didn't seem irritated or upset. I'm sure discovering his boss was dating my mom had thrown him, but he seemed to have already recovered from that unexpected surprise.

"How'd you end up teaching and not working in your family's business?" Evette pried.

"My parents do eventually want me to take over," Mathais explained, "but for now, to appease my soul, I champion literature."

I stared at him, enchanted by this new information. We talked all the time but we never talked about family or the future or really anything more pressing than the *now.* I was curious and my mind was becoming riddled with questions that I wanted to ask next time we were alone.

Evette smiled warmly at him.

"You and Piper certainly have that in common. I want her to take over *Galaxy* too one day. Do you plan on keeping your family's legacy going?"

"Depends. I have a sister, Mariah, and she loves everything about our family businesses. I figure either we'll duel at dawn or I'll let her take over our dynasty."

Phil roared with laughter, my mother giggled, and just like that, Mathais won Evette over. She probably liked him more than she liked me. The rest of the dinner went smoothly; the food was great, my mom seemed extremely happy. Even though I'll admit, it was irritating to see my mom so girly and very odd to watch her blush and flirt, the fact that she was so happy kept me from being too critical. Maybe it was really possible for things to be different.

"How long do you think they've been..." Mathais asked me, with a devilish smile as we walked out of the restaurant, hand in hand.

"Oh God," I said, feigning a dry heave.

Mathais wrapped his arm around my shoulder.

"It was just as awkward for me as it was for you. I'm going to have a lot of quality time with Phil now. He's nice, but no one wants to spend that much time with your boss. You're not tired yet, are you?"

"Not at all. Are you ready for some *alone* time?"

"Of course—and we can still make it."

"Wait—aren't we just going back to your apartment?"

Mathais' expression shifted from baffled to hurt.

"If you just want to go back to your place or mine we can," he said slowly. "I figured we'd eventually make our way there but I had something else planned that feels a little foolish."

"I didn't mean to offend you," I said quickly. "I just misunderstood what 'alone time' meant. Whatever you have planned is fine."

"There's more to us than just alone time."

"Wait," I said poking him in the chest, "you can't switch the meaning of alone time back and forth like that. I'll never know what you mean."

"Good, it'll keep you on your toes."

I honestly had thought we were just going to romp tonight and I was content if that was all this was. I hadn't let myself overthink. I had been focused on enjoying, but did he want more? Did I want more? Were we already *more?*

Stop, my mind screamed. I didn't need to think like this now. All I needed to do was enjoy his company and the easy way we could fall into each other's rhythms. Whether it was dinner with my mom and his boss, playing video games, or really good sex, I deserved some good times and I was not going to let myself ruin it by analyzing Mathais' every move.

"So," Mathais asked, "what do you want to do?"

"I want to go wherever you want to take me."

Mathais brushed a light kiss against my cheek and hailed a cab.

I scooted in first and Mathais followed, telling the cabbie an address I didn't recognize. Then, he pulled me to him for a greedy kiss that was unlike our normal smooches. His hand trailed up the inside of my thigh; his tongue pushed between my lips as we dipped back into the leather cushions. I was enjoying this more domineering side of him. He was hungry and his energy excited something primal in me. I was willing to give him whatever he needed and our embrace intensified until I was breathless and completely focused on him.

"NO SEX IN MY CAB!" the taxi driver bellowed at us.

The quick snap of the driver's voice broke the spell. We sat up properly in our seats. Mathais' arm curled around my waist; his head lightly kissed along the line of my neck. The cab driver glared at us in the rear-view mirror.

"I missed you all week," Mathais whispered in my ear.

"What did you miss?"

"Everything," he said into the curve of my shoulder.

"Tell me," I insisted.

"The way your skin flushes when I touch you."

"Come back with me tonight," I whispered suddenly, turning around to him.

His eyes widened and he nodded slowly in agreement. I wondered how he could be surprised with that offer. Didn't he know that this was where our friendship was leading to? To me, sex with him felt as natural as breathing. Why wouldn't we go further than just the petting and oral sex we'd done? After the kiss we'd just shared, I couldn't fathom him *not* wanting just as much from me as I wanted from him, so I couldn't understand why he'd be hesitant or nervous.

The taxi driver slowed and I leaned forward, grabbing my wallet out and paying the fare. Mathais' hands had been wrapped around me and he couldn't untangle himself fast enough to beat me to the punch.

"Piper," Mathais grumbled unapprovingly as he jammed his wallet back in his pockets.

I gave him a quick kiss.

"You're not the only one who can be chivalrous," I reminded him.

Mathais smiled, grabbed my hand and helped me out of the cab. The night air was a little crisp but not cold. Couples and groups of people fluttered down the street. It was night and already the nightlife was ramping up. I was curious to know where Mathais had brought us. I quickly took in my surroundings and the large lit sign over the building we moved towards. My face paled and my stomach dropped.

I recognized instantly where we were.

24

Tippin' and Sippin' Bar and Grille. Levi had brought me here my first night in Las Vegas. I felt frozen in time; stuck in some weird deja-vu loop between the past and present. I didn't want to see Levi and I did not want to go in that bar.

"Piper? Are you all right?" Mathais asked. His voice had a twinge of urgency. "What's wrong?"

"Nothing," I said, with a quick shake of my head. *Get your shit together.* This was *not* the same bar that Levi took me to. He's not here, you're not there. Just breathe.

"You do like to dance, don't you?" Mathais asked. "I was kind of assuming but I think I'm starting to know you well and this bar seemed like something you'd like."

I pulled him into a quick hug that was really more for me than him. Feeling his strong arms curl around my waist soothed my anxiety down a bit.

"I was just surprised," I said into his shoulder. "I love dancing."

"Are you sure? We can just go back to your place if you want."

I released him from my impromptu emotional hug.

"No—it's fine," I insisted. "Let's go in."

"You're a bit up and down tonight. Are you sure there isn't something bothering you? You can talk to me, Piper."

I could tell him and it would make me feel better to vent but it wasn't worth ruining his night.

"It's fine. Let's go in, Mathais."

He held my hand.

"They have delicious food, the DJ is great and I promise it's not like any bar you've ever been to."

We walked through the doors and to my great surprise (and relief) it looked entirely different than the one in Nevada. The whole interior was done in a rainbow neon 80's theme. Cyndi Lauper's "Time After Time" was blaring through the speakers. The lights were dimmed and black spotlights lit up everything.

Mathais pulled me close as we walked.

"Every month is a different theme," he explained, "but the 80's is always one of my favorites."

I grinned ,completely enchanted by the neon, glitter, side ponytails and off-the-shoulder shirts.

"This is amazing," I said.

"There's more. Let me show you," Mathais said. He led me towards the right and into a shop whose sign read: *Tighty Whities*. It was a little boutique with a one-curtained changing room.

"We're closing in about twenty, but we're not going to rush you out of here or anything," a tall clerk said.

Mathais nodded and told me to pick out an outfit. I was already rifling through the racks.

"We should split up to save time. I want to look just as fly as you," Mathais said, smirking.

We spread out and I quickly found the perfect flash dance replica outfit.

"How do you feel about matching metallic silver glitter fanny packs?" Mathais asked from across the shop.

"I'm down to clown," I said.

"I'm done! Hurry up so I can pay the lady."

I practically ran to the small register.

"We're closed, but if you want to change you can use that dressing room over there. I'm sure you two won't mind sharing," the cashier said with a broad, knowing smirk.

"Not at all," Mathais said smoothly. "I bought this little duffle bag for us to put our 'present time' clothes in."

"Clever girl," I praised.

"*Jurassic Park* references? I am touched by your commitment to tonight's theme," Mathais said, clutching his heart.

"That was in the *nineties*," I corrected.

He laughed, pulling his shirt off over his head.

"Well fuck me for trying to be knowledgeable. That movie felt like it was in the eighties."

"At least you got my reference," I commented as I slipped my bra off and my off-the-shoulder thin sweatshirt on. I probably looked a bit skanky, my jugs were way too large to go bra free, but fuck it—it was the eighties tonight. I'd bought some tie-dyed leggings too, along with some slip-on Keds. I let my hair down and fluffed my curls. I caught Mathais admiring me and our eyes locked in the mirror.

"There's nothing about you I don't like," Mathais said in a saucy, deep seductive tone that made me shiver in delight.

"Everything?" I echoed.

A teasing smile lit up his face as he moved towards me.

"Everything," Mathais confirmed.

"Hurry up," the shopkeeper called to us, "we closed five minutes ago!"

I stifled a squeal as Mathais' hand slipped upped my thigh to my ass. He gave me a firm squeeze.

"Let's get you and your fanny pack a drink," Mathais said.

I gathered up what I'd worn in and jammed it into the neon paint splattered bag on top of Mathais' clothes. I strapped my glitter fanny pack over my hips and loaded it with my wallet, phone, lip balm and the lotion I never went anywhere without. When we stepped out of the dressing room, the cashier hooted approvingly.

After Mathais paid, I sprinted up the stairs. The music was even better now. "Material Girl" was just starting and I couldn't stop my shoulders from wiggling to the iconic beat.

We snagged a corner booth and Mathais slid in beside me.

"You look amazing," he said.

I leaned in to kiss his cheek as a thank you, but he turned, catching my lips instead. It was just a quick, soft peck but it still made my toes curl.

"Are you hungry?" Mathais asked.

"We just ate," I said, laughing.

He grinned and shrugged. "I'll order something and you can help yourself if you feel like it."

As if on cue, the waitress appeared and Mathais gingerly ordered cheese sticks and classic boneless wings. Then serendipity continued to have its way with us and the theme song from *Dirty Dancing* began to ring through the speakers.

"Since you're dressed like Swayze, does that mean you know the dance that goes with this song?"

"I don't know this dance," Mat confessed with a not-so-apologetic grin.

"You can't be serious?" I said, crossing my arms.

"Completely, but I'll still dance with you, if you want."

I eagerly took his hand and Mathais willingly followed me out onto the floor.

The song wasn't far from the beginning. Mathais pulled me close, his lips grazing against my neck in his familiar way that made me shiver and smile. His fingertips were light on my hips and we swayed slowly, like enamored prom dates.

He smelled wonderful and I buried my head in his neck, enjoying the world we'd created when we were this close. I knew the rhythm would change soon, becoming faster, but I didn't care if we just swayed like this all night.

The song transitioned into the beat the end scene was famous for and Mathais surprised me; he quickly twirled me around, my body gracefully spinning in the motion he'd propelled me in until he halted our momentum and I fell into his ready arms. Just like that, I was Jennifer Grey doing a mamba with my hazel-eyed Patrick Swayze.

I laughed in surprised delight.

"You're such a liar," I said, shaking my head.

"I don't know all of this dance, but I've seen the movie and I know *how to* dance."

"All right," I encouraged, show me what you got!"

Mathais was fantastic. He improved a few moves and we kept going, feeding off of each other's energy. The DJ was amazing and he quickly changed the song to "Push It" and Mathais kept going; god, he could really move. His energy packed with a ridiculously joyous spirit was infectious. I let myself go and we danced through a few more songs until the music finally slowed again and Mathais took me back into his arms.

Kissing my hand lightly, he held it against his heart and trailed his other one from my waist up to the middle of my back. We were sweaty and our fanny packs were smooshing together but I didn't want to be anywhere else. It was perfect. When the song turned fast again, he led me off the floor and back to our table.

Mathais grinned at me.

"I bet you'll eat some of my food now."

The food looked cold; I was sure it'd been sitting there for a while but I was sweaty, starving and not in the least picky. I blew him a kiss and took a liberal bite out of a freshly dunked cheese stick.

"Shit, this is so good," I praised.

"Are you having a good time?" Mathais asked as he split the food up between the baskets.

"I am," I said. "Do you come here a lot? The pack would love it."

"No, this was my first time."

"What?" I said in disbelief.

"I googled it, thought it'd be a fun place to take you."

"It's fantastic," I assured him. "So, how is everyone?"

"They're jealous that I wouldn't share you with them this weekend."

I smiled, enjoying the fact that I had a place with his friends. I hadn't realized how lonely I'd been until they'd taken me in.

"Thank you," I said quietly, re-dipping my already sauced stick.

"For what?" Mathais asked, confused.

"For coming up to me the second time we met in the coffee shop, for not judging me for bailing on the expose, for sharing your friends, for bringing me here—really just for existing."

Mathais sat back in the booth with the dopiest smirk on his face; he was gawking at me as if he didn't believe me.

"I mean it," I insisted.

"You're welcome, Piper. God, you're so fucking sexy right now. I hope you take me home with you tonight like you promised."

I wiggled my eyebrows at him and popped a boneless wing in my mouth.

Mathais grinned at me.

"Pure sex appeal," Mathais hummed approvingly.

25

We danced until my legs felt like jelly and I had to finally concede. Mathais didn't look tired at all and apart from my squishy feeling legs, I was wide awake too. As soon as my butt hit the leather seat of the taxi, I groaned with relief and kicked my sandals off.

"Are your dogs barking?" Mathais asked.

I smirked, knowing full well—for a reason unknown to me—that he was talking about my feet.

"They're howling and you sound like some eighty-year-old southern man."

"Keep sassing me and I won't rub them."

"I had no idea that was where this was going."

"Move over to the opposite side of the cab and put them between us," Mathais instructed.

"They might smell," I warned as I scooted our duffle bags and fannies to the cab floor.

"I'm a *man's man*," Mathais boomed, "I can take it."

"Love your woman, love her stench?"

"A good man wouldn't have it any other way."

I closed my eyes with the first stroke of his thumb down the arch of my right foot.

"What really happened with Cordelia?"

The words just slipped out of my mouth before I'd even realized that was the sentence my lips were formulating. I opened my eyes, studying him as best I could through the streetlight shadows that striped the cab interior. I'd thought it would get a bigger reaction but Mathais only smiled and I was relieved that I hadn't upset him.

"I'll agree to talk about it, under two conditions," he bargained. "You have to tell me what happened with *your* ex and the conversation stops as soon as we're out of this cab."

I nodded yes; I could live with those terms. I'm sure eventually I would have told him about Levi anyway, so the fact that it was now didn't really matter to me. Might as well rip the Band-Aid off, right?

"Cordelia and I met in college," Mathais started. "She was sweet, quiet, hardworking and I really liked her. We had good chemistry—"

"Like us?" I butted in, unable to ignore a twinge of ridiculous jealousy.

Our eyes locked and then mine darted away to watch his hand slide from my foot up my calf and down again.

"No, not like us," Mathais answered quietly.

His words were a comforting, reassuring caress and combined with his hands made me feel a delicious mixture of hot, unfocused and, even, less jealous.

"Nathaniel was the first person I met in college," Mathais continued. "Our dorm room was a four-person suite. He and I moved in first, then Henry and Orlando. Nathaniel wasn't around much when Cordelia and I started dating but eventually they met and anyone could tell they both liked each other, but Nathaniel wasn't *that guy* and my relationship with Cordelia felt strong. Life went on, everyone seemed happy and then three years later, I went home for summer break, Nathaniel didn't and I got dumped."

"That's bullshit," I told him passionately. "I'm sorry, Mathais, we all deserve loyalty and honesty."

"After that I finished out my college and just sort of did the stag routine—a couple girls here and there, nothing too serious."

"Are we serious?" I asked as he worked my heel.

"You know we are," Mathais said in a quiet voice. The thought of being *serious* with him made me this nervous kind of excited and I wasn't sure if that made being serious with him the right thing or just another very wrong thing.

"Your turn," Mathais reminded me. "I want to know about the guy who messed up your expose."

"A porn production company found out about my project and wanted me to meet their recently signed star. They knew my connection to *Galaxy* and flew me out to interview him. They looked at the interview as free exposure, you know? A classic win, win. We went there and I clicked with the guy I was scheduled to interview. Everything felt fine, until his mom got admitted to the hospital for congestive heart failure. We drove through the night from New York to Michigan but she died before we could get there. I woke up the next morning in the hotel room and he was gone. He did leave me a letter dumping me and a prepaid ticket back to New York though, so at least I wasn't stranded."

"Fuck," Mathais said in shock.

"It messed me up bad; I'm really just starting to recover from that *experience.* I got way too emotionally deep with him—he was the first man to—" I froze. Why the hell was I telling him *that?*

"Tell me," Mathais said. "Once we're out of this cab we'll only talk about it if you bring it up, I promise."

I pulled my feet away from him and began putting my shoes back on. I was already embarrassed that I was going to tell him this. I liked the image he had of me, a whole person without some bizarre complicated pass. I hoped the truth wouldn't damage what he thought of me, but, if it did, I'd rather know how it affected us now rather than later. We'd only be in the cab for another five minutes, if that. I took a deep breath and just told him.

"I use to have this *problem,*" I said slowly. "Until him, I'd never been able to orgasm during sex. I could with him which was huge for me. I think it bound me to him faster, if that makes sense."

"Piper, you *are* normal. Did you ever think that maybe you just weren't ready for that level of intimacy with someone? Socially we over-sexualize everything but when it comes down to having sex, it's just you and that other person. You have to really want them and you have to trust them to take care of you."

I stared at him in disbelief and he gave me a small, almost invisible smile.

"That's not what you thought I'd say?" Mathais asked.

Mathais moved across the cab seat to me and pulled me into his arms. I was too stunned to formulate a response and honestly not sure what I had expected him to say if I'd expected anything at all. We stayed that way, silent and close, until the cab stopped.

"Don't you dare try to pay," Mathais warned.

I smiled, gathered up our belongings and scooted out of the car *without* trying to pay.

We walked up the stairs to my apartment quietly, both of us probably wondering what the other one was thinking about. When I went to unlock the door, Mathais moved behind me, lightly kissing the curve of my shoulder. The affection made me clumsy, barely able to focus as I unlocked my apartment door. His palms glided under my shirt too, cupping a breast in each of his large hands and I dropped the entire set of keys. His lips trailed up my neck and behind my ears. I swayed back into him.

"Mathais," I moaned quietly, "I can't think."

His hands sunk to my waist and he turned me around to face him. He pushed me hard against my door and I lost track of space and time. I didn't mind and I didn't want it to end. It did end, of course, when I heard a not-so-discreet cough from behind the adjacent door. I blushed, knowing full well my neighbor was creepin' on us.

"Let's go in," I mumbled awkwardly as I untangled myself from Mathais.

I opened the door as quickly as I could, my hands a little shaky from the adrenaline rush of getting caught making out in my apartment hallway. Once the door was opened, Mathais was barely a foot inside before I could hear him clucking his approval.

"This is so you!" he concluded at the end of a handful of compliments.

"How so?"

"I don't know *exactly*, but it fits what I'd imagine you'd like in a place, decor, furniture, everything really."

I smiled, pleased that he was pleased. I took his hand and led him across the open floor space to a screened-off area where my bed was.

Mathais chuckled.

"No tour?"

I smirked and shook my head no.

We stripped each other quickly before tumbling half-naked down onto my bed. His chest was bare and I ran my hands up and down any skin I could reach. Glitter from the fanny pack was all over his stomach. It flickered, catching the light, with every slow breath he took.

Mathais gave me a charmingly crooked half-smile, his hands resting on my thighs as he studied my face. I wonder what he saw. When he looked at me like that, it felt like he knew everything I didn't want anyone to know. Time stilled as we looked at each other and I wondered how there could have been anyone else before him. The heat between us crackled in the quiet air and Mathais sat up quickly, encircling his hands around my back and pulling me close enough to share the same breaths. He kissed me, such a needy, hungry kiss that left me breathless and dazed by emotion I couldn't begin to fathom I'd had stored in me. I let go, letting myself be vulnerable to the way he could make me feel.

We fell back again, this time with his hips pressing me down into the mattress. His lips wet my skin—throat, stomach, chest, cheek—he drenched me in affection and my heart thundered between us. Our stormy love was feverish and completely took over my senses. I have no idea when the rest of my clothes, or his, vanished, but that first push, that first hard thrust, was a delicious eternity that had me gasping.

I stretched my arms above my head gripping the bunched-up sheets and realized I was at the foot of the bed. Mathais' hands found mine and our fingers wove together as we moved. His voice quivered against the side of my neck where he'd buried his head and whispered my name against my skin.

His hands moved back down my body to my waist, where he wrapped them around me and pulled me up closer to him. He slowed his pace, the depth increasing. The angle made my back arch, which allowed his lips to reach my stomach as he held me. I tightened, retracting around him and then my body crackled to a million pieces with each wave of pleasure that racked over me. I heard Mathais growl into my stomach, finding his own release, while I trembled beneath him.

"Did I earn some breakfast in the morning?" Mathais asked, reaching down through the blankets to lightly hold my hand.

"'Definitely," I said, between pants, "I'll even make you hash browns."

Covering my face with my hands, I laughed.

26

"Here are your choices," I said the next morning as I squatted down to see what was crammed in the bottom drawer of my fridge. "I can make you a ham and cheese omelet, chocolate-chip pancakes, scrambled eggs, toast, bacon or even my own version of a bagel sandwich."

"You're not going to judge me? I can have *whatever* I want?"

Amused, I turned around to see Mathais looking at me earnestly, like some handsome man-child.

"You can have whatever you want," I promised.

Mathais came up and moved beside me. His face scrunched as he tried to be decisive.

"God, I don't even know," Mathais said.

"How hungry are you?" I asked.

"*Famished.*"

"I'm hungry too. I'll tell you what I want to eat and you can tell me what you think. I have these thin bagels and cream cheese. I can make this delicious breakfast sandwich with ham and cheddar. I think I could also go for a little bit of scrambled eggs, hash browns and bacon."

Mathais shifted his position so he could hug me from behind.

"Never leave me," he whispered dramatically.

"I'll always be around. We're in a *pack* now, remember?"

He playfully nipped my ear.

"I don't want you cooking breakfast for those animals—only me!"

"When did you become so territorial?" I teased.

"After I found out you could cook—it's a territorial game changer."

"What if my cooking tastes horrible?" I asked, feigning concern.

"It's impossible for you to do anything badly," Mathais countered sweetly. "Can I use your computer?"

"Sure, it's on the coffee table."

"I need to check my work emails. A paper is due this Monday, which promises me a lot of crisis emails."

"What type of English classes do you teach?"

"It's a 'then and now' themed class. First half of the semester is current, second half is filled with classics."

"So like *Herland* versus *Hunger Games*?"

He stared at me with a bewildered expression.

"What?"

"Nothing—that's just a really good idea—but yes, that's the general theory behind my class."

I thought of Mathais teaching; a sexy fantasy of him dressed up like an urban Indiana Jones flashed through my mind. The bacon grease began to sizzle and I snapped back into reality.

"How much bacon do you want?" I asked.

"You look so natural in the kitchen. Why is this password locked? You live by yourself."

"You never know when bitches be tryin' to snoop!" I said. "The password is SecondBreakfast29. You never told me how many pieces you want."

"I trust your culinary judgment."

Mathais grew quiet and then I heard the ferocious pounding of his fingers against my keyboard. I put my full focus on breakfast. I cooked the eggs, made the ham and cheddar bagel sandwich, all while he responded to emails. I gathered our feast of a brunch and organized it on the table so I could eat even if he wasn't ready to yet, all the while sneaking peeks at his profile. Working-Mathais was just as enticing as Weekend-Mathais. I caught myself licking my lips and then felt like a creeper.

"Lots of emails?"

Mathais leaned forward, groaning into the computer screen.

"So-many-emails," he said.

I began eating without him, letting him keep on working. His nostrils flared like a bull as I chewed and his focus quickly shifted to the overstuffed plate set in front of him.

"This looks fantastic, love. Thank you."

I smiled and I knew my face was beaming with pride. I unashamedly loved being praised by him and I only got prouder as I watched him scarf down the breakfast I'd made like he hadn't eaten in days.

"How'd you learn to cook like this?"

"Don't you know? A true feminist like Evette doesn't cook. That would be a social stereotype created by the very literal and spiteful *man* we are sworn to fight against!"

Mathais smiled with puffy cheeks and asked an unexpected question that made me blush.

"When did you transition from 'Mom' to 'Evette?'"

I knew it was a very bitchy thing to not call my mom, *mom,* which was why to her face I either called her nothing or consented to appropriate social norms, but to hear him ask that question reminded me just how spiteful I could be. Had Evette really done anything that bad? Hadn't she just raised me the best she could? I kept saying I wanted to let go and start fresh but I couldn't even make a simple change in how I referred to her.

"When I felt like she was more of a live-in boss than my mother," I explained. "Our relationship is strained. Last night was the nicest she's been to me in years."

"Maybe last night was a sign that it will get better sooner rather than later."

"I hope so," I said, sighing.

"When did you and she co-found *Galaxy?*"

"I was a teenager and she was contemplating getting a third job. I suggested it as a joke, but like they say: in every joke there's a bit of truth."

205

Mathais scraped his fork across his plate, catching the last remnants of food.

"I can understand how you feel," Mathais said as he chewed." My father was out of my life before I even knew him. When I was seven or so my mom met Thomas and everything changed for the better."

"Was he nice? My mom has never dated anyone—that I know of at least—until Phil."

"He was more than nice; he's my father."

A sad smile shadowed my face. I thought about when I was younger and how I'd always wanted to have a *family*. A real one; the correct kind of family, but when a parent rejects you it creates scars so jagged and deep that if you do manage to get over it you're not in the least interested in tearing through that scar tissue. It was done. Choices were made and ultimately people moved on to survive.

"There are a few good men out there," I said.

"Do you remember your dad?"

"No, but I think it's better that way. I'd rather have him gone permanently than constantly in and out."

Mathais' phone buzzed on the table. He leaned over to look at it and let out a long curse.

"What?" I asked nervously.

"Forgot about this garden party my mother is throwing for my sister. She's getting married six weeks from now. This party is a compromise of wills between my sister and mother. Mariah wanted a small wedding—my mom can't imagine offending anyone ever. Passivizing my mother's need to people please became the most viable solution."

"I'd elope," I said.

"Yeah?"

"Hell yes—or I'd have the smallest wedding ever."

"I'm going to have to leave for Michigan this Thursday and I won't be back 'til late Sunday."

I looked away, fiddling with my food, trying to hide my surprise at him being gone.

It was just a weekend, I reassured myself. *It wasn't a big deal. He'd be back.*

"Has it been a while since you visited your family?" I asked politely.

"Yeah, I don't visit enough."

"I'm sure they'll be happy to see you," I said.

"You know, you do owe me an awkward family gathering."

My stomach flipped; mind scrambling to decide if not wanting him to go meant I was willing to go with him.

"I thought this brunch I just made you had us square on that debt?"

"No—we're even for the back rub but you still owe me one awkward family dinner. Come with me, Piper."

I got up and grabbed the empty plates from the table. God, had my face been that pathetic? Would every emotion I felt always be right at the surface? I didn't want to guilt him into anything. I just really, truly enjoyed his company and, well, I'd miss him.

I turned back towards him and leaned against the sink. He looked excited, eager for me to go with him. It was going to be hard to say no.

"We've spent a lot of time together. You know it'll be fun," Mathais insisted.

Mathias came to me and slipped his hands into the back pockets of my jeans and pulled me close. I closed my eyes, breathing in his familiar scent and knew immediately that I didn't want to get left behind. I just wasn't sure if I was brave enough to go. A weekend was way different than a dinner. His lips trailed down the line of my neck.

"I'm pretty sure that's your favorite spot," I murmured.

"Second favorite," Mathais corrected. "If you come with me I'll give you another massage and consent to two more family events of your choosing. Plus, I'll have you back by Sunday afternoon."

"Your family is going to ask questions about us," I reminded him.

It was one thing for us to be together here in New York, but bringing me home to meet his parents was a big deal. We were drifting into new, very romantically serious territory. I wasn't sure how I felt about it until I knew what was going through his mind.

His arms curled around my waist, securing our chests flush together.

"Let them ask," Mathais said.

I snorted at his unexpected candor.

"Just think about it, all right?"

"All right," I said after a moment.

"I'm behind on papers, emails and basically everything work related. I'd better get going."

"I'm behind too," I confessed.

"I very selfishly like that you look sad when I leave."

I shook my head at him but pulled him closer for a long kiss.

"Come with me to Michigan and we'll spend the whole weekend together."

"I'll think about it," I said.

I desperately wanted to go but it terrified me a little. The last time I'd gone to Michigan it was so *awful.* I couldn't imagine if something just as crazy happened again. What if we fought? What if he realized he *didn't* want to continue down relationship lane? I knew that's where this was headed and I wanted it, but maybe he felt differently. Maybe this was just what it was like when you had a mutual attraction to your best friend. Everything about us was so easy; the idea of an *us* had evolved unknowingly to us all on its own and now here I was, on the fringe of love, once again. I could handle the sex stopping if that's what *he* wanted, but the idea that we would no longer talk at all felt devastating, like getting a limb cut off or having your best friend move away. I was so attached to him; maybe I should hit the brakes and make sure my heart could take it.

I didn't know if I could break twice and put myself back together again.

27

"Your mom is dating your lover's boss and he asked you to go away with him," Berea summarized in quick rambled disbelief.

I nodded, unable to verbally confirm Berea's recap of this weekend's events due to a mouth full of the lunch we'd picked up from a deli down the street.

"My weekend barely tops yours," Berea boasted. She whipped her hand on to the table, dazzling me with a traditional princess-cut solitaire on a rose gold band.

"Clyde proposed!" Berea squealed excitedly.

I immediately hopped out of my chair and hugged her.

"How did I *not* see that rock before? Berea, I'm so happy for you!" I said.

"I deliberately hid my hand so I could dramatically show you, *duh!*"

"Tell me *everything,*" I insisted, as I sat back down.

"I found the ring by accident. It was in one of our dresser drawers. I was trying to put it back, but then Clyde came in and the next thing I knew I was saying yes! We didn't come to dinner because—well—we were too busy, gettin' busy!"

While we ate, Berea told me about their plans, her wedding ideas, when they were telling his family, and I listened. I did my duty as best I could, but I couldn't erase the nagging feeling that if the ring was hidden, Clyde hadn't been ready to propose and that was not a good sign.

You're such a bitch, my inner monologue spat at me. I was right. I was a bitch but I couldn't just be jealous; there had to be some validity to my bitchiness. I couldn't possibly be that callous. I could have had him, but I hadn't *wanted* him; so why couldn't I just stop over-analyzing and be happy for my best friend who after all my shit still wanted to be my best friend. I had to let the past go. We were all adults. As long as Berea was happy, I should be happy—bottom line. I'd be supportive and I would not ruin this for her with my uncontrollable propensity to be negative, mistrusting, pessimistic and judgmental.

Berea's soft curse brought me out of my ponderings back to the present.

"We'd better get back."

I glanced at my phone and quickly shoveled down the rest of my food. We'd have to power-walk to make it back to our desks on time. Working for your mother didn't really have any perks.

We said our goodbyes at the entrance. Berea had to hurry into a meeting she was running with the two staff photographers and an intern; I was knee-deep in editorial work for the upcoming issue, plus creating the website *Galaxy Publishing.* I headed to my desk, mentally creating a battle plan for how I could get all of my work done so I could sneak away with Mathais this weekend if I wanted to. I rounded the last corner before my desk and, to my horror, Clyde was waiting for me. I turned on my heel ready to book it back to safety, but Clyde saw me.

"Piper, can we talk?" he called out.

I knew it was about Berea—there wasn't anything else he'd want to talk to me about. I didn't want to talk to him one-on-one; new me was too fragile, he'd say something dumb, I'd get annoyed and then Berea would be upset that things weren't mended between Clyde and me, but there was no way I could get out of it without being rude. I gritted my teeth and took a deep breath.

"Don't tell me you have the jitters already," I teased, forcing what I hoped was an easy smile and not a snarl. "We both know Berea can be intense when she is excited. Just give her some time to let it all sink in and she'll—"

"It's not that," Clyde said, cutting me off. "Things between Berea and me are fine. Really, they're better than fine, they're perfect; but no matter how hard I try, I always come back full circle *to you.*"

No, no, no, no, no! My mind blared like a fog horn.

"That ring wasn't meant for her," Clyde confessed.

My stomach dropped instantly; I was going to throw up.

"That ring was my grandmother's and I'd just been holding on to it."

I held up a hand, silencing him.

My voice came out in an angry whisper.

"Don't you fucking *dare*," I warned.

I took a moment to collect myself, desperate to get a grip on my rapidly firing mind. Clyde looked just as uncomfortable. In fact, he looked downright miserable. *That fool really is in love with me,* I realized in horror.

I lowered my voice as much as I could while still being sure Clyde could hear me.

"Be a fucking man. If you don't love her, if you don't want to marry her, if you need more time—whatever the fuck it is—you do it. But leave my name the hell out of it. She deserves more than this, Clyde, much more. Fix it."

"God, Piper," Clyde groaned. "You don't have any empathy for me. You weren't just Berea's best friend, you were mine too. This shouldn't be so easy for you. You just decided our friendship hadn't ever existed. I can't—I can't just turn it off like that. "

"I know," I said, trying to soften my tone.

"I didn't plan this! Honestly, I do love her. I just can't get *you* out of my head."

"That's not enough. Either be what she needs or end it. Don't lead her on, and for fuck sake don't marry her if—"

"Did I just hear you tell Clyde *not* to marry me?"

I spun around. Berea was just a few feet behind me, wide-eyed, pale and clearly livid.

I didn't have an answer. Clearly she'd heard me correctly, but I didn't mean it in the context that she thought I had. I was trying to defend and protect her; yet once again Clyde was putting a wedge between us.

"Berea, it's not what you think," Clyde started, moving towards her.

She cringed and he froze mid-step.

"Evette wants to see you in her office," Berea said coldly and then she was gone.

"Fix this! Right, the fuck, now," I said violently to Clyde.

"I don't even know what I want."

"Well, it shouldn't be too hard of a decision because I am *still* not even a fucking option."

"You're such a bitch," Clyde muttered.

"You're fired."

"What?" he said.

"Pack your desk and leave within the hour."

"You can't do that," he insisted.

"I fucking own half this god-damn company. Pack your shit. Clearly we can't be co-workers or friends anymore."

"Piper, you can't be serious."

"One hour," I repeated without inflection and then I left.

When I got to Evette's office, I was too wired from everything that had just happened to even remember to knock.

"Let me call you back, Phil," Evette said as soon as she saw me. When she was off the phone, she instantly asked me what was wrong.

"Berea got engaged to Clyde, who just came by my desk and told me he had been saving that ring for me. I yelled at him, Berea overheard. Clyde called me a bitch and I fired him."

"Firing him was a bit harsh, but I'm impressed to see you show some authority."

I was dumbfounded.

"I'll back your decision to fire him, but I'll have to insist that we postpone it until we have a replacement. I'm looking to bring in new talent for *all* the departments and I think you have earned yourself a slight reprieve from *Galaxy*. You're only twenty-nine, Piper, and this is all you've really known. Last week Berea mentioned your interest in starting a small sister publishing company to *Galaxy*. I like it—in fact, I think it is a really good idea. Take a month off and find a few authors you'd be interested in working with and a concrete plan for production, advertisement, royalties."

"Am I still a partner in this company?"

Evette's eyes widened but her face stayed neutral.

"Of course," Evette said quickly.

"Legally?"

"Yes, on paper we are partners. It was your idea to start this company and I want you to one day run it. Even while you work on this sister company, I'd appreciate being able to consult with you and keep you up to date with *Galaxy*."

"Then I need to start shadowing you. You need to mentor me," I insisted.

"All right, are you opposed to taking a month off?"

"I'd rather it be shorter. Three weeks should be enough."

"Let's start with three weeks, and when you get back we'll discuss next year's plans for *Galaxy*. Phil has really opened up a lot of doors for us, and I'd like us to create a real internship partnership with Hayes University."

I nodded in excitement.

"I can still do some editing even while I'm gone."

"No, delegate that work out and start having all the editors in all departments send you the proofs of their work to approve."

"You're not going to be having the final word anymore?"

"I think it's time I shared the crown, don't you?"

"Thank you, Mom. I mean it."

"You're welcome, Piper. Oh, and by the way, I really liked that young man you brought to dinner."

"I liked the old man that you brought to dinner," I said with a smirk.

"Ha! Well, Phil is not as young as Mathias, but he's just as *lively*."

I groaned in shocked disgust.

"Really, honey, I did like Mathais. You two seem to have things in common but you're opposites in some ways too—which is good, perhaps even necessary—you'll balance each other out. You want your partner to be strong where you're weak. You want someone in your life who makes you better."

"Wow, if I had known how much you liked getting flowers, I would have gotten them for you years ago."

"The flowers definitely didn't hurt," my mom said with a smile, "but I like the way he *looks* at you, the way he focuses on everything you say. He's a good, genuine man."

"He wants me to meet his parents this weekend," I said. I was surprised by my urge to confide in her, but instead of overthinking it, I went with it.

"Are you going to go?"

"I want to, but I'm not sure, you know?"

"You should go. Where are his parents from again?"

"Michigan."

My mom flashed me a snarky Evette smile.

"You seem pretty fond of that state."

"That's mainly why I don't want to go."

"It's a completely different situation this time," she reminded me.

"Just because Levi and I didn't work out doesn't mean my relationship with him wasn't real. You don't even know what happened."

"I know *enough.*"

And just like that, the nice talk with my mom turned back to a coaching opportunity for *Evette*.

"It disgusts me how judgmental you are."

"I didn't mean to make you upset, Piper, but why are you even defending Levi?"

"I'm not defending him. I'm upset because you're a stuck-up, horrible person who is bossy, controlling, self-centered and, until *Phil* materialized, didn't do anything that even remotely classified as 'mom-like.'"

"That was incredibly harsh."

I leaned back in the chair, feeling tired. I couldn't remember ever being that blunt with her before and she looked really upset. She grabbed a couple of tissues and swiveled her chair away from me.

"You never cry," I said in disbelief. A part of me had honestly believed that it didn't matter what I said to her. She never acted upset, let alone vulnerable. Now, watching her sniffle and wipe at her eyes, that notion felt childish. Of course she had feelings.

"Not in front of you, but I do cry," my mom assured me.

"Mom—I—I'm sorry. I shouldn't say any of that."

"No, it's fine. It's all true and I deserve to hear it."

"Maybe, but not all bundled up like that at one time."

She laughed as she dabbed the rest of her tears dry.

"I'm going to take the rest of the day off," I announced.

"You don't need my approval but I think that's a good idea."

"I'll be back in tomorrow morning and begin delegating the smaller projects I've been working on.

"Yes—let's meet tomorrow after lunch again and touch base. In fact, why don't we go get lunch?"

"All right," I agreed. "I promise I won't have a tantrum and list all the things I don't like about you again."

We laughed and I could feel the weight lessen in the room.

"You are my daughter, after all, and let's be honest, respect is a two-way street. I know I need to make some changes and I'm willing to put the work in, Piper."

I was stunned and had to choke back the emotion that erupted as the meaning of her words really sunk in. Evette's days were finally numbered.

I cried the whole train-ride home and then again once my head hit the pillows; so many feelings, way too many. Once I was alone it just all came out and I couldn't seem to stop feeling once I started.

My biggest concern was that Berea was going to hate me. That she was going to think that I'd ruined her relationship with Clyde. It was true, but I hadn't intentionally done it. I wanted to call her, but I didn't. It was all too fresh, and she might be with Clyde and I'd just be interfering. I'd have to wait for her to reach out to me. Hopefully she would.

I must have fallen asleep mid-cry because I woke up, groggy and confused, around six that evening.

The first thing I did was call Mathais. He answered by the third ring.

"Hey—how was your day?"

That was all he got out before I started blubbering incoherent sentences and having a completely new meltdown. Sometimes kindness makes you cry more than anything else.

"I'm leaving work right now. I'll be over as soon as I can."

"No—" I said between ugly hiccup cries, "I'm fine."

"Piper, I'll be there within the hour," Mathais said in very a stern, serious, no-argument tone I'd never heard from him before.

"All right."

And thirty-five minutes later he was. I didn't realized how horrible I probably looked until I opened the door and was reminded of how handsome he was. Mathais had on dark khakis and a charcoal crew-neck sweat and of course, those professor-looking tortoise-rimmed glasses. He immediately dropped his bags inside my door and took me into his arms. Being consoled by him was heaven and I felt better just from one hug.

"What happened?" Mathais asked.

We sat on the couch and he listened with a calm expression as I rambled like a mad woman. I told him everything. Starting with lunch, and ending with Evette. I mean, I really told him everything. Including what my mom said about liking him, about us complementing each other, to my role changing, to starting the publishing company—everything.

"You've got to work on a better relationship with your mom and as far as patching things up with Berea, well, that's going to take some time, but for now give her some space. She knew what she was getting into when she started dating Clyde. He clearly still had feelings for you and she chose to set those aside to pursue a relationship with him. That's not your fault, Piper. I think with time she'll see that you were only trying to help a helpless situation. I'm glad you'll have a more pivotal role in *Galaxy*. That's long overdue and the publishing company is an exciting idea that you can really make your own. Firing Clyde was a bit rash only because you've established such a casual tone with your subordinates and that doesn't always work. You can be friendly but you can't be friends. With that being said, he was out of line and it was appropriate for you to fire him. Everything will be fine though, love."

Mathais' arm dropped over my shoulders and he kissed the crown of my head. I curled up on him like a worn-out cat and was ever so thankful I hadn't talked him out of coming. I needed him here.

"You're right," I agreed simply.

"About what?"

"Everything."

"I'm selfishly excited that you're coming to Michigan with me."

"When did I say that?"

"You haven't, but I'm being optimistic."

"I would like to get away from the city," I said.

"Michigan *has* cities too, you know."

I tilted my head up and nipped the side of his neck.

"Don't sass me," I warned.

"I wouldn't dare," Mathias replied.

Mathais shifted and our faces became just inches apart. His eyes were a warm hazel. He tilted my face up to his and gave me the sweetest kiss that would make you agree to practically anything.

"Say you'll come with me to Michigan, Piper," he urged.

217

The door buzzed.

"Yes, I'll go," I said, ignoring the ringing of the downstairs lobby door. It buzzed a few more times and then stopped.

Our innocent couch kiss turned into a delicious bout of foreplay. My hair had been set free and Mathais' pants unbuckled.

"I'd like to properly thank you for coming over to check on me," I said.

I slid his pants and boxers below his hips and down to his thighs.

Mathais leaned back into the couch, his eyes quickly closing as I took him in my mouth.

"I got you pizza rolls too," he murmured.

I stopped sucking.

"Really? What kind?"

He opened one eye. "Pepperoni?"

There was a pounding knock on the door and I jumped in surprise. My feisty mood evaporated, leaving behind a fog of anxiety.

"What if it's Clyde?" I said nervously.

"It better fucking not be. I'll answer it," Mathias said, buckling his jeans back up as he strode to the door."

I pulled my hair up into a quick bun, anxiously watching him peer through the peephole. I turned back around and I held my breath.

"It's Berea," Mathais said quietly.

I exhaled in relief but then realized that she was probably knocking on the door because she was so angry. I stood there, watching Mathais unpack the bag he'd brought with him. He placed the pizza rolls, chocolates, and a hand-sized fluffy white alpaca on the counter.

"You got me an alpaca?" I said, completely endeared by its cute ears and fluffy long face.

"I raided the little grocery store on the corner. Answer the door, love."

Fuck, I was all over the place today. I scrambled to the door in time to see that Berea was pulling a carry-on behind her."

"Wait," I screeched, running into the hall.

Berea stopped, turning at the waist with a look that wasn't quite sure if she wanted to come back down the hall. Her eyes were red, her face puffy, and I hated myself.

"I didn't think you were home," Berea said hesitantly, "I shouldn't have come, but I didn't know where else to go."

"Call me," Mathais whispered, giving my hand a quick squeeze before leaving.

Berea turned away from me, watching him leave. Even from as far away as I was, I could see that her bottom lip was trembling.

"I really shouldn't have come," Berea repeated.

"I'm glad you're here. I wanted to call but I thought you wouldn't answer. Please, come in. You can stay here as long as you want."

"You're not going to ask what happened?" Berea said bitterly as she came in.

"No—you can tell me if you want, but—just know I wouldn't intentionally mess anything up. I love you and I feel horrible and I'm just so sorry."

"I heard more of that conversation than you telling him to end the relationship, but when I heard that string of words, I saw red."

"I fired him."

"What?"

"We argued more after you left and I realized he will never get over me if he's still working for *Galaxy,* so I fired him. Plus, he did call me a bitch."

"What a little shit!"

I laughed and hugged her.

"Did you hear Clyde say how much he loves you?" I asked.

"Yes, but I also heard him say he couldn't get over you."

"If I knew how to fix this, I would."

"It's not something you or anyone else can fix. I ended it," Berea said. "I've just liked him for so long, I wasn't thinking clearly. I should have never started anything romantic with him."

"How long have you had feelings for him?"

"College," Berea said, sighing. "I knew he really liked you and I wasn't sure until you moved on with Levi whether you liked him or not. I know you *said* you didn't, but Clyde and you always seemed to be together. Then Levi happened, Clyde started paying attention to me and it just—happened."

Berea really did love him and I'd been the self-centered friend who never bothered to realize. I didn't know what to say or do, so I fell back on what I knew we both liked in hard times.

"You want some pizza rolls?"

"Yes," Berea said, laughing, as she wiped away a few stray tears, "and please tell me there's some type of reality TV marathon on!"

Berea and I spent the rest of the night brainstorming about the publishing company, watching reruns of various shows and eating the entire 80-count bag of pizza rolls.

I was just clearing our plates and getting us refills of the sangria I'd made when Berea's phone buzzed.

It was Clyde.

I knew because Berea bit her lip, as she stared at the screen of her phone, clearly torn between whether she should let it be over or listen to what he had to say.

"If you want to talk to him, talk to him," I said.

"Really? You don't think it's a bad idea?"

"It's not a good idea, but when is being in love ever a good idea?"

"True," Berea said smiling.

"He really does love you," I said. "He just lost his job and his two best friends. Plus, who knows how long he had that ring. It was an heirloom, he couldn't just get rid of it, you know? I'd at least listen to what has to say."

"I'll text him. I don't want to talk to him—really I shouldn't talk to him at all, because I clearly love him more than he'll ever love me and that just isn't good enough anymore."

"Just let him know you need some time to think."

Berea nodded. She stared down at her phone for a long time before finally typing a message.

28

The rest of my short week flew by. Berea's and my excitement about our publishing company grew exponentially. We teamed up with marketing, drafted ideas for features we could include in the online and e-book versions of the literary journal, created an ad, virtually anything you could imagine doing we thought up and hashed out until it was, in our eyes, perfect.

Things with my mom were going pretty good too. We'd flushed out my job description with *Galaxy* and she helped me streamline my goals for *Galaxy Publishing*. My mom suggested redoing our floor plan a bit, shifting some desks around so Berea and I could still be a part of the company but have some privacy as well. She was actually helpful and I found that when I wasn't already in defensive mode, her ideas were really good, even when they were different from my own. By the time Wednesday night came, I felt more confident about *everything*. It wasn't perfect, but it was progress and I was extremely thankful for it.

Berea was dozing off on the couch with her laptop perfectly balanced on her crossed legs. I had just finished eating a light dinner when my phone rang. I scooped it off the table and retreated to the bathroom (the only walled room in my quaint studio) where I could talk freely. I was smiling before I even heard Mathais' voice.

"Still coming with me this weekend?" he asked.

"Are you kidding? Of course I'm coming. What time is our flight?"

"Decided to drive. I thought we could make a road trip out of it. Is that all right?"

My stomach flipped. I had this odd deja vu feeling. Another road trip to Michigan, fuck, I wasn't sure my nerves could take it. *No.* I chastised myself. Mathais wasn't Levi, they were not the same person. I knew Mathais. We'd spent way more time together. There was no way he would abandon me like that. We were *friends.* My relationship with Mathias was different. He was steady, dependable, consistent.

"Piper?"

"Sorry—I'm still here."

"We can fly, if you'd rather."

"No, driving is fine," I insisted.

"Are you sure?"

"Positive."

"Great. I'll pick you up tomorrow at 7 AM."

I clicked my seat belt in place and looked over to a very overzealous, giddy Mathais. I hadn't slept too well the night before. Between being worried and excited, it'd taken me forever to get my brain to shut down and even when I slept I kept stirring awake. But I was always happy to see Mathais; nerves couldn't dull my growing affection for him.

"I have plans," Mathais told me excitedly. "Our charted course navigates us through a couple of cute places for lunch and snacks, even dinner if you want."

"You've really thought this out," I said.

Mathais looked over at me, his demeanor shifting from excited to slightly self-conscious.

"I've just never had anyone plan things for me like you do," I explained awkwardly. "I think it's sweet."

"I'm not normally this detail-oriented."

"I like it and I appreciate it."

Mathais gave me a quick smile and I felt confident that he no longer felt *unconfident.* I really hadn't meant to sound like a condescending snob—that just happened when I was nervous or out of my comfort zone. Whether I liked it or not, this road trip to Michigan was a creepy parallel to the final days of my relationship with Levi. It was logical that I'd be a bit edgy. I just had to remind myself that Mathais was *not* Levi and I was *not* that same girl anymore either.

223

Different time, different place, different person. Everything would be fine.

"Ready to meet my family?"

Fuck. I'd forgotten exactly why we were going on this trip in the first place. I avoided eye contact and tried to give a cool, non-panicked response.

"How many people will be there?" I asked.

"Everyone," Mathais said with a sly smile, "my parents, sister, extended family, friends, neighbors—the whole brood."

"It practically is a wedding."

"Just about, my parents love a party."

"It's really okay that I'm coming?"

"Of course," Mathais said, reaching across the car to lightly take my hand reassuringly. "Unless you don't want to; I didn't mean to spring this whole trip. We're not too far out; I can take you back. Really, love, I won't be upset."

"No, I'd like to get away from the city for a while. I'm just nervous. What do you want me to say when people ask about *us?* Be honest. I just want to make sure our stories match."

Mathais paused and the silence thickened between us by the second. I couldn't look at him, not directly anyway, but in my peripheral vision I could see that he wasn't looking at me. His face was straight on the road.

"Do you want to be just friends?" Mathais finally asked.

"Do you?" I countered back, unwilling to be the first to brave this new territory revealing between us.

I felt his body shift in his seat and dared to take a quick glance at him. He smiled, giving my hand a little squeeze before finally releasing it and turning back to the road.

"That's obvious. I've invited you to a large family gathering, planned the ultimate road trip when we could have easily flown, just so I can get a chance to have all of your attention and time. I don't just like you, I *adore you,* Piper, but I can reel it back into the friend zone if I have to, if that's what you want."

"No, it's not what I want."

"You just want to be friends?" Mathais asked. Clearing his throat, he added, "I just want to be a part of your life, Piper. If that means *just* being your best friend, I'll take it.

"No! That's not what I meant. I want more than just friends."

We both let out a loud sigh of relief that made us laugh at how ridiculously cautious we were both being. We hadn't been *only friends* for a long time. I couldn't pinpoint exactly when the shift had happened, but we were a duo and it was exactly what we both needed.

After one oversized chai, a double chocolate chip cookie, two hours of car Karaoke and a nap (for me), we'd traveled six hours into our journey. We had just five hours left to go.

"Ready to eat?"

"Yes," I purred, stretching.

"Have a good nap?"

"Yes, I feel a little guilty for falling asleep."

Mathais laughed.

"No you don't," he teased.

"I do, I do!" I insisted.

"You've got good timing, though, I'll give you that! This is our exit."

We veered off the highway and the road began to descend down into a little town-valley. We'd been traveling through the mountains just on the edge of West Virginia. I'd loved—when I'd been awake—watching the scenery change. I hadn't really noticed the first time I'd made the trip to Michigan. It was nighttime and I was a ball of nerves and anxiety. This time around was completely different. It'd always been so easy being with Mathais.

"I wish they'd open these in New York, but I doubt they'd stay open," I commented as we pulled into the parking lot of Rob Selvan's Family Restaurants.

"Don't let the lack of sophisticated curb appeal fool you," Mathais said, reading my expression perfectly.

The building looked like a barn turned restaurant. It was a wide, red and white building that had an old-homey feel to it. I probably would have never gone into one on my own, but the parking lot was packed. They must be doing something very right in the kitchen.

"I trust your judgment in all things."

Mathais raised an unbelieving eyebrow at me.

"I *do,*" I insisted sincerely.

"Will you let me order your food then?"

Fuck.

He watched me closely, smirking smugly while he waited for my response.

"Well played, Mathais."

"I'm starting to know you very well," Mathais said.

We were greeted by an elderly hostess, Anita, who led us through the restaurant to a booth tucked away along the far side of the room.

"So," I said, as I opened the menu, "I know we talked before briefly, but tell me more."

"Mariah is my younger sister. She's sweet, quiet, almost shy, even well after she's gotten to know someone."

"The closest thing to siblings I have is Berea and she is definitely not shy."

"Did things get resolved with Clyde?"

"Somewhat," I answered.

"That's good."

"I just hope he doesn't fuck it up again."

"He's never been *pushy,* has he?"

"You mean, like sexually aggressive?"

"Yes," Mathais said.

"No, he's just an ass."

Mathais nodded; his jaw tightened and his eyes hardened.

"If he ever crosses *that* line, let me know."

"Been my boyfriend for a few hours and you're already territorial?"

Mathais' eyes warmed a little with my teasing, but the way he reached across the table and took my hand let me know that he wasn't even remotely joking.

"If anything were to ever happen to you I'd go mad."

"Ready to order?" Anita asked.

"You're the hostess and the waitress?"

"A girl's got to eat," Anita said brightly. "What can I get you both?"

Mathais went first, ordering a country-fried dinner, swapping the coleslaw for a salad and adding extra gravy on the side. The waitress brought out our salads and two country-style biscuits first. I greedily ripped mine in half and smothered it in honey.

While we waited for our food, Mathais told me about Isaac, his stepfather who'd raised him from a young age. He told me stories about him and Mariah, the family store and his friends in high school. I enjoyed every bit. His voice was soothing.

"Ready to eat?" Anita asked rhetorically as she arrived back at our table with our dinners.

"Your parents know I'm coming, right? It's not a surprise or anything?"

"Why? Are you nervous?" Mathais teased.

"Hell, yes!"

"Don't be," he said reassuringly. "You're the first person I've ever brought home to meet them, so they won't be comparing you to anyone else. You'll set the bar."

My eyes shot up to his and the panicked look in my eyes made him chuckle.

"It'll be fine," Mathais insisted. "I'll admit, I think it's sweet that you're so nervous."

"I don't want them to hate me."

"No one in their right mind could hate you."
I hoped he was right.

29

For the rest of the journey, I drilled Mathais with family questions and also got to know him a little bit better. He told me about the antics he and Mariah use to get into—digging up toads and racing them in the living room, sneaking around campsites and putting out fires, transplanting dog poop through a catapulting method that involved a shovel and a lot of forward momentum; but I also learned about some of the heartache. We were both mixed and that came with a lot of awkward moments where people were idiotic and treated you more like a *thing* to pet rather than a child to be kind to. At least for Mathais, his mom had been the black one so even when she remarried he still had some of that culture. Me, I was this freak-show invention that acted one way—unintentionally, I might add—but looked another. Mathais didn't care. He understood, he could relate, and he reminded me that we were cut from the same cloth. I wished I'd known him growing up. He would have been such a rock in my life.

Even with all that bonding, as the car rolled forward through the dark my stomach was queasy with nerves. My gut felt heavy, my legs almost frozen to the floorboards of the car. Suddenly, I didn't feel ready to meet his parents *at all*.

"Let's go in first, then I'll come back out and grab our bags."

I got out of the car and started down the lit driveway. The air was still and the night was quiet and dark. The brightness of the little lights gave off the ambiance of an abandoned runway strip. Mathais guided me forward to the front door. The familiar weight of his hand on the small of my back only eased my nerves a little; my heart felt like it was going to thud right out of my chest.

Before we'd even knocked, the porch light was on and the front door opened, revealing a middle-aged man with smooth brown skin.

"Here's our boy!"

Mathais was immediately engulfed in a hug.

"Hey, Isaac!" Mathais greeted

"Oh my god, she's beautiful," added a woman from the doorway.

Mathais laughed.

"Hi, Mom!"

His mom had instantly swept me into a hug and I felt the ice in my veins melting.

"Do you need help with your bags?" Mathais' mother asked.

"I'll help him," Isaac said quickly. "Go ahead and get Piper inside, Ada; fix her a plate, too!"

"It's so good to meet you," Ada said sincerely. "I'd heard a little bit about you and I was just thrilled when Mathais said he was bringing you to the wedding this weekend."

"I appreciate the invitation," I said. I tried to say it smoothly but I'm sure my voice was squeaky. *Wedding?* I thought this was just going to be an engagement party.

Ada wrapped an arm around my shoulder and walked me into the house.

"You're always welcome here," Ada assured me. "Are you hungry?"

"A little," I admitted.

My head was reeling and I was having a rapid-fire inner monologue in a desperate attempt to calm myself down. Breathe, *Breathe.* He'd never throw you to the wolves. I could wear my same dress I packed. It's not that much different than an engagement party. I could handle this.

"Are you all right?" Ada asked me.

"Yeah—just tired."

"Understandable! We have leftover quesadillas or I can just whip up a grilled cheese if you just want a snack?"

"Either is fine. Thank you, Mrs. Parker."

"Ada is just fine."

"Your home is lovely," I commented quietly as I followed Ada through the foyer. I took a deep breath, willing my mind to steady itself as I took in my surroundings. The house was furnished similarly to the lake house but this felt lived in. The rugs, the accent tables, the paintings, they felt more like pieces than furniture. The house was immaculate but it still managed to have an inviting, cozy ambiance.

"That's the last of it!" Isaac boomed from the entrance way. "Mathais and his girlfriend packed light. It's a godsend compared to when we go anywhere with Mariah. Any woman who can pack for a weekend in one medium-sized suitcase is a *keeper.*"

Ada winked at me and then replied, "Is that a request for a divorce I hear?"

"Just an observation," Isaac insisted.

"Would you like some tea? I have decaf."

"Yes, thank you."

"Of course," Ada said warmly. I watched her fill a silver kettle and melt some butter in a skillet. She was curvy, fit and quite lovely. Her very presence had a calming, almost soothing, effect; it was an instant commonality between her and Mathais.

"Have a seat at the bar and tell me how you met Mathais," Ada said as she worked.

Oh shit. Lie or tell the truth? Lie? Truth? Maybe a hybrid lie-truth?

"We actually had two first meetings," Mathais said, materializing. He wrapped an arm around my shoulder.

"I have to hear this!" Isaac exclaimed, excited.

Mathais sat on the barstool beside me.

"Piper is a writer and she posted a request to meet with people to discuss their modern understandings of sexuality and culturally imposed gender roles. We met up but it was all strictly business."

I gawked at him. Half horrified that he'd told the truth and half in awe that he made the truth sound so *articulate.*

"About six or so months later," Mathais continued, "we had a second encounter at the same coffee shop and we became quick friends."

Mathias looked over at me for confirmation, and the look in his eyes was so sincere.

"Best friends," I correct.

Mathais smiled.

"Best friends," Mathais repeated. "Everything else just fell into place."

Isaac roared with laughter.

"You old dog!" Isaac said between breaths.

"Isaac!" Ada scolded sharply. "Mathais, did you want two grilled cheese sandwiches or one?"

"Two."

"That's my boy!" Isaac said enthusiastically. "Make me one too, Ada!"

"Two for you, Piper?"

Isaac turned to me.

"Can you hang? You don't look like you eat that much."

"I wouldn't be with any woman who can't throw down," Mathais said.

I blushed. It was a weird compliment-complaint sort of thing parents said. If you tried to be modest then you cared too much about your weight; if you ate with too much gusto you were a glutton. Clearly, Mathais appreciated my gusto but it still made me feel a little bit like a pig as he confirmed that I could indeed *hang*.

"Well damn," Isaac exclaimed. "She packs light and she's not afraid to eat? I'm practically in love with her myself, Mathais!"

"Ignore them," Ada said, handing me a mug of tea, "and forgive us if we make you feel awkward, Piper. We're just excited to meet you."

"Is Mariah still up?" Mathais asked.

"Probably, but she shouldn't be since she's getting married tomorrow."

"Married! I thought it was an engagement party!"

"Mathais Lawrence Parker! I specifically told you—"

"Ma! I swear if you did I didn't hear you."

232

"Now, don't get upset, Ada," Isaac piped in. "This just means you'll get to squeeze in some shopping tomorrow. The ceremony isn't until dusk, remember?"

"I'm sorry," Ada said to me directly. "I did specifically tell Mathais it was a wedding."

"No, it's fine. I think my dress will work for a wedding too."

"Oh, that's perfect and you can join us tomorrow when we go to the salon. I was planning on that anyway, but now I realize that you came under *false pretenses*."

Ada shot Mathais a glare that made me sit up straighter in my chair.

"Ma, I *swear* you said party, not wedding."

"Well, a wedding is a party," Ada retorted back.

"It's fine," I said, addressing all three of them, "I would have come either way."

"That's sweet of you, Piper," Ada said. "I just imagine it would be a little overwhelming to not know you were going to meet someone's entire family on a first visit."

"Mathais says she can hang, so she can *hang*," Isaac said with confidence. "No harm done."

"It really is fine, " I insisted.

"I don't mean to be snippy," Ada said, apologizing, "I'm just a little on edge. My baby girl is getting married and—"

"Oh lord," Isaac said, getting to hug her. "It's all right. You know Mariah can't go a day without calling you, let alone a weekend without seeing you."

Ada wiped away a little tear.

"God, Piper, I swear we're a *normal* family," Ada said with an awkward giggle. "You don't mind going with us tomorrow when we get all dolled up? We'd love to include you."

"I don't mind going," I said.

"Good! I've jabbered so long the food is ready."

"Thanks for the late night snack, Ma."

233

Ada smile warmly, any annoyance with her son already evaporated. "I'm just so glad you're both here!" Ada said.

I sipped my tea and ate while the light chatter kept going between Mathais and his parents. I watched them, a little envious of the easy openness they shared. Mathais leaned forward while he ate, smiling as his mother told some story about Mariah when she was young. My heart twitched. I wanted to belong to Mathais, to be a part of his world, be something that really mattered to him and that felt very dangerous.

"Why didn't we just fly?" I asked a little while later. We were settling into the guest room Ada had prepared for us.

"You didn't like driving?" Mathais asked as he pulled back the spread.

"No—I loved it! I always have a good time with you, no matter what we're doing."

He reached across the cream-colored duvet and took my hand in his.

"Me too, Piper."

"But still, you never even asked me if I wanted to fly."

He looked away as he answered me, focusing on rolling the covers down to the foot of the bed.

"I guess I just wanted the excuse to be alone with you. I care about you and I wanted our trip here to be a good memory. I thought if we could drive here, have a good time, I could show you that I'm not *him*. I can't erase how he's hurt you but I thought, maybe, I could repair it a little. "

I blushed. That was so sweet and thoughtful. I wasn't expecting his reasoning to be focused around me.

"Thank you," I said.

"I'm glad you came here with me," he grinned.

"I'm glad you invited me," I said, smiling back.

I left Mathais sleeping soundly as I tiptoed out of the room early the next morning. Ada was already in the kitchen brewing coffee and cooking something that smelled delicious.

"Morning, Piper! Have a seat," she instructed, motioning toward the island's barstools. "We have a few things planned. We're getting massages, brunch, manicures, pedicures, and then we'll all go get our hair and makeup done at the actual venue."

"Thank you for bringing me along," I thanked her sincerely.

"Of course! Do you like breakfast burritos?"

"Never had one, but I'm sure they're delicious."

"I'll wrap these to go and then we'll go pick up Mariah and her maid of honor. She's having a small, intimate wedding, which is fantastic, I think. We can do so much more for her and we really wanted to pamper her today."

"I can pay for—"

Ada cut me off with a wagging finger.

"Don't you even *try*," Ada warned.

I relented immediately with a shy smile.

"Now that it's just us," Ada started, "I wanted to ask you a few things."

My stomach lurched and I braced myself.

"How long have you and Mathais been dating?"

It was a simple, innocent question but the answer was complicated.

"Just a little while," I answered hesitantly.

"Did you want coffee to go? I have an extra thermal travel mug."

"Sure, thanks."

"Did Mathais tell you about his father?" Ada asked.

I nodded yes and Ada studied my face. I knew she *knew* what had happened between them all, but telling her what Mathais thought felt like a violation of my relationship with him. His feelings were private. If she wanted to know how he felt about something, she should ask *him*.

"I'm glad you're close. It's fantastic to see him so happy, but it's a bit eerie too."

My stomach knotted.

Even without making a verbal response, Ada read me like a book.

"It's just that his father used to look at me the same way Mathais looks at you."

"Oh," I murmured. I wasn't sure how to feel about that; his father wasn't a savory character.

"I loved him, but when I found out he had a wife," Ada shook her head, "I just couldn't. His wife and I were pregnant at the same time too; such a selfish man."

"It wasn't your fault."

Ada smiled sadly and patted my hand.

"You're kind for that," she said. "I ended it as soon as I knew but that never absolved me from feeling guilty. I do take a little solace in the fact that he stayed with her. It makes me feel like I didn't cause too much damage. Haven't broken the news to Mathais, but Mariah invited their half-brother to the wedding. Isaac is going to tell him today. "

I didn't know what to say so I just kept nodding.

"Sorry for the mini-ramble, Piper. You just have the kind of quiet soul that makes people want to tell you all their problems. We'd better get moving."

It was a quarter to five in the afternoon when I was finally alone again. Today had been surprisingly fun. There hadn't been any more questions or confessions. Mariah was beautiful and so very kind. They included me in everything easily as if the plan had always been for me to be there. Ada did have a few moments of spontaneous crying, which was expected and understandable, but the spurts always ended in mutual laughter and the mood always stayed joyful.

The wedding was in just under an hour; I smoothed out my slip underneath the formal dress I'd found today and leaned close to the mirror to check on my makeup. I felt so elegant in the dressing room under the soft yellow lights.

I heard the doorknob to the room turn and Mathais poked his head in.

He let out a little whoop as he came in.

"Yes, finally," Mathais cheered, "I've been looking for you." He had his arms wrapped around my waist before I could even speak.

His lips trailed across my shoulder and I tipped my neck to the side in anticipation.

"You smell divine," I said with a sigh.

"You look divine."

"How was your day?"

"I should be asking *you* that," Mathais said, pulling me closer.

"It was fun. Your family is fantastic."

"No, weird stories or questions?"

My eyes snapped open.

"Actually—"

Mathais groaned.

"It wasn't that bad, but your mom did mention that Mariah invited your brother to the wedding tonight."

I felt him stiffen and I turned quickly around.

"Your mom said Isaac was going to tell you."

"It must have slipped his mind."

I kissed his cheek.

"Are you okay?"

"I don't know," Mathais said.

"Have you ever met him before?"

"Yes and there's actually two of them; we went bowling once. Mariah means well, but she's always been a 'fix-it' person. Some things can't be fixed. You can't force a bond that isn't there, you know? But, it's her day and I'll be supportive."

I held him tight, willing my energy to seep into him so he could feel just how much I cared for him. Mathais exhaled hard and tightened his own grip around my waist."

"I can think of a few things we could do instead of leaving this room," Mathais said.

I turned my head to the side and nipped his ear. He gave a sexy growl that made me shiver. I felt a needy, restless hunger that was completely inappropriate. His family liked me—at least, I was pretty sure they did—but being late to his sister's wedding or not showing up at all would definitely sway them into *not liking me.*

"You're so beautiful and if we don't go now we'll only make it to the reception."

Mathais's words enveloped me like a warm glove, and in that moment I knew two things: he was the only one I wanted to be beautiful to and that I was in love with him.

30

The ceremony was short but meaningful. The reception was just a room away and now that I was seated with a drink in hand, I was feeling more relaxed and a little like myself again. I'd more than just survived—I actually liked everyone *and* had had a good time. Before Mathais I'd had two friends; now it felt like I had a whole family. I was humbled by how easily his people took me in. I felt as if I was exactly where I belonged. Dinner would be served to our table soon, there was an endless bar, the DJ was amazing and Mathais' brothers hadn't shown up; I felt safe and free to let loose—just a little.

"Ready for a *real* drink?" Mathais asked.

I giggled.

"Cranberry sours don't count? What is a *real* drink then?"

"I'll get one for you. Hang tight. I'll be right back."

I watched Mathais walk away, licking my lips like a hussy as I admired the way his ass looked in his suit pants. *Mine. Mine. Mine.*

"Piper?"

My body went rigid with surprise. I could never forget that voice. *Levi.*

"What are you doing here?"

"Mariah invited me. What are you doing here?"

"I'm here with her brother," I stammered.

He looked stunned.

"As a couple?" Levi asked.

I just stared at him. My brain felt like mush. I couldn't believe that we were talking after all this time. Everything was good. Everything made sense. Levi was the embodiment of chaos. I had no control over the tidal wave of emotions that were rushing back: abandonment, anger, hurt, attraction. I didn't want him to make me feel anything at all, but he still had such an effect on me. I wanted *this* to be dead but it wasn't.

"Dance with me, Pi."

I began to protest but Levi pulled me slowly into his arms and I still didn't seem to have the ability to speak. I was too overwhelmed, too confused. Levi held me too close and I was quivering against him with so many emotions—conflicting emotions—that my brain couldn't even function properly.

I thought I'd never see him again, and here he was. I was so angry and so happy. We shouldn't be dancing. He couldn't just come in and out of my life when he pleased. Hell, I didn't even *want* him here. I had something completely different now. I had Mathais and I had myself.

"I'm so sorry, Pi" Levi whispered.

Four words and I was crying. Levi cracked right through my defenses and set free everything I'd been bottling up since the night he'd abandoned me. I didn't even know if we were dancing anymore. I couldn't breathe. I couldn't open my eyes. All I could do was stay in his arms and let the world swirl around us.

"Baby, please," Levi moaned. "Don't cry, please, Pi. I know I was horrible to you. I shouldn't have ended it at all, let alone like that. I knew it then, but I was just so—"

I finally gained some control over myself. Shaking my head, I pushed myself out of his arms and away from him. I couldn't bear it. Hearing Levi say the words I'd needed to hear so badly for so long. It didn't soothe me like I'd thought it would. It burned and after everything that *hadn't* happened, it felt hollow and meaningless.

"I can't listen to this," I sobbed.

I ran, rushing off the dance floor as fast as I could and smacked right into Mathais.

"What the fuck is wrong?" Mathais asked desperately as he caught me. His eyes darted between me and the space behind me which I knew led to Levi.

I couldn't answer, I just kept crying.

240

Mathais quickly took me into his arms.

"What's wrong?" he asked again, his tone less urgent this time.

"I'm sorry," I whispered raggedly. "I never cry, I swear, I just can't stop."

"Don't apologize. Let's just go, okay? I think we should talk."

31

Mathais was very solemn as he drove us back to his parents'. Was he that mad at me? I couldn't tell. He didn't seem like the jealous type, but maybe seeing me dance with someone else had sparked something in him. Now we'd have to come to an understanding that either left us together or snapped us apart. I watched him anxiously but his body language gave nothing away. I couldn't take not knowing what to expect.

He caught me staring at him and he sighed.

"We can talk now, but I should pull over."

My stomach twisted; my mouth went dry instantly.

"If you want to end this, then we will. I don't need some big explanation."

"What? No!" Mathais said quickly. He pulled off to the side of the road and turned on the hazard lights.

"I know Levi," Mathais blurted out. "He's one of my half-brothers."

I started hyperventilating. *I fucked his brother. I fucked his brother.* I couldn't even think straight. This meant so many things. The worst was that they both *knew* me. There was going to be a permanent rivalry between them and I'd never be free of Levi, *ever.*

I felt him reach across the car to me and take my hand in his. I looked up at him but he wasn't looking at me. He couldn't muster it. Mathais was staring blankly down the road ahead of us.

"Piper, it's all right. There was no way you could have known. But I—" Mathais paused, clearing his throat. "You mean more to me than anyone ever has or will, do you understand? I'm not running. I want us to work through this."

I couldn't speak. I could barely breathe. My mind was a whirl of self-disgust, fear and confusion.

"Say something, Piper."

"I feel cheap," I whispered.

"Don't, this isn't your fault. Our relationship is built on our bond, our friendship. I don't give a flying fuck about what you did or who you were with before me. If you want to end this and go back to Levi, I won't think ill of you because I care about you. I want you to be happy, even if it turns out that you choose him."

"I just want to go home," I whispered.

"We can leave tonight. I'll drive you back."

"Your parents—shit—your sister, Mariah, will want an explanation."

"I'll deal with that."

Suddenly I felt so tired and we were both out of words. Mathais started up the car and pulled back onto the road.

We gathered up our things in silence. Mathais had the car loaded and we were driving away in the dark night before anyone had even noticed we were gone. About fifty miles in, he broke the silence that seemed to be devouring the intimacy between us. I was glad he'd spoken because I was afraid I'd never have the courage to and he'd take my embarrassment for indifference which is something I knew in my heart I could never, ever, feel towards him.

"You ready to talk about us now?"

I nodded. I still hadn't told him anything about my past with Levi. I owed him that.

"You want me to go first or you?" Mathais asked.

"I'll go first. Levi was the really intense relationship that I told you about. That was almost a year ago. I hadn't seen or talked to him until today."

"Did you love him?"

"I did," I confessed, "and it ended horribly and abruptly."

"Do you still love him?"

243

I thought about the way I'd reacted when I'd seen him. Everything had come rushing back. It was like I had no power over it. I didn't want to still love him, but did I? Had I just tricked myself into thinking Levi and I were finished?

"I don't know but I don't want to," I said honestly.

"I know I'm going to sound crazy saying this to you, but I want you to go see him."

"That's a very odd request."

"I'm going to be brutally honest with you, Piper. I'm in love with you. I should have told you the first time I felt it, but—I don't know, it just didn't seem like the right time. I'm telling you now. I love you and it'll kill me to not know if you're really choosing to be with me or if you're just too scared to leave me. What we have is safe, it's consistent and it'll last, but I need you to want me, to choose me."

Mathais leaned across the car console and kissed me. It was the slowest, sweetest kiss I could have imagined ever getting and it reminded me of everything we had together—how real it was, how easy it was. Inside, my heart was terrified.

I couldn't think about anything else the entire car ride back—all fourteen hours of it. I couldn't stop looking at Mathais either. He was quiet and he was *never* quiet.

He doesn't think he has a chance, I thought, turning my eyes away from him.

Mathais dropped me off in front of my building. Offered to help me carry everything in but I declined. We didn't hug, kiss or even touch again, and he couldn't even look at me as the car pulled away.

I stared until the car was gone.

I got my phone out. I had a missed call and message from Levi.

ADONIS: I want to talk. Please don't avoid me. I'm in New York. I flew back Sunday.

ME: Text me your address.

Levi replied almost instantly and I quickly picked up my suitcase and went inside my apartment.

I was nervous the whole drive, and even though I knew the cabbie was speeding, I couldn't help myself from wanting him to drive faster. I didn't want him to think for a minute longer that I didn't want him.

I raced up the stairs and pounded unnecessarily hard on the door. The door opened quickly.

"Piper, what's wrong?" Mathais asked.

I tackled him in a hug, wrapping my legs around him as he scooped me up.

"You don't know how relieved I am," he whispered into my hair. I felt tears wet my cheek and neck. "God, woman! You've turned me into a sap."

"Are you crying?" I said as I climbed down.

"No," he lied, trying to dodge me.

"Let me see!" I squealed, reaching for him.

He laughed, turning towards me and allowing me to examine his face.

"I'm an ass," I confessed hugging him again.

"Keep going," Mathais teased.

He ran his hands under my shirt and up the bare skin of my back.

"I love you, Mathias Parker."

"I love you too."

We kissed and the feeling sunk deep down into my soul. *Love.* It was everything. He was everything.

"What happens now?" I asked.

Mathais smiled. "*Us,*" Mathais said softly. "We're what happens now."

246

Acknowledgments

Writing has been one of the most rewarding uphill journeys of my life, and anyone who encourages me, backs one of my crowdfunding campaigns, reads my work, shares or retweets a post, is helping to push me up that hill. You know who you are and I hope you know how greatly I appreciate your support! You remind me to keep on keeping on and that is more valuable to me than I can accurately articulate on any acknowledgment page. There have been a few of you that have sought me out with tips, events, ideas or just offering to read my work and spread the word. I'd like to give an extra special thanks to the kind souls who were able to back The 29 Publishing Project on Kickstarter:

Kendyl Braynt
Andrea Cummings
Erin Gienger
Amy Lokker
Kyle Ray McBride
Tracy Melfi
Sheri Meltzer
Lyanna Moore
Amber Nesan
Charlotte Odea
Shakisha Ogburn
Patricia Lucia Reed
Aubrey Slotman
Ryan Smith
Andrea Stringer
Julie Taylor
Bountom Vongkaysone
Carla Wilson
Nicholas Wilson
Cynthia Zack

About the Author:

Vera West resides in the Midwest where she is furiously working on her next novel with her family and her best-pup, Stark. West prefers to wind up with coffee and down with tea. She also recently accepted that she is a Hufflepuff and not a Gryffindor. Acceptance is the first step. Future works include a Banguri(s) the final installment in the Soul(s) Series, a new collection of poems and quite possibly a new novel written in the 29 universe.

Made in the USA
Columbia, SC
16 November 2017